ESCAPE TO EDEN

ESCAPE TO EDEN

TONY SQUIRE

CONTENTS

Dedication   viii

1 WELCOME TO KABUL   1

2 AN UNCERTAIN JOURNEY   19

3 THE KNOCK   38

4 WHERE ENLIGHTENMENT ONCE STOOD   58

5 HUNTED   73

6 BETRAYED   84

7 SOME THINGS ARE NOT MEANT TO BE
FOUND   104

8 SUSPICION   116

9 PERFUME   144

10 THE WATCH TOWER   157

11 WE NEED A MIRACLE   174

12 THE TREE SHALL GUIDE THE WORTHY   190

13 PARADISE FOUND   203

14 SHADOWS OF RETRIBUTION   221

15 THE ESCAPE   232

16 TOO IMPORTANT TO BE LOST   252

About the Author   267

More Books By This Author   268

For my beautiful wife Sheila.

CHAPTER 1

WELCOME TO KABUL

The flight into Kabul felt like a voyage through time itself, each minute bringing Evelyn Kane closer to a land of ancient secrets and untold beauty. She leaned toward the window, captivated by the view below, gazing out at the undulating ridges, marvelling at how such rugged beauty could cradle a history so ancient and mysterious. The mountains surrounding the Afghan capital rose like ancient sentinels, their uneven peaks dusted with snow, defying the summer heat. Valleys, carved by millennia of wind and water, snaked through the rugged expanse below, their depths shrouded in a haze of golden dust. Civilisation clung to the edges of this unforgiving terrain, small villages and winding roads stubbornly carved into its rocky walls.

Evelyn, a historian and archaeologist, had spent her career chasing whispers of lost civilisations and unravelling the myths that history had shrouded in mystery. A Cambridge graduate, she'd honed her skills in both academia and the world of espionage, having been recruited as an MI6 Analyst on completion of her studies, emerging not just as a scholar but as someone adept in political intrigue and weaponry - a skill set few in her field could claim. But now she had settled for the quiet life, or so she thought, working as a historian and occasional treasure hunter at the British Museum.

As the aircraft droned steadily toward its destination, she thumbed through the journal balanced on her lap, running her fingers over its worn leather cover, a bequest from the professor who had first ignited her fascination with lost civilisations. Within its pages lay the fragments of a puzzle, its pages filled with sketches, annotations, and cryptic notes - clues painstakingly pieced together from her late mentor, Professor Hallam's final letter, a trail that, if followed correctly, could lead her to The Garden of Eden itself. Hallam had been more than a mentor; he'd been a guide to the mysteries of the world and it was his insistence that she follow the threads of myth surrounding Eden that had brought her here. The professor's notes mentioned everything from ancient gardens to the Buddha statues that once towered in Bamiyan, their cultural significance a painful reminder of what had been lost in recent decades.

She flipped to a sketch of a crumbling stone tablet, its surface etched with faint lines of Aramaic. The professor's translation was scrawled in the margins: *"Sanctuary of life hidden from the hands of man where enlightenment once stood".* This was the first clue, the fragment found near the ruins of the Bamiyan Buddhas, a fact unbeknownst to Evelyn. She had traced the partial map engraved on its surface, but it hinted at a path leading west - its destination tantalisingly incomplete.

Another page held a copy of an ancient Persian parchment, discovered in the citadel of Herat. The faded script described a verdant valley *"where the waters bring life eternal"*. It was maddeningly poetic, but the professor had linked its language to Genesis, particularly the description of the four rivers flowing out of Eden. Evelyn had spent hours cross-referencing this with historical accounts and maps, narrowing down the possibilities.

Further in, she paused at a charcoal rubbing of a temple carving from the Hindu Kush. The image depicted angelic figures wielding flaming swords, standing guard before a gate flanked by rivers. Beside it, Evelyn had noted the translation of an inscription: *"Only the pure of heart may pass through the Veil of Creation"*. Beneath that, the professor had added his own cryptic remark: *"Is this gate metaphorical, or could it truly exist?"*

A loose page slipped out from between the journal's leaves - her notes on a Nuristani tribal song. The melody, passed down through generations, spoke of a place "where the stars touch the earth". The professor had speculated that the lyrics encoded directions, perhaps tied to a celestial alignment visible only from specific coordinates in the mountains.

Evelyn's pulse quickened as she reviewed the final clue: a hand-drawn map of a river junction, marked with a warning carved onto a stone slab: *"Beyond lies the realm of the divine. Turn back, lest you be unworthy"*.

"The heavens will be your guide," the professor had noted.

Each clue felt like a breadcrumb on a perilous trail. And yet, for all her scholarly preparation, there was so much she couldn't control.

For a moment, Evelyn closed the journal and leaned back in her seat. The professor's words echoed in her mind: *"The greatest discoveries are never without risk, Evelyn. But remember, some mysteries are meant to remain unsolved"*. Her mind was racing now as she hastily turned the pages again, until she found it, her fingers lingering on a particularly intriguing passage: "Eden's truth lies in its persistence, not as a single place but as a symbol of harmony. Follow the rivers, and you may find its echoes in the land where myth and history entwine".

In her heart she knew that not all of the clues were genuine, placed there by the professor as an insurance policy, just in case his journal fell into the wrong hands.

"But which clues were real?" she thought to herself.

As the aircraft banked slightly, revealing another sweep of jagged peaks, Evelyn allowed herself a fleeting thought: What if the Garden of Eden was truly out there, hidden in the folds of these ancient mountains? And what would it mean - for her, for the world - if they found it?

Her attention shifted back to the landscape below. She could see the winding path of the Kabul River but no other obvious waterways. Perhaps *"follow the rivers"* just referred to any waterway or stream, for surely a garden requires water. Somewhere in this desolate, awe inspiring land, she hoped to uncover a truth hidden for millennia. The stakes were high, but Evelyn was prepared for the challenge ahead. She closed the journal, and placed her hat on her head, its wide brim casting a shadow over her determined expression. As the aircraft began its descent, she took a steadying breath, ready to meet the land and the people who would shape her journey, the city revealing itself - a sprawling collection of beige and sun bleached buildings encircled by mountains, a harsh reminder of Afghanistan's precarious existence. Evelyn knew the significance of what lay beneath her; the ancient Silk Road, the crossroads of empires, and the birthplace of countless myths and civilisations. But beneath the allure of history lay the ever present spectre of unrest. Kabul was tense, on edge with whispered fears of a Taliban resurgence. The country stood at a fragile crossroads, where every shadow seemed to carry a threat.

Evelyn was 34, with deep and inquisitive blue eyes that missed little, and a strong, sporty build that spoke of someone who kept herself fit. Her shoulder length blonde hair was pulled back to keep it out of her face. She carried herself with quiet a confidence, accustomed to standing her ground in unfamiliar places.

When she arrived at the airport, she looked every bit the seasoned adventurer - a military style jacket with deep pockets, a well worn cowboy hat shielding her face, and sturdy hiking boots laced tight for whatever lay ahead. There was nothing delicate about her, yet beneath the rugged exterior was a woman who had seen enough of the world to know when to push forward and when to be cautious.

The airport was bustling but subdued; an odd mix of activity and unease. Passport control was slow but methodical, the officers scrutinising every document and stamping each one with deliberate finality. Evelyn's credentials as a historian and archaeologist were noted and added to a growing database - a reminder that she was an outsider, her movements carefully logged.

Her single piece of luggage, a well worn backpack, passed through the scanners without issue. Evelyn had packed light, as always, her gear suited for an expedition. As well as her jacket and hat, she wore a pair of sturdy Cargo trousers built for practicality, a Norwegian shirt, and a fleece, which all completed her look. The contents of her pack included everything she might need: survival gear, notebooks, a change of clothes, and a meticulously curated toolkit for archaeological digs. She was prepared.

When she stepped into the Arrivals section, her sharp blue eyes scanned the crowd. It didn't take long to spot him: a tall Afghan man with an athletic build, his posture relaxed but alert. His kind eyes, framed by a friendly face and neatly trimmed facial hair, seemed to soften the edges of the bustling terminal. He was dressed in a blend of local and practical attire, neither fully Western nor traditional, offering both function and respect for his heritage.

He held up a simple white card bearing her name: *Miss Kane*.

She approached; her stride purposeful despite the weight of her pack.

"*I* am Evelyn Kane, but my friends call me Eve," she introduced herself with a bright smile, "you must be Tariq. You come highly recommended".

Tariq bowed his head, a polite smile forming on his face, the warmth in his expression putting her slightly at ease.

"Yes, Miss Kane. Welcome to Kabul".

He extended a hand toward her luggage, but Eve waved him off, shifting the pack on her shoulders with the ease of a veteran hiker.

"Thanks, but I've got it".

He led her outside to a weather beaten Toyota Land Cruiser, its faded paint and worn tyres speaking of years of hard use. The scent of diesel and dust hung in the air, mingling with the hum of engines and distant voices. Tariq opened the boot and gestured toward it. Evelyn dropped her pack inside with a thud before slamming the hatch shut.

The city awaited. The streets buzzed with chaotic energy - car horns, vendors calling out in sharp Pashto and Dari, children darting between rickety carts piled high with colourful goods. Evelyn caught glimpses of towering minarets in the distance, the domes of mosques gleaming faintly in the sun, and heard the wailing voices calling the faithful to prayer. The air carried a mix of spices, exhaust fumes, and the unmistakable dryness of a land long untouched by rain.

Evelyn settled into the passenger seat, her curiosity aroused. Kabul was not just a destination; it was a gateway to something ancient, something hidden. And she was ready to find it.

As he drove, Evelyn gave Tariq a quick smile.

"I'm famished. Can we stop and get something to eat?"

He raised an eyebrow, his eyes darting toward the edges of the bustling market.

"You want to eat *now*?" Tariq replied, in a surprised tone.

"Yes. I haven't had a proper meal since London. And let's just say aeroplane food isn't exactly satisfying".

Tariq couldn't believe his ears as he scanned the crowd, the lines of vendors, and the labyrinth of narrow alleys beyond.

"Stopping here isn't safe," he said, his voice low.

Evelyn frowned.

"Surely it can't be *that* risky? I need to eat...just something quick".

He hesitated, clearly torn between her request and his own instincts. Finally, with a reluctant nod, he stopped the vehicle at the side of the road and clambered out, gesturing for her to follow.

"Stay close, and do not linger. I will find something fast".

Tariq moved quickly, weaving through the crowded stalls, his presence commanding just enough authority to part the throng. Evelyn struggled to keep up, her curiosity momentarily eclipsed by the tantalising aroma of grilled meats and spices. They stopped at a small vendor where skewers of marinated lamb sizzled over open flames. Tariq spoke quickly in Pashto, his tone curt as he exchanged a few coins for food.

Moments later, he handed her a warm naan bread filled with spiced lamb and fresh vegetables.

"Here," he said tersely, "eat quickly".

Evelyn took a bite, and the burst of flavours made her pause.

"This," she said between mouthfuls, "is heaven".

Tariq didn't respond but just thought that if she didn't hurry then she would be closer to heaven than she expected. His eyes continuously searched the marketplace, his body tense, as though he expected trouble at any moment.

Evelyn took another bite, savouring the rich spices, the warmth of the naan, and the sounds of the market around her. For a brief moment, she allowed herself to enjoy the sensation of being immersed in the heart of Kabul.

"Tariq, you should try this," she said, holding up the bread.

But Tariq barely looked at her.

"We do not have time," he muttered, his tone sharp as his hand clamped firmly around her arm.

Without waiting for her to finish, he began to steer her forcefully through the throng of people.

"Finish it now - we need to leave".

The serious tone in his voice snapped Evelyn out of her momentary reverie. The vibrant colours of the market, the rich smells, and the lively chatter of the vendors faded into the background as the intensity of Tariq's urgency took hold. She stumbled slightly as he quickened their pace, practically dragging her through the narrow alleys.

"Tariq, I can walk on my own," she said, trying to keep the annoyance from creeping into her voice.

She took another hurried bite of the naan, barely able to taste it as she struggled to keep up with his determined stride.

"Quiet," he hissed without looking back.

His grip on her arm tightened briefly, a silent warning. Evelyn swallowed hard, not just the last bite of her meal but the lump of unease growing in her throat.

The bustling market had thinned by the time they returned to the car. The once vibrant chatter of merchants and shoppers now faded into the distance, leaving behind the occasional echo of footsteps and the rustle of wind through dusty alleys. Tariq turned his head left and right constantly, his keen gaze scanning every shadow, every passerby, as though he expected someone to step out and block their path. His hand hovered near his jacket, as though ready to grab something concealed beneath it.

Evelyn trailed slightly behind, acutely aware of the tension radiating from him. She quickened her pace, the crunch of gravel beneath her boots unnervingly loud in the quiet. For the first time, she wondered if she had underestimated the risks she was taking - or if Tariq was simply overreacting.

As they approached the old Toyota parked against a crumbling stone wall, Tariq's pace slowed. Evelyn followed his gaze and froze. A man was leaning into the backseat, his upper body almost entirely inside the car. Something about his posture - the deliberate way he moved, his quick, darting glances over his shoulder - set alarm bells ringing in her mind.

"Hey!" Evelyn's voice rang out, loud and commanding, "what do you think you are doing?"

The man jolted upright, startled, his face partially hidden by the brim of a weathered baseball cap. In his hand, a small camera gleamed, its lens reflecting the fading sunlight. Without a word, he turned toward her, shoving the camera into his pocket and pulling out a knife in one fluid motion.

Evelyn held her breath as the blade glinted menacingly. Tariq, standing a few steps away, tensed and instinctively moved closer to her, his body slightly shielding her from the man.

"Stay back," Tariq muttered, his voice low but angry, as he turned his head to Evelyn, "move slowly. Just step aside and let him go".

But Evelyn didn't move. Instead, she tilted her head and laughed - a soft, almost mocking sound that caught both men off guard.

"Do you have children?" she asked the knife-wielding man, her voice confident and calm.

The question hung in the air, strange and disarming. The man's grip on the knife tightened, he obviously understood, and though his dark eyes narrowed in suspicion, he didn't answer.

Evelyn's expression hardened.

"I'll take that as a no then shall I?" she said, her tone angrier now.

Without warning, she lashed out, the toe of her boot connecting with the man's groin in a swift, brutal motion. His face contorted in agony and surprise as he doubled over, the knife slipping from his grip. Before he could recover, Evelyn brought both fists down hard on his back, sending him sprawling to the ground, his camera spilling from his pocket.

Tariq stared, momentarily stunned.

"Get in the car!" Evelyn ordered Tariq, stepping back as the man groaned on the dusty pavement.

Snapping out of his shock, Tariq nodded, circling around the fallen man. As he passed, he delivered a swift kick to the man's stomach, eliciting a pained grunt, and scooped up the camera.

"That is for the knife," he muttered under his breath, his usual composure returning.

Evelyn had already climbed into the passenger seat, her breathing quick but controlled. Tariq slid into the driver's seat, the keys jangling as he shoved them into the ignition. The Toyota roared to life, and Tariq wasted no time pulling away from the curb, the man shrinking into the distance behind them.

For a moment, the only sound in the car was the hum of the engine and the rhythmic bump of the tyres over the uneven road. Tariq glanced sideways at Evelyn, his expression one of annoyance. Without warning he pulled the vehicle to the side of the road, coming to an abrupt halt.

He didn't bother with pleasantries or small talk, slamming his palm against the steering wheel, his voice quiet but seething with anger.

"Do not *ever* do that again," he snapped, his accent sharpening his words.

Evelyn blinked, startled by the intensity in his tone.

"Do what?"

"Stop. Linger. Wander," Tariq said, each word delivered like a warning shot, "this is not a city tour, Miss Kane. It is not safe. Every second we stay there, you put both of our lives at risk".

She opened her mouth to argue but stopped herself. Tariq's expression was one of anger and disappointment, his knuckles white as he clenched the steering wheel.

"You do not understand," he continued, his voice softer but no less fierce, "in this place, danger does not announce itself. It comes from the corner of your eye, from the man who isn't looking at you, from the car parked too long on the street. The market is alive, yes, but it is also full of eyes - and some of them are not friendly".

"I just needed to eat..."

"You think I do not know that?" he interrupted, his frustration boiling over, "I agreed out of politeness, but next time, you listen to me. When I say we do not have time, I mean it. No more stopping unless I say it is safe. Understood?"

Evelyn stared at him, her initial defensiveness melting under the force of his words. She nodded slowly.

"Understood".

Tariq exhaled sharply, running a hand over his face.

"Good...you did not mention you could do that," he said finally, his tone laced with both admiration and irritation.

Evelyn shrugged, brushing dust from her knuckles.

"Didn't think I'd need to, but perhaps I should have".

Tariq shook his head, a faint smile tugging at his lips despite himself.

"Remind me not to make you angry".

Evelyn grinned, leaning back in her seat.

"Don't worry. I only fight dirty when I have to".

Tariq chuckled softly, the tension between them easing as he shifted the car into gear and pulled onto the road, his eyes still flicking toward the rear view mirror.

Switching on the camera, Evelyn quickly saw that the man had been photographing her map.

"Cheeky sod," she muttered as she forced the camera in front of Tariq's eyes, "look...he was taking pictures of my map...but why?"

Tariq shrugged.

"Hopefully we will not find out".

As the city began to fade into the distance, Evelyn remained quiet, the earlier warmth of the market now replaced by a cold realisation. This wasn't just a journey to uncover ancient secrets - it was a battle for survival, and she wasn't sure if she had truly grasped the seriousness of the situation until now.

The Land Cruiser rumbled away from the city, the business of the urban sprawl giving way to open roads, the noise replaced by the hum of the engine and the occasional rustle of the wind through the dry landscape. Tariq kept his eyes on the road, his grip firm on the wheel.

The tension between them began to ease the further they drove.

"It is not safe for you to stay in Kabul," he said, breaking the silence, "the city has its dangers, and the situation here is...unstable. I will take you to my home in Bektut. It is quieter there...safer".

Evelyn nodded, trusting his judgment. She had read enough classified reports about the region to know that danger often lurked in plain sight, especially for an outsider.

The drive took them westward, the terrain gradually transforming as they entered the Paghman district. Evelyn was struck by the change. Here, at the foothills of the Hindu Kush, the landscape softened, as though the mountains themselves had gifted this place a rare generosity. Fruit trees lined the roads, their branches heavy with promise, and small plots of farmland stretched out in patches of green amid the dry earth.

As they bumped along the narrow, dusty road leading to Bektut, Evelyn noticed Tariq's hands tightly clenching the steering wheel, causing his knuckles to turn pale. His eyes scoured the horizon, alert and cautious. The burden of his thoughts seemed to stifle the air.

"You seem troubled," Evelyn said, breaking the silence.

Tariq glanced at her briefly before returning his focus to the road.

"The times *are* troubling," he replied, "the Western soldiers - your soldiers - are preparing to leave. For many of us who worked with them, it feels as if the ground beneath our feet is crumbling".

Evelyn leaned forward slightly, her interest aroused.

"You worked with the Army?"

He nodded.

"For many years, I was a translator for the British. I helped them understand the land, the people, the languages. It was dangerous work, but I believed in it. I believed in what they were trying to build here. But now..."

He trailed off, his lips pressing into a grim line.

"And now you're worried for your family," Evelyn finished gently.

Tariq's shoulders slumped slightly, the anxiety easing into resignation.

"Yes. Those of us who helped the foreign armies are seen as traitors by many. The Taliban remembers names, faces. They have long memories. When the Westerners go, those of us who remain will have no shield".

Evelyn scowled, the gravity of his words sinking in.

"Do you have a plan?"

"I have many plans," Tariq replied, a trace of bitterness in his voice, "but plans require more than will; they need time, resources. Both are running out. For now, I bring my family here, to this place, hoping it will be far enough, hidden enough. The British tell me they will get us out, but how?"

Evelyn looked out the window, taking in the serenity of the village as they approached. It was hard to reconcile the idyllic landscape with the apprehension in Tariq's voice. Yet, she understood that beneath the calm surface lay the constant undercurrent of danger.

"You're brave to stay," she said after a moment, "braver than most".

Tariq gave a small, humourless laugh.

"Bravery, Miss Kane, is often just another word for having no other choice".

Evelyn didn't reply. She could only imagine the choices Tariq had faced, the risks he had taken to protect his family. For all her preparation and excitement for this journey, she realised she was stepping into a world far more complex and precarious than she had imagined.

Bektut, a suburb of the main town, appeared like an oasis, nestled in the foothills where the Kabul River began its journey, fed by mountain springs and snowmelt. The village seemed untouched by the harshness of the surrounding land, its modest homes shaded by the greenery of Paghman's fruit orchards. Evelyn marvelled at the resilience of this place; how it thrived despite decades of turmoil.

As they wound their way through the narrow lanes of the village, Evelyn glimpsed women tending to small gardens, children playing near ancient stone walls, and men gathered in quiet conversation. The air carried the scent of fresh earth and blooming flowers, an undeniable contrast to Kabul's dust and diesel.

"This area here is Paghman," Tariq said, his voice carrying a note of pride, "it has always been a place of beauty, though its history is not without pain".

He pointed toward the distant hills where the remnants of Paghman's past could still be seen.

"The gardens here were once the pride of Afghanistan, a retreat for kings and poets. King Amanullah Khan made it a symbol of change, a way to welcome a new era, with the Taq-e Zafar, villas, and wide avenues. But wars have left their scars. The Russian bombings destroyed much of what was here. What remains is a memory of what was lost".

Evelyn's gaze followed his gesture, imagining the grandeur that once graced this land. Even in its current state, with ruins scattered among new growth, the area held an undeniable charm; an affirmation to its lasting spirit.

As Tariq drove Evelyn through the winding village streets, his home came into view - a modest structure of mud, timber, and clay that seemed to blend effortlessly with the earth around it. The design was practical and purposeful. Evelyn noticed the windows, carefully placed to face south, likely to draw in as much winter sunlight as possible. The flat roof above bore evidence of its utility, with baskets of drying fruits and vegetables neatly arranged.

As Tariq parked the tired Land Cruiser in the courtyard of his home, Evelyn unfastened her seatbelt and turned to him. His face was shadowed by a weariness that went beyond physical exhaustion, a burden borne from years of conflict and uncertainty.

Evelyn hesitated, and then said softly, "Tariq, you must put your family first. If it ever comes to choosing between helping me and protecting them, you don't need to think twice".

Tariq met her gaze, his dark eyes steady but tinged with resignation.

"I am thankful for your words, Miss Kane; truly. But for now, life must go on. My family is here, and until we know what the future holds, I will do what I can to keep them safe while helping others, including you. Work is survival. Hope is survival".

Evelyn felt a pang of guilt ripple through her chest. She had arrived in this country with grand ambitions; ready to uncover its past, but Tariq's reality was one of navigating an uncertain present.

"Still," she insisted, her voice firm, "if the situation changes, promise me you'll do what's best for them".

Tariq offered a faint, reassuring smile.

"The Taliban are not yet in power, and no one knows what tomorrow will bring. Many of us still hope the Western powers won't abandon us. There's no certainty, but there is still hope. Until then, we live, we work, and we trust that better days will come".

His optimism, though cautious, settled something within her. Evelyn nodded, her strength of will hardening.

"Then let's make the most of the time we have. I won't waste the effort you're putting into helping me".

Tariq stepped out of the vehicle and opened the boot for her backpack. Evelyn followed, taking in the sights and sounds of the small village. Children's laughter echoed faintly from somewhere nearby, mingling with the rustle of leaves in the trees and the soft murmur of flowing water.

Life here had its own rhythm, its own strength. As she hoisted her pack onto her shoulders, Evelyn made a silent vow - to tread carefully, to respect this land and its people, and to ensure that her work here wouldn't endanger those who had welcomed her.

CHAPTER 2

AN UNCERTAIN JOURNEY

The wooden door to the house creaked open, and a woman stepped out into the pale light of the courtyard, her movements graceful yet purposeful. Her face lit up with a subtle, but unmistakable, warmth as her eyes settled on Tariq.

The woman, her head covered with a patterned scarf, approached with quiet elegance. Her eyes softened, lingering on Tariq for a moment longer than necessary, the corners of her mouth lifting in a tender smile meant only for him. Without a word, her hand brushed his arm lightly as she passed, a fleeting gesture that spoke of shared affection and understanding.

"My wife, Miriam," Tariq said, his voice filled with a note of fondness as he gestured toward her.

Miriam turned to Evelyn, her calm demeanour never faltering, and offered a polite, welcoming smile. She wore a traditional dress in soft, earthy tones that seemed to mirror her composed and kind nature.

Evelyn extended her hand.

"Evelyn Kane, but please call me Eve".

Miriam clasped Evelyn's hand in both of hers, her voice gentle as she greeted her in Dari.

Tariq translated.

"She says you are most welcome here".

Evelyn smiled.

"Thank you. It's a beautiful place".

Miriam smiled and nodded her appreciation.

"Thank you, Eve, you are very kind," she said softly, her voice carrying the warmth of a quiet but assured hostess.

"Oh... you speak English?" replied a surprised Evelyn.

"Yes, I do, but not very often," said Miriam.

"Well, you speak it very well," Evelyn acknowledged.

Though Miriam's movements were reserved, there was kindness in her eyes. She exchanged quiet words with Tariq before gesturing for them to enter. Evelyn followed, glancing back at the verdant hills and the faint shimmer of the Kabul River in the distance. Despite the uncertainty of her journey, she felt an odd sense of calm. This place, with its deep history and quiet determination, seemed the perfect starting point for the adventure ahead.

Inside, the house revealed its thoughtful layout. The central courtyard bustled with hushed activity. The scent of cooking wafted through the air as the faint sounds of children at play echoed quietly from beyond. Evelyn's curiosity was aroused when, from around the corner, two small figures came running toward Tariq, their faces lighting up with excitement.

"Baba!" the boy and girl exclaimed in unison, their English accented but clear.

Tariq crouched down with a rare, wide smile, catching both in a warm embrace. The boy, aged seven, had a mischievous twinkle in his eyes, while the girl, two years younger, carried herself with a shy but bright demeanour.

"Baba, who is this lady?" the girl asked in English, peeking curiously at Evelyn from behind Tariq.

"This is Evelyn...Miss Kane," Tariq said, standing and resting a hand on each child's shoulder, "she is our guest, and she has travelled a very long way".

The boy grinned and gave a small wave.

"Hello! I am Omar!"

"And I am Asmaan," the girl added politely, offering a little bow that made Evelyn smile.

"Hello, Omar, Asmaan," Evelyn said warmly, "you both speak excellent English".

"They have been practising," Miriam said softly from behind, her voice filled with maternal pride, "they love to learn new things".

"And they must be prepared for the future," Tariq added.

"Well, they're naturals; you should be very proud," Evelyn replied.

Miriam smiled.

"Yes. Yes we are".

Asmaan blushed slightly at the compliment, while Omar, brimming with energy, pointed toward the courtyard.

"We were helping Mama with the herbs. Do you want to see?"

Before Evelyn could answer, Tariq gently steered the children toward Miriam with a firm but kind tone.

"Later, perhaps. Right now, Mama needs your help to finish the meal".

"Yes, Baba," the children chorused obediently, though their enthusiasm didn't wane.

Evelyn watched as Miriam guided the children back toward their tasks, their footsteps light and their chatter playful.

"The mehmankhana," Tariq explained, noticing Evelyn's attention focussing toward a detached room, "it is a guestroom for male visitors, separate from the rest of the home to maintain privacy for the women".

Evelyn nodded her understanding. Everything about the house, from its layout to its materials, spoke of history, toughness, and tradition. The thick walls, adorned with woven tapestries and family photographs, exuded a sense of strength that mirrored the lives of its inhabitants.

Evelyn settled onto a cushion near a low wooden table, observing the balance of old and new around her. A Quran rested on a shelf beside family portraits, hand carved wooden bowls sat on the floor, and a sleek laptop lay closed but ready on a nearby side table - a lifeline to the outside world.

Moments later, Miriam reappeared with a tray, her movements dignified. She placed a teapot and delicate porcelain cups on the table, her children following with smaller plates of dried fruits and nuts, carefully balancing their contributions.

"Thank you," Evelyn said with genuine gratitude, taking in the warm glow of the family dynamic, feeling the care and quiet discipline that held the household together.

As Omar and Asmaan shyly watched from the corner, Evelyn couldn't help but smile. It was a household built on tradition but alive with the playful energy of youth - a perfect complement to the vibrant land beyond its walls.

"Please, drink," Miriam said in soft but confident English, gesturing towards the tray set before Evelyn and looking towards her husband.

Tariq nodded at her with a small smile, gratitude in his expression, then turning his attention to Evelyn.

As they sipped the tea, Tariq leaned back, his gaze thoughtful and his curiosity clear.

"Miss Kane, I know that you study history, the past, but I still do not fully understand. Why are you here? What is it you are truly searching for?"

Evelyn hesitated for a moment, her fingers tightening around the delicate cup. She met Tariq's gaze, deciding there was no longer a reason for vague explanations.

"I'm looking for the Garden of Eden," she said, her voice balanced but quiet, as if the significance of her words might change the air in the room.

Miriam and Tariq exchanged startled looks. Miriam's hands hovered over the tray as she set down the teapot.

"The Garden of Eden?" Miriam echoed, her voice cautious but curious.

Evelyn nodded.

"I believe it might be a real place. It could be here, in Afghanistan. The legends point to a place in the mountains, near where rivers converge. If it does exist, it is a place of immense historical and cultural significance, not just to Christians and Muslims but to humanity as a whole. It is part of all of our stories".

Tariq leaned forward, his voice quiet.

"And you truly think this garden is here, in Afghanistan?"

"The clues lead here," Evelyn explained, "the writings, the geographical hints; even some ancient texts that haven't been fully translated. If I'm right, it could change how we understand history, faith, and our shared humanity".

Miriam's hands rested on the edge of the tray, her face a mixture of wonder and concern.

"But why now, and why in such dangerous times?"

Evelyn sighed, setting her cup down.

"That's precisely why. The world is on edge. People are divided - by nations, by beliefs. Imagine what finding something like this could mean. A place that connects us all. It's more than history; it's hope".

Tariq rubbed his chin, a concerned expression on his face.

"You must know that the Taliban will not see it that way. To them, your search is not about unity or discovery. It is about invasion, desecration. They fear what they do not control, and they will stop at nothing to keep you from succeeding".

"Well, what they don't know won't hurt them will it?" Evelyn replied defiantly.

Tariq laughed.

"They have spies everywhere. Do you not think that they were not aware of you as soon as you stepped foot in the country...and what about the man in Kabul?"

"I know the risks," Evelyn said firmly, "but some things are worth the risk. This isn't just about me; it's about all of us. History, hope, unity. It's too important to give up now".

The room fell silent for a moment, the faint whir of electricity the only sound. Miriam broke the quiet.

"If you find it, what will happen to us, to this land?" Miriam's voice trembled slightly, but her gaze was steady, locking onto Evelyn's.

Evelyn looked at Miriam, understanding the seriousness of her question.

"I don't have all the answers. But I promise you this; I'm not here to exploit or harm. I'm here to learn, to protect, and I'll do everything I can to make sure the people here are not forgotten in the process".

Tariq nodded slowly, but before he could speak, Miriam turned to him, hesitating.

"Tariq, do you mind if I speak freely?"

He leaned toward her, his expression softening.

"Miriam, you never need my permission. Your thoughts, your opinions...they are always valued".

Miriam drew in a deep breath and then spoke, her voice confident yet filled with emotion.

"The Taliban... they twist everything that is good, everything that is holy. They take our faith and turn it into something distorted, abominable, evil. If they gain more power, Tariq, they will destroy this land all over again. Women will be silenced, children robbed of their innocence, and the beauty of Islam turned into a weapon of fear".

Her words hung in the air, laden with truth. Evelyn felt the depth of her pain and fear.

"And now," Miriam continued, her eyes moving to Evelyn, "this journey, this search... I fear it will draw even more danger to us. To you, Tariq. You have already sacrificed so much for this land, and I cannot bear the thought of losing you".

Tariq reached out and took her hand gently.

"Miriam, my love, I hear your fears. And I share them. But we cannot let those who twist the truth win. This land, its people, its history; they deserve better. If there is even a chance that Evelyn's journey can bring hope or healing, I must be part of it".

Miriam nodded, though tears glistened in her eyes.

"Then promise me, Tariq, that you'll remember why you are doing this. For Afghanistan. For our family. And come back to me".

"I promise," he said softly, squeezing her hand.

Tariq turned back to Evelyn, his tone serious.

"Miss Kane, you need to understand something. This is not just your journey anymore. The risks are higher than you realise...for all of us".

Evelyn swallowed hard, the gravity of the moment pressing in. The warmth of the home seemed to dim as the shadows of an uncertain future loomed closer.

Miriam placed her hands in her lap, her face drawn with worry, then looked directly at Evelyn.

"If Tariq goes with you, he may not get out. We're waiting for news of an evacuation. An e-mail from the British could come any time. If he stays, he can leave with us".

Evelyn nodded, meeting Miriam's worried looks.

"I understand your fear. And I promise, before we leave, I'll give you some clues about where we're going. But ultimately, Tariq has a choice. He doesn't have to go".

She turned to Tariq, her expression solemn.

"This journey is dangerous. You've already risked so much. If you choose to stay, I will understand. Besides, I have my maps and journal to lead the way".

Tariq sat in silence for a moment, his kind eyes fixed on the rugged terrain visible through the window. Finally, he shook his head and spoke firmly.

"This land is in my blood, Miss Kane. If there is even a chance this garden exists, we have to find it; for Afghanistan, for my people".

His voice lowered as he continued.

"But you must understand something. The mountains are unforgiving, not just because of the terrain but because of those who call them home. Tribal people live there, fiercely independent and deeply suspicious of outsiders - especially foreign women. Even with your maps and journal, nature itself will fight you. The cold, the lack of water, and the animals...you would not survive alone".

Evelyn hesitated, hearing the concern in his words. The determination in his voice left no doubt: she needed him.

Miriam looked away, then sighed.

"If you must go, go. But promise me this - if it becomes too dangerous, come back to us. Don't lose yourself out there".

Tariq reached across the table and took her hand gently.

"I promise, Miriam, my love, I will come back".

Evelyn watched the exchange, the substance of their words settling over her. The garden felt closer than ever, yet the cost of finding it was becoming clearer with each passing moment.

Tariq turned his gaze back to Evelyn, breaking the silence.

"Miss Kane, do you have a gun?"

Evelyn straightened in her seat, caught off guard.

"I can handle myself, if that's what you're asking," she replied, her tone firm.

"So I have seen, but that is not what I mean," Tariq said, his kind eyes steady, "do you *have* a weapon?"

"No," Evelyn admitted, "but I'm trained. I know how to use one".

"Trained?!" replied a surprised, yet curious Tariq, "were you a soldier? I have seen many brave women soldiers with the western armies".

Not wanting to reveal her MI6 past, Evelyn hesitated for a moment before replying.

"A soldier? No. I used to shoot for pleasure, you know, a gun club and all that".

Tariq nodded, although not entirely convinced by her explanation, then stood and walked over to an old sideboard. Miriam, watching with quiet apprehension, grasped her scarf. Tariq opened a creaky drawer and rummaged through its contents before pulling out a 9mm Browning pistol. He placed it on the table along with a few boxes of ammunition.

"This is from my time with the British," he said, "it is reliable, and it will serve you well. You will need it out there".

Evelyn reached out, lifting the pistol to inspect it, automatically pointing the weapon upwards, checking the safety catch, removing the magazine and finally cocking it to ensure the chamber was empty. It was a familiar weapon to her. The cold metal felt heavier than she remembered from her training days, but she nodded.

"It's perfect. Thank you, Tariq".

Tariq gave her a knowing look then nodded smugly.

"There is more to this woman than appears," he thought to himself.

She glanced at him.

"What about you? What will you carry?"

Tariq's expression softened as he replied.

"I have an AK-47 and enough ammunition to last a good while. Do not concern yourself with me Miss Kane".

Evelyn raised an eyebrow, clearly impressed.

"An AK? You don't mess around, do you?"

Tariq chuckled, though the tension in the room remained evident. Miriam stood silently, her worry etched into every line of her face.

As Tariq handed Evelyn the ammunition boxes and a cleaning kit, he cast a reassuring look at his wife.

"I will take care of her, Miriam. I will take care of us".

Miriam nodded but said nothing, her silence a hefty reminder of the dangers that lay ahead.

The dusty plains of Afghanistan stretched endlessly before them as Tariq coaxed his aging Toyota Land Cruiser along a narrow, rutted road. The vehicle groaned in protest at every jolt, its suspension squeaking with the strain of the uneven surface, but Evelyn barely noticed. Her eyes were fixed on the mountains in the distance, craggy peaks that seemed to cut the sky in half. Somewhere beyond them lay the answers she was now chasing.

Tariq was quiet beside her, his hands firmly gripping the steering wheel as they bounced along the pot holed highway. He had not spoken much since they had left the town two days prior, but

Evelyn could sense the turmoil behind his silence, as she thought back to the farewell he had shared with Miriam and their children.

The sun had barely risen when they stood at the door of the small, sturdy home. Miriam's hands trembled as she clutched Tariq's arm, her eyes shining with tears she refused to shed. She had whispered words of caution, her voice wavering but serious.

"Come back to us, Tariq my love".

Tariq had kissed her forehead, and gently hugged their son and daughter, his own voice trembling with emotion.

"I promise. Allah, Glory be to Him, the Exalted, will keep us safe. I am sure of it".

Before stepping out into the cool morning air, Evelyn had taken Miriam aside. Quietly, she had handed her a folded piece of paper.

"If anything happens to us, these are the clues to where we're headed. They're vague, but they should help if someone needs to find us".

Miriam had stared at the paper for a moment before taking it, her fingers brushing Evelyn's as if to ground herself.

"Thank you. But I pray it will not be necessary".

Now, as the Land Cruiser rattled along the roadway, Evelyn looked over at Tariq. He was concentrating on the road ahead, but his eyes betrayed the pain of the parting. She wanted to say something comforting but wasn't sure how to bridge the gap between their worlds; their burdens.

In the streets of Bektut, she had noticed the worrying presence of onlookers. Men lingering in doorways, staring at their every move, and children pausing their play to watch the vehicle as it rumbled past. The directness of those stares had been oppressive, a reminder that their journey was already drawing unwanted attention.

Evelyn shifted uneasily in her seat.

"Did you see the people watching us?" she asked, breaking the silence.

Tariq nodded grimly.

"I saw them. It is hard to say whether they were simply curious or something more".

He cast a glance in the rear view mirror, his shoulders tense.

"From now on we must stay alert".

Evelyn clenched her notebook tightly, the familiar leather cover grounding her in the present. The mountains loomed larger now, their rugged beauty both a promise and a threat. Whatever lay ahead, there was no turning back. While the Taliban's grip hadn't yet tightened into the vice it would become, whispers of their resurgence were already spreading fear. As a British historian and archaeologist specialising in Middle Eastern cultures, she had always prided herself on navigating volatile regions, but something about this venture felt different.

The truck continued to rumble steadily along the bumpy dirt road, its tyres sending up plumes of dust that hung in the air like ghosts of the past. Evelyn adjusted the knot in her headscarf, ensuring it stayed secure against the drafts slipping through the cracked window, taking a quick glimpse at the barren landscape outside – a combination of endless mountains and plains dotted with huge rocks and boulders, and clusters of shrubs clinging stubbornly to life.

The rhythmic purr of the engine filled the silence between her and Tariq. He sat behind the wheel, his expression calm but alert, his keen eyes scanning the horizon for any hint of danger. Evelyn, however, was lost in thought, her mind drifting back to the cramped safety of Tariq's modest home just days earlier.

The dim room had smelled of wood smoke and spices, a huge contrast to the sterile offices she was used to. Spread across the low table between them had been her collection of weathered documents - faded maps, brittle papers covered in unfamiliar script, and the most puzzling of all, an inscription that seemed to hold the key to everything: *"Sanctuary of life hidden from the hands of man where enlightenment once stood"*. She had wondered about this whilst on the aeroplane journey, trying desperately to solve its meaning, to break the code; if indeed it was a code.

Tariq too had studied the words with an intensity that only deepened the lines of worry on his face.

"Enlightenment," he had said slowly, as if testing the definition of the word, "in our region, that can only mean one thing...the Buddha statues in Bamiyan".

Evelyn had nodded, a sense of relief flowing over her thoughts, the pieces of the puzzle clicking into place.

"The Buddhas were symbols of enlightenment. It fits, but what about the sanctuary part? That one still baffles me".

"If the clue is pointing to Bamiyan, it must be where we start," Tariq replied, "but the area is not as it was before. The statues are gone, destroyed by the Taliban years ago. We will have to search carefully. I think being there will lead us to the next part of the puzzle, do you not agree?"

Evelyn nodded.

"Yes...yes I do".

They had packed quickly after that and now, in the Land Cruiser, Evelyn could still see his determination as he drove, his focus unbroken despite the monotony of the road, as he worked to try to solve the clues.

Evelyn's thoughts too were racing, as she turned her attention back to the horizon, the words of the second part of the clue echoing in her mind.

"Sanctuary of life hidden from the hands of man..."

Bamiyan was a place of loss, its towering statues obliterated, leaving only scars in the mountainside. But if the clue was right, it might also hold a secret; a thread leading them closer to the sanctuary they sought.

Evelyn pulled the scarf tighter around her head as the wind seeped through again, carrying with it the faint scent of dust and dry earth. The truck bumped over a rock-strewn patch of road, jolting her thoughts back to the present.

"Are you all right?" Tariq asked without taking his eyes off the road.

"Yes," she replied, forcing a small smile, "just thinking about what we'll find in Bamiyan".

He nodded, flicking on the wipers to clear the windscreen of dust.

"Whatever it is, we will find it together Miss Kane, but remember, the mountains are as dangerous as the men who seek to control them".

Evelyn didn't need the reminder. The Taliban's resurgence hung over their journey like a storm cloud, its shadow dark and foreboding. But for now, the road ahead stretched clear, carrying them toward a destination neither could fully predict but both were determined to reach.

Despite his curiosity, and a hint of excitement about their quest, Tariq was still concerned.

"Are you sure about this?"

The former translator's dark eyes flicked to her briefly before returning to the road.

"Afghanistan...it is not safe. Not anymore".

"I'm not here to be safe," Evelyn replied, her voice calm, "I'm here to find the truth".

Tariq sighed and rolled his eyes at her bravado, muttering something in Pashto that Evelyn didn't catch.

She knew he didn't fully approve of her quest, but for him, finding the garden was hope for his country, and perhaps even the world.

They passed through a small village, its mud brick homes clustered tightly together as if seeking comfort from the desolation around them. The villagers paused to stare at the vehicle, their expressions wary. Women in burqas shuffled quickly out of sight. A few men stood by the roadside, their eyes stern and unwelcoming.

Evelyn caught sight of an older man who suddenly stood up as if trying to get a better look at her. His face twisted in disapproval, as he spat on the ground, as the car passed.

"That is a very bad sign," Tariq muttered.

"Why do they hate me?" Evelyn asked, though she already suspected the answer.

"They hate what you represent," Tariq said bluntly, "an educated woman, a Westerner. For some, that is plenty good reason".

Evelyn bit back a retort. She knew Tariq wasn't being unkind - just honest. Still, the hostility stung. She had come here to learn, to understand, to uncover a piece of history that could unite people. But instead of curiosity, she was met with suspicion and fear.

Evelyn wasn't in Afghanistan for the adventure - though she often joked otherwise when filling out endless forms for her research permits. Officially, she was here to document ancient trade routes and study local traditions of craftsmanship. Unofficially, her reasons ran far deeper. Somewhere in these mountains, the echoes of a legend whispered to her, a tale of a garden that defied time and decay.

The Land Cruiser groaned as it climbed higher into the harsh mountains northwest of Kabul. Evelyn held onto the door handle, the vehicle jolting over ruts and stones on the dirt road, as she bounced up and down in her seat like a jack in the box, whilst Tariq navigated the treacherous road with a mix of skill and caution.

Around each bend the scenery was breathtaking. Steep ridges rose like ancient fortress walls, their pointy silhouettes framed against a blue green coloured sky. Far below, a river glittered like a silver thread, winding through a valley lush with spring growth. Goat herders, dressed in traditional clothing, waved from rocky outcrops, their flocks scattered like white patches against the scrubland.

"This path is not on any maps," Tariq explained, "few dare to travel it now, but it is safer than the main roads with...everything going on".

Evelyn nodded, glancing momentarily at the journal open on her lap. One of the cryptic clues, a faded sketch of a river carving through mountains, seemed to match the terrain. She made a note, her fingers brushing against the smooth leather cover.

The truck bumped its way along the uncompromising dirt road, the headlights casting long shadows over the dry Afghan plains. Evelyn sat, gripping the seat with both hands, trying to steady herself against the jerky motions, whilst Tariq calmly drove on, oblivious to her discomfort. The wind outside was biting, whipping up dust and the faint scent of burning wood, but inside the vehicle, the air was teeming with anticipation - and something else.

Fear.

Evelyn could sense it in Tariq, even though he didn't speak of it. He had grown up in the mountains, knew the trails and villages like the back of his hand, but this journey was different. There were whispers that the Taliban were everywhere, and Tariq was worried that they would soon be on their trail, spurred on by tales from frightened and suspicious villagers. The risk was high, but there was no alternative. Tariq had been adamant that they would reach the mountain pass before dawn, but Evelyn knew that time was not on their side.

Unbeknownst to them, the situation in Kabul had deteriorated dramatically since Evelyn's arrival. The Taliban had entered the city with astonishing speed, meeting little to no resistance from the new Afghan Army, which had fled without a fight. Despite outnumbering the Taliban over ten to one, the soldiers had melted away, leaving Kabul, and the country, to its fate. Pandemonium gripped the city as ordinary Afghans flocked to the airport, now held by Western armies, desperate to escape before the Taliban reinstated their harsh laws and brutal punishments.

The Taliban, meanwhile, had not been idle. Having taken over parts of the terminal, they had begun sifting through records of arriving foreigners. It was here that they discovered Evelyn's presence, her name standing out as a Westerner who had entered the country at a precarious time. For the Taliban, she was not only a woman, but an anomaly - a potential threat - and they needed to stop her.

Oblivious to this, Tariq and Evelyn continued their journey, unaware that the noose was tightening.

The first stop on their journey had been a small village a few hours from Kabul. It was the last place where they could rest before heading deeper into the mountains, but even here, Evelyn felt the weight of the world bearing down on her. The village had been quiet, too quiet, and the villagers had seemed to avoid eye contact. Even the children, usually eager to approach strangers out of curiosity, had remained out of sight, their laughter replaced by an uneasy silence.

There had been whispers - low murmurs between the men gathered at the edge of the village square - about Taliban patrols spotted nearby. Tariq had spoken to a local elder briefly, his tone and his words blunt as Evelyn stayed near the vehicle. When he returned, a worried expression covered his face, though he had tried to reassure her with a forced smile.

"There is nothing to worry about," he had said.

But Evelyn knew better.

CHAPTER 3

THE KNOCK

The knock came, soft but deliberate, breaking the oppressive silence of the house. Miriam froze in place, her ears straining against the quiet of the night. Even the embers in the stove seemed to still. She momentarily held her breath, her heart hammering so loudly she was certain it would wake the children. Omar, stirred on the woven rug near the stove, his eyes fluttering open, his small body curling instinctively closer to the warmth.

Hassan, Miriam's brother, stepped into the entryway, his hunting rifle cradled in his hands. His face, lined with worry, betrayed his unease.

"Stay back, Miriam," he whispered, his eyes darting toward the door, "if this is a trick..."

His tone carried no expectation of an answer.

Miriam clutched at her shawl, her mind racing. Another knock, louder this time, broke his sentence. A voice followed; calm and authoritative, muffled by the heavy door.

"Miriam. Tariq. This is Sergeant Jake Allsop of the British Army, we are here to help. Open the door".

Hassan stiffened, his grip on the rifle tightening.

"How do we know this isn't a trick?"

Jake's voice came again, this time in Pashto, steady and assured.

"Tariq worked for us. You've been warned about the danger. I have a word for you...Bongo. We must move quickly".

Bongo was the code word sent in the e-mail.

Miriam took a shaky step forward, her eyes locking with Hassan's. She had prepared for this moment, but now that it had arrived, her will power wavered. Her paperwork sat ready, the bag by the door packed with every necessity she could gather. Yet her thoughts clung to Tariq, wondering if she would ever see him again.

"Hassan," she whispered, her voice trembling, "it is them. We have to go".

Hassan hesitated, his finger curled around the trigger of his rifle.

"And if it's not? If this is the Taliban...?"

The voice outside spoke again.

"Your family is in danger. We have intelligence that *they* are coming. We must move now".

Miriam took a step forward, her hand brushing Hassan's arm.

"Tariq trusted them. We must trust them too".

Hassan was reluctant, his suspicion clear, but after a tense moment, he lowered the rifle and unlatched the door. It creaked open, revealing five figures cloaked in shadows. Their black combat uniforms helped to conceal them in the darkness, whilst their faces, streaked with dirt and sweat, were partially obscured by helmets and scarves. Their weapons were ready, but their movements were measured and deliberate, designed to reassure.

Jake stepped forward, his piercing green eyes scanning the room. Tall and lean, with an air of quiet authority, he exuded the calm confidence of a man accustomed to danger.

"Miriam," he said, his voice firm yet friendly, "we don't have much time. We need to leave now. Are you all ready?"

Behind him stood Sergeant David Leck, Lecky to his friends, a towering broad-shouldered American with a rugged face and a Montana accent that coloured his Dari as he addressed Hassan.

"We're here to keep you safe," said Lecky, his voice deep and steady, "but we've got to move before the Taliban get here".

Lecky radiated quiet strength, his eyes softening slightly as he saw Omar clutching a threadbare blanket.

Miriam's heart sank as she stepped forward.

"But Tariq is not here," she said, her voice quivering with emotion, "he left with a British woman - a historian, Evelyn Kane. They went into the mountains a week ago".

Jake gave a quick nod.

"Understood. We'll deal with that later. Right now, we need to get you and the children out of here".

Lecky exchanged a glance with Jake before turning his attention back to Hassan.

"Gather up your stuff...no more than you can carry".

The team moved swiftly, two soldiers taking positions at the windows, their rifles aimed into the night. A third, Corporal Mackie, a wiry young man with an easy grin, crouched by the door, keeping watch, whilst another, Taylor, a solemn looking medic, knelt beside Omar, offering a quiet reassurance that the boy barely seemed to hear.

Miriam turned to her children, kneeling beside them as tears pricked her eyes.

"We are leaving," she whispered, her voice trembling, "stay close to me, my loves. Do not let go of my hand".

Omar nodded, his wide eyes glistening with fear.

"Where are we going, Mama?"

"To a safe place," she said, forcing a smile she didn't feel, "somewhere the bad men cannot hurt us".

"Bad men? What about Baba?" the boy enquired.

Leck crouched down to Omar's level, his large hands resting gently on his knees.

"Hey, buddy," he said softly, "you've got to be brave for your mama, alright? We're going to take you to a safe place".

Omar nodded, his wide eyes brimming with fear. Miriam's heart twisted as her son clung to her side, his small hand clutching her shawl, whilst her youngest, Asaam, whimpered in her arms. Miriam kissed her forehead, her tears soaking into her hair.

Hassan picked up the bag of possessions.

"Let's go".

Jake motioned for the family to follow.

"Stay between us. Move quickly, but keep quiet".

The group slipped out the back door into the frigid night, the soldiers forming a protective circle around them. Miriam clutched the sleeping Asaam tightly against her chest, whilst Omar walked beside her, his head turning nervously. Hassan carried the bag, a stalwart expression covering his face. The village, so familiar by day, now felt alien and hostile. Every shadow seemed to breathe, every sound a potential threat.

Each soldier wore night vision goggles. Lecky led the way, his large frame moving with surprising stealth. Behind him, Mackie scanned the rooftops and alleyways, while Private Carter, a quiet man, brought up the rear, staying close to the family, his rifle ready.

The children's fear was evident. Omar tripped on a loose stone, falling hard onto his hands and knees. Before Miriam could react, Taylor was there, lifting the boy with gentle hands.

"It's alright," he whispered, his voice soothing, "I've got you".

Miriam stumbled on the uneven path, her body heavy with exhaustion and fear. Omar struggled to keep up, his small legs faltering on the steep incline. Without a word, Taylor scooped him up, carrying the boy as if he weighed nothing.

Miriam's chest tightened as she watched Taylor carry her son, the boy's small arms wrapped around the soldier's neck. Asaam whimpered in her arms, her tiny fingers clutching at her shawl.

"Shhh, my love," she murmured, kissing her forehead, "we are almost safe".

A distant rumble broke the silence - the sound of motorcycles growing louder. Jake's voice crackled over the radio.

"Mackie, eyes up. Lecky, cover the ridge".

Leck turned, motioning for the family to move faster. His voice was calm but firm.

"Keep going. Don't look back".

Miriam stumbled, her legs shaking with exhaustion and fear. Carter was at her side in an instant, steadying her with a firm hand.

"You're doing great," he whispered softly, "not far to go now".

Leck turned to Miriam.

"We've got to move faster".

They reached the ridge at the edge of the village, where an SUV waited, its engine idling. The driver, Parks, had the doors open and ready, motioning for the family to climb in.

"Get in!" Jake ordered, his voice cutting through the silent confusion.

Miriam helped Omar into the vehicle, her hands trembling as she held Asaam close. Hassan hesitated, quickly looking back to the distant village as if memorising every detail before stepping into the car.

As soon as the doors closed, the SUV sped off, bouncing over the rough terrain. Miriam clutched her children tightly, her heart pounding, whispering prayers under her breath.

An hour later, they arrived at a small airstrip, where the roar of a transport plane filled the night. In the darkness they could see that many more Afghan families and their rescuers were gathered on the airfield. The allies had indeed been busy that night, fulfilling their promise. As the soldiers began to guide the refugees aboard, Miriam turned to Jake and handed him Evelyn's clues.

"Here, these are the clues left by Miss Kane. Do you think you will find them?" she asked.

Jake looked her in the eyes, his expression softening.

"We'll find them," he said, "you have my word".

As the last refugee boarded the aircraft the loadmaster signalled for the ramp to be closed. The engines roared to life, and the plane began its journey along the taxi way before beginning its ascent. Miriam sat beside her children, holding them tightly as the land she had always known disappeared beneath them. Her mind was a storm of worry and hope, her heart torn between the family she had saved and the husband she had left behind. She closed her eyes, whispering a prayer for Tariq, praying and hoping that their paths would cross again, somewhere safe, somewhere far from the shadows of war.

As the special forces team clambered aboard their SUV for the journey back to Kabul Airport, Lecky pondered for a moment then looked over to Jake.

"That was a huge promise to give," Lecky uttered.

"Yeah, but in this awful shitty mess something good has to happen mate," Jake replied.

As dawn broke, the Taliban convoy thundered into the village, the trucks grinding to a halt in a cloud of dust. Their leader, Rashid, a rough looking man, stepped down, his boots sinking into the dry earth. Tall and wiry, with a grizzled beard and piercing, hawk-like eyes, Rashid was a veteran of countless battles, his face marked by the scars of Soviet shrapnel. He gripped his rifle that was slung across his chest, his eyes drilling deeply into the terrified villagers who had already begun to gather in the square.

"Round them all up," Rashid ordered, his voice as cold and biting as the mountain wind.

Vakil Khan, his second in command, growled instructions to the men. Shorter and stockier than Rashid, he carried a perpetual scowl and a battered notebook tucked into his belt, ready to record any detail that might aid their hunt. While Rashid burned with ideological fervour, Vakil was purely pragmatic - tracking, capturing, and eliminating threats was *his* trade. The Taliban fighters moved with ruthless efficiency, pulling men, women, and children from their homes. The villagers were herded into the centre of the square, forced onto their knees in uneven lines. One of the Taliban, Faheem, the youngest among them, clutched his Kalashnikov with trembling hands. Barely in his twenties, he lacked the hardened cruelty of the others. His darting eyes refused to meet the villagers' pleading stares, and under his breath, he muttered prayers - whether for himself or the people before him, even he wasn't sure. He wanted to prove himself, to silence the doubts that gnawed at him, but deep inside, he felt the cold grip of uncertainty.

Rashid stepped forward, his scarred face shadowed under the rising sun, as he surveyed the captured villagers. Somewhere among them, or perhaps beyond this village, was the woman; a foreigner, an opportunity. If she was involved in anything against them, she would serve as an example. If not - well, that was of little consequence. In his hand, he held a folded printout - the scanned passport page of a western woman. He unfolded it deliberately, holding the picture aloft for the crowd to see.

"This woman," Rashid announced, his voice carrying over the uncomfortable silence, "her name is Evelyn Kane. She arrived at the airport days ago. We have her records".

He handed the paper to one of his men, who moved down the line, thrusting it into the faces of the kneeling villagers.

"Who has seen her?" Rashid continued, "who knows where she went?"

The villagers exchanged frightened glances but said nothing. Mothers clutched their children tightly, shielding them with their bodies. A young boy whimpered, silenced by a sharp glare from his father.

Rashid's lips curled into a humourless smile.

"You think you can protect her? Or perhaps you think we are fools?"

He walked slowly along the line of villagers, his boots crunching on the dirt. Stopping in front of an elderly man, he crouched, holding the printout close to the man's face.

"You've lived a long life," Rashid said, "tell me what I want to know, and you might live to see another day".

"I swear, Commander, I don't know anything!" the man pleaded, his voice trembling.

Without hesitation, Rashid drew his pistol and shot the man in the head. Blood sprayed onto the villagers beside him, eliciting screams and cries of horror. The old man's body slumped forward, lifeless, the blood from his head wound oozing onto the stony ground.

Rashid stood, wiping the barrel of his pistol with the hem of his scarf.

"Let us try again," he said calmly, "who has seen her?"

Another man was dragged forward, shaking so violently that he could barely kneel. The Taliban fighter thrust the copy of the passport photo into his face.

"Speak!" Rashid commanded.

"I...I haven't seen her," the man stammered, "I don't know who she is!"

Rashid sighed, shaking his head.

"Lying is a sin," he said, raising his pistol again.

This time, he shot the man in the chest, the force knocking him backward into the dirt. The man gasped for air, his hands clawing at the wound. Rashid stared at the him as he struggled for life, a smirk on his face as if he was proud of his actions; finally ending his suffering with a second shot.

"Enough!" a voice suddenly cried.

All eyes turned to a frightened young man, his face pale and streaked with sweat. He was shoved forward by the crowd, his knees hitting the ground hard.

"Please," he begged, "I'll tell you what I know!"

Rashid crouched before him, his eyes narrowing into a squint.

"Good. Speak".

"Tariq," the young man said, his words tumbling over one another, "Tariq left days ago with a western woman. They took his Land Cruiser and headed northwest, into the mountains. That's all I know, I swear".

Rashid studied him for a long moment.

"And why should I believe you?"

"It's the truth!" the young man insisted, his voice cracking, "I saw them leave with my own eyes. Please, I don't know anything else".

Rashid stood, nodding slightly.

"You've been very helpful," he said.

Relief washed over the young man's face, but it was short-lived. Rashid turned to one of his men.

"Execute him".

The fighter raised his rifle and fired a single shot into the young man's head. His skull exploded from the force of the point blank shot and his body crumpled to the ground, lifeless, as the villagers screamed in unison.

"Silence!" Rashid shouted, his voice cutting through the terror.

He then gestured to his men.

"Kill them...kill them all. Leave no witnesses".

The fighters raised their automatic weapons, the barrels glinting in the morning light. The sound of gunfire erupted, deafening and almost never ending. Bullets tore through flesh and bone, cutting down the villagers in a gruesome spray of blood and dust. Mothers shielded their children, only to fall together in a macabre heap. The air was filled with the acrid smell of gunpowder and the cries of the dying.

When the last rifle fell silent, the square was a scene of utter carnage and devastation. Bodies lay sprawled in pools of blood, the once vibrant village reduced to a grotesque tableau of death.

Rashid surveyed the gruesome scene with cold satisfaction.

"Burn the bodies, burn the village" he ordered, climbing back into the lead truck, "we have a long journey ahead".

As the convoy rumbled away, Faheem sat in the back of one truck, his face pale and his hands trembling. He clutched his rifle tightly, muttering prayers under his breath. Behind them, smoke began to rise from the ruined village, a dark plume that would haunt the mountains for days to come.

In the city the air was choked with dust and desperation as the SUV rolled to a stop near the gates of Kabul International Airport. Outside, the chaos was obvious - families pressed against the barriers, waving documents, passports, and desperate pleas written on scraps of paper. Shouts and cries filled the air, mingling with the distant thrum of departing aircraft.

Sergeant Allsop stepped out of the vehicle, his eyes scanning the scene. Behind him, Lecky climbed down, his towering frame instantly commanding attention. The rest of the team followed, moving through the tumult like a wedge, their black combat kit and calm demeanour setting them apart from the turmoil.

A young woman clutched a baby to her chest, sobbing as she waved a tattered passport toward Jake.

"Please! My family...we have papers!" she cried in English.

Jake said nothing. He wanted to help, but their orders were clear. He raised a hand, signalling her to stay back, and forced himself to keep walking.

"We can't stop," he said under his breath to Lecky.

"Doesn't get easier," Lecky muttered, his eyes flicking to a boy clutching the leg of an older man near the fence.

The team made their way inside a hangar in the secure zone, where the noise was muffled by the reinforced walls. The contrast was jarring; inside, the building buzzed with organised urgency. Refugees being brought through the barrier in small groups were processed in hurried but methodical lines, and soldiers called out instructions to overwhelmed aid workers.

Jake led the team to a sparsely furnished briefing room near the operations centre. A single table dominated the space, surrounded by mismatched chairs. Maps of Kabul and the surrounding regions were tacked to the walls, along with whiteboards covered in hastily scrawled notes.

Their commanding officer, a Lieutenant Colonel Paul Salloway, a long time veteran of the Middle Eastern campaigns, was already waiting. A tall, thin, bald man in his early forties, he exuded a quiet authority. His stern features were softened only by the weariness in his eyes.

"Team," Salloway began, nodding as they entered.

He gestured for them to sit.

Jake remained standing.

"Mission only partly complete sir. Miriam and her family are safe. In the air as we speak".

"Good work," Salloway replied, though his tone suggested little room for celebration, "and Tariq?"

Jake exchanged a glance with Leck before answering.

"Not with them, sir. Miriam said he went into the mountains with a British national. A woman named Evelyn Kane".

The Colonel's forehead wrinkled as he raised his eyebrows, but he didn't seem surprised. He tapped a folder on the table.

"I already know about Miss Kane. She arrived about a week ago on a civilian visa, listed as an archaeologist. And she's not just some random scientist digging in the dirt. She's former MI6".

The team exchanged surprised looks, but Jake simply crossed his arms.

"MI6? That explains a lot. Tariq's wife said she was looking for something and gave me this," he replied as he unravelled the paper and placed it on the table, "bloody hell!"

"What?" Lecky asked, his curiosity ignited.

"There's a lot of scribble here, but the words Garden of Eden are underlined...look," replied Jake.

The colonel's interest was suddenly ignited as he stood next to Jake and examined Evelyn's notes.

"Ancient ruins, secrets in the mountains...whatever it is, the Taliban are now aware of her, and they're on the move," Salloway added.

"They'll kill her," Leck responded, his deep voice cutting through the room.

Salloway nodded, his face expressionless.

"They will if they find her. And if she's compromised, she risks exposing whatever mission she's on - and putting more people in danger, including Tariq. In the end we are here to save *him*, so we can't let that happen".

He turned to a map on the wall, perused it for a few moments then circled areas near the Paghman Valley.

"We've got intelligence placing her last known location in this region as heading north west. No doubt Tariq's skills as a former interpreter and tracker are keeping them alive for now, but it's only a matter of time before the Taliban close in".

"Her notes mention Bamiyan as their first stop. What's our play boss?" Jake asked.

"You find them and bring them back," the Colonel said firmly, "alive".

Jake nodded.

"Understood. Any support?"

"You'll have artillery and some air cover if needed," Salloway replied, "but this is a retrieval, not a search and destroy, so keep it quiet".

The colonel paused for a moment.

"And Jake..." he locked eyes with the team leader, "if you can't bring them out, destroy whatever it is she's after. We can't risk it falling into the wrong hands".

The importance of the mission settled over the team.

Jake glanced at his men, and thought to himself.

"Hmmm...destroy the Garden of Eden...who'd have thought that would ever be a thing to do?"

"Righto boys," Jake said, his voice calm but determined, "we move fast and light. We find Miss Kane and Tariq, and we bring them home".

Leck clapped a hand on Jake's shoulder.

"Let's get to it."

The team rose as one, their mission clear. Outside, the chaotic scenes of the airport continued, but inside the room, there was nothing but purpose.

The de-brief was over, but the mission was just beginning. As the team exited the briefing room, the noise from the crowds seemed even louder. Jake spared one last glance toward the throngs of desperate people pressing against the fences, and then he turned his focus inward.

"Right, let's get sorted," he ordered.

The joint British and American team moved swiftly to the makeshift barracks near the secure zone, where rows of camp beds and stacks of military crates were crammed into a converted hangar. There, they shed their black urban gear and donned camouflage uniforms more suited for the harsh mountain terrain - lightweight but durable, with shades of grey and brown to blend in with the rocky landscape.

Lecky strapped on his tactical vest, securing magazines of 5.56mm ammunition. His towering frame seemed to shrink slightly under the weight of the equipment, but his movements were smooth and deliberate. Taylor, the medic, another American, double checked his medical kit, ensuring he had enough supplies for any wounds or injuries the team might sustain.

Although a team, each man had his role. Carter sat cross legged on the ground, his focus entirely on the sleek weapon laid out before him. The L115A3 sniper rifle was more than a tool; it was a precision instrument, a companion honed for the art of long range warfare. He gently ran a cloth along its barrel with the reverence of a craftsman tending to his finest creation. To him, and all others who had used it, the rifle was a marvel of engineering, firing a heavier 8.59mm round designed for unparalleled accuracy at extreme distances.

"Everything good, Carter?" Jake asked, as he tightened the straps on his vest.

"As good as gold sarge," Carter replied without looking up, his voice calm, almost detached. He adjusted the scope, its x3-x12 magnification ensuring he could track targets with precision whether in daylight or under the cover of night.

The weapon was designed for first round hits at 600 metres and harassing fire up to 1,100 meters. Carter had pushed those limits before, and he intended to do it again if needed.

A laser range finder rested next to him, along with a spotting scope and a compact tripod - all essential elements of the kit that had seen action in Afghanistan since its deployment in 2008. The rifle itself was an example of British ingenuity, withstanding harsh conditions while maintaining its lethality.

Carter leaned back, satisfied, and gave the rifle a final pat.

"Ready," he said, standing and slinging the weapon over his shoulder.

The others exchanged glances. They knew Carter's reputation; cool under pressure, a marksman who turned impossibly long distances into fatal certainty.

The team worked methodically as the mission preparations hit full stride. Amidst the activity, two figures stood out, Mackie and Parks, engrossed in their usual banter even as they loaded extra ammunition belts for the mounted weapons.

Mackie, a wiry Englishman with the unmistakable accent of a Liverpudlian, handled the belts like an expert, his expertise honed during his years in the Parachute Regiment before joining the SAS. Parks, in contrast, was bulkier, his hands rough and oil stained from years of tinkering with engines. A Green Beret and veteran of the Middle Eastern wars since they began in 2001, Parks had seen more than his fair share of action, and his hobby and knack for keeping vehicles running under the harshest conditions had saved countless missions - and lives.

"Are you sure you tightened the mounts this time, Yank?" Mackie teased, slinging a belt of 7.62mm rounds over his shoulder as he nodded toward the lead vehicle, "we don't want one of your machine guns flying off the back when we hit a bump our kid".

Parks grinned, his easygoing nature showing through.

"Don't worry, Limey. Everything's locked down. Just make sure you don't forget how to aim, huh? I don't want to do all the work again".

Mackie snorted, tossing another belt into the rear of the vehicle.

"You wish mate. Last time I checked, it was me pulling your American arse out of trouble in Iraq," said Mackie as he leaned closer, a mock serious expression on his face, "and don't forget, you're only here because we let you...Britain's satellite state and all that...if you know what I mean?"

"Satellite state, huh?" Parks retorted, laughing as he tightened the latch on the bonnet of the vehicle, "keep dreaming bud. We both know who calls the shots".

The two mens friendship had been forged over years of joint operations, and despite the constant ribbing, the respect between them ran deep. Parks had learned to trust Mackie's razor sharp instincts in battle, just as Mackie relied on Parks' ability to keep any vehicle running no matter how dire the situation. Parks' background as a Green Beret meant he brought a wealth of experience in unconventional warfare to the table, and his presence was as reassuring as it was practical.

"We're looking pretty good," Parks said, giving the front of the lead vehicle a satisfied slap.

Each of the three military all terrain vehicles was ready; spare jerry cans of fuel, mounted machine guns, tactical communications, and enough ammunition to take on a small army.

Mackie joined him, surveying their handiwork.

"Smashin' mate, but remember not to crash this time. I don't know if I like you that much to drag you out of another ditch".

Parks shot him a sidelong glance, shaking his head.

"Go home, Limey".

Mackie smirked.

"I think that's my line mate, but I can't anyway," Mackie replied, "someone's got to teach you how to do this job right".

The two shared a laugh as they returned to their tasks, their banter providing a moment of humour amidst the tension.

The team replenished their supplies - rations, water, night vision goggles, grenades, and communication devices. Jake and Lecky walked along the vehicles, inspecting every detail. They were both sergeants and although Jake was the patrol commander, he and Lecky had an understanding and mutual respect, each sharing command.

Once the vehicles were loaded, the small convoy rolled out of the hangar, heading for the flight line where a waiting Chinook helicopter loomed like a giant steel bird. The double rotor craft hummed loudly, its ramp lowered to receive the convoy.

Jake's headset crackled with the voice of the Chinook pilot.

"Ramp's down Alpha 21. Ready to embark".

"This is Alpha 21. Roger. Loading now, out," Jake replied.

One by one, the ATVs drove up the ramp and into the belly of the Chinook. Inside, the team worked quickly to secure the vehicles with heavy duty straps, the thudding roar of the rotors growing louder as the helicopter prepared for takeoff.

As the last strap was tightened, Jake climbed into the cockpit to speak directly with the pilot. The man, a wiry American captain with a patch reading *Callsign: Falcon*, gave him a nod.

"LZs are limited, but we'll put you down as close to Bamiyan as we can without attracting too much attention".

"Good luck with that one sir. Just keep us under the radar," Jake replied, "and we'll do the rest".

Moments later, the ramp lifted, sealing the team inside. The Chinook shuddered as it began its ascent, the roar of its engines drowning out the noise from the airport below.

Inside the cargo bay, the team sat silently on fold down benches, their expressions a mix of calm and focus. The dim red glow of the cabin lights cast shadows on their faces. Jake stood near the vehicles, doing one last check.

Leck broke the silence.

"Mountains at night. Always a party".

"Let's hope this one's quiet," Mackie replied, though his grip on his weapon suggested he didn't believe it.

Jake looked at his team, his voice only just heard through the low noise of the engines.

"This isn't just a retrieval, Evelyn Kane is MI6, and whatever she's after is important enough for people to kill over. We do this right, or not at all. Understood fellas?"

The raising of five individual thumbs was answer enough.

The Chinook dipped slightly as it gained speed, heading into the jagged embrace of the mountains. Below, the sprawling mayhem of Kabul was left behind, replaced by the dark, unwelcoming landscape of the Hindu Kush. The soldiers, who hadn't slept for over 24 hours, closed their collective eyes trying to grab as much rest as they could before touching down on terra firma again.

CHAPTER 4

WHERE ENLIGHTENMENT ONCE STOOD

Tariq eased the Land Cruiser to a stop on the dusty plateau overlooking Bamiyan. The sun had set but the glow from the full moon lit the area up like a huge flood light, casting long silvery shadows over the rugged cliffs, their pockmarked faces still bearing the wounds of the Taliban's destruction. Evelyn stepped out of the vehicle, a look of disbelief on her face as she gazed at the immense niches carved into the rock, the hollowed recesses in the cliff where the Bamiyan Buddhas had once stood. The statues, for centuries towering symbols of faith and enlightenment, were now gaping voids in the rock face, courtesy of the Taliban's ruthless campaign against cultural heritage.

"This is where they stood," Tariq said softly, his voice tinged with sorrow, "the Buddhas of Bamiyan, now reduced to just memories and rubble".

Evelyn approached the larger of the two niches and stood before them. As she tilted her head back, the sheer scale of the empty cavity filled her with both awe and despair, a lump suddenly coming to her throat as she gazed at the emptiness.

"To think these stood for over a thousand years," she murmured, her voice laced with sorrow, "witnesses to so much history, destroyed in an instant...a moment of hatred".

Tariq's expression was one of sadness and disappointment, his hands curling into fists.

"It was not just stone they destroyed," he said, "it was a piece of all of our souls".

His voice was low but seething with restrained anger.

Evelyn nodded.

"But, even with all of their hatred, they couldn't erase everything. There is still history here, hidden in the shadows".

"The clue said *where enlightenment once stood*. This has to be the place, but there is nothing here. You should have come years ago when the statues were still here Miss Kane," said Tariq.

"But what about the second part of the clue, *the sanctuary of life hidden from the hands of man*?" Evelyn asked as she and Tariq clicked on their torches.

"There are many caves here. *They* could be the sanctuary of which you speak," Tariq replied.

Their torch beams cut through the darkness as they began to explore the cliff side, moving behind the largest recess where the tallest Buddha had once stood. Along the rock wall, dozens of small caves revealed themselves; simple, unadorned openings that had once housed monks, artists, and pilgrims.

But as they scanned the caves, something caught Evelyn's eye. She stopped abruptly, raising her torch higher. Above one of the entrances, partially obscured by time and dust, was a faint Buddhist carving. It depicted a lotus blossom encircled by a halo, a symbol of enlightenment and purity.

"Tariq," she whispered, her voice trembling with anticipation, "this one".

Tariq turned, his torch beam joining hers as they illuminated the symbol.

He nodded.

"Yes...this is different. It must be important".

Together, they climbed the short narrow path which led to the cluster of ancient caves hidden at the rear of the larger statue's niche. Inside, the air was cool and bathed with the earthy scent of ancient stone. Shadows danced wildly across the walls as their torches flickered. Tariq moved ahead, ducking under the low entrance.

The moment they stepped inside, a shrill screech echoed from the darkness. Evelyn barely had time to register the sound before a flock of bats exploded from the shadows.

Evelyn screamed, throwing her arms over her head as the bats whooshed past, their wings brushing against her hair. Tariq stumbled back, shielding his face and flailing his arms.

"Alqarf! What was that?" he exclaimed, his usual calm shaken.

When the chaos subsided, Evelyn leaned against the wall, catching her breath.

"Well," she said, her voice still shaky, "that was... unexpected".

Tariq brushed himself off, regaining composure with a faint smile.

"Unexpected? I think I just lost ten years of my life... and my pride...but let us keep this between just the two of us...yes?"

Evelyn smirked despite herself.

"Only if you don't mention my scream".

"Agreed," Tariq replied with a small laugh.

They steadied themselves and pushed on along the passage. The torch beams swept across the cave walls, revealing faded murals, etched symbols and carvings that had somehow survived the centuries - many indecipherable, others clearly Buddhist in nature. The passage extended deeper than they had anticipated, its end shrouded in shadow. As they moved further along Evelyn's torch light revealed, in the far corner of the cave, a small alcove. She knelt beside it, finding what appeared to be fragments of a scroll, a stone tablet etched with inscriptions, and a collection of weathered relics.

"Is that anything of use?" Tariq enquired.

"No...no I don't think so," replied Evelyn, "let's carry on a bit further".

After several minutes of careful exploration, their lights fell upon a section of the passage blocked by collapsed debris. Above the obstruction was another carving - a more elaborate Buddhist symbol, glowing faintly as their beams lingered.

"This *has* to be it," Evelyn said, stepping closer.

Tariq crouched to inspect the pile of rubble.

"It is definitely blocked, and it looks unstable. We must be careful moving it. A wrong step could bring the whole thing down".

Evelyn tilted her head upwards, studying the barrier.

"If we start with the smaller rocks at the top we might be able to make a hole big enough to crawl through".

"Yes...you could be right," agreed Tariq.

They worked methodically, the occasional clang of stone against stone punctuating their efforts. At one point, Tariq paused, wiping sweat from his brow.

"If this does not work, maybe we should go and find some dynamite".

Evelyn shot him a dry look.

"Right, because blowing up the entrance we're trying to open is a brilliant idea".

"What is it you people say...I am just thinking outside of the box?" Tariq replied.

"With dynamite in the equation I have no doubt that a box or boxes will have *some* role to play," joked Evelyn.

Hours seemed to pass as they chipped away at the blockage, alternating between serious concentration and light hearted banter to keep spirits high. At one point, Evelyn sat back on her heels, brushing dust from her hands.

"What if this isn't even the right place?"

"It has to be," Tariq replied firmly, shifting a larger stone, "that carving is not there by accident. Trust yourself, Miss Kane. You have brought us this far".

Finally, after a particularly stubborn boulder gave way, the blockage crumbled enough to reveal a narrow opening. A rush of cool air greeted them, carrying with it the scent of ancient stone, as they scrambled through the hole.

Inside, their torches illuminated a hidden chamber, its walls covered in intricate carvings, Biblical pictures intertwined with Hebrew inscriptions, their meanings lost to time. Buddhist symbols and depictions of the lotus flower adorned the higher sections, suggesting an extraordinary fusion of cultures and beliefs.

Evelyn stepped forward, running her hand gently over the carvings.

"This...this is incredible," she murmured.

Tariq brushed his hand along the rough stone, searching for anything unusual.

Evelyn's pulse quickened as she recognised familiar elements from the professor's notes.

"Here," Evelyn called, her voice echoing in the dim chamber.

She pointed to a faded carving on the wall, lit up by a shaft of sunlight streaming through a crack in the rock. It depicted a constellation - a serpent coiled around two figures, a man and a woman holding a fruit. Beneath it, a series of inscriptions in a mix of ancient Persian and Sanskrit wound like a flowing river. A charcoal rubbing of a temple carving from the Hindu Kush was also replicated here, chiselled into the stone wall. Angelic figures with flaming swords stood guard over a gate flanked by rivers, eerily similar to the biblical imagery of Eden. Below the carving, she noticed a faint inscription, weathered but legible. Translated it read: *"Only the pure of heart may pass through the Veil of Creation"*.

"Look!" she whispered excitedly, her fingers tracing the words, "this matches the professor's notes".

Tariq looked closer at the first carving.

"The constellation of Adam and Eve," Tariq said, his voice flushed with wonder, "the serpent, the forbidden fruit...it is written that it is symbolic of humanity's origins".

Evelyn ran her fingers over the worn symbols beneath the carving.

"This script," she said, "it's a map of sorts. Look at the patterns - those aren't just rivers. They're pointing to a specific place".

Tariq bent closer, tracing the lines with his finger.

"The Euphrates and Tigris perhaps?" he muttered, recognising the ancient names embedded in the text, "and here, look, it mentions the Pishon and Gihon, the four rivers told of in Genesis. This could be the guide to the Garden of Eden".

Evelyn's heart raced.

"We're getting closer," she said, the realisation and excitement of their discovery bearing down on her, "but why would it be here, in a Buddhist site? And why the connection to Adam and Eve?"

Tariq shrugged.

"Perhaps these caves were once a sanctuary for knowledge, a crossroads of faiths and ideas. Buddhism flourished here, but this region was always a melting pot. Someone must have preserved this clue for future seekers like us".

Evelyn nodded, taking a photo of the carving and the inscriptions.

"Let's document everything and compare it to the maps we have. If this leads us to the rivers, we'll be one step closer to finding Eden".

Tariq crouched beside her, examining the cave walls with equal intensity.

"It confirms the direction," he said, pointing to a rough map carved onto a stone slab.

The depiction of a river junction was unmistakable, and beside it, the ominous warning: *"Beyond lies the realm of the divine. Turn back, lest you be unworthy"*.

Evelyn searched the walls in and around the alcove, eventually finding another map, chiselled into the cave wall, which mirrored the professor's diagram. To the outer edges were faint marks that appeared to correlate with stars, hinting at a celestial alignment above a mountain peak.

"This has *got* to be it," Evelyn said, her voice a mixture of wonder and hope, "every clue leads here. The mountain, the constellation - it all fits".

Tariq's eyes scrutinised the symbols with a quiet admiration.

"It seems your professor was right," he said softly, "but this is only the beginning. We must tread very carefully from here".

Evelyn turned to him, her torch casting a warm glow on her face, and nodded her agreement as they stood together.

"The heavens will be your guide," she murmured, recalling the professor's final note.

Tariq leaned back, his expression contemplative.

"The clues are leading us toward the rivers. If these are tied to the Garden of Eden, then we are on the right path. But the Tigris and Euphrates flow through Turkey and Iraq?"

Evelyn nodded, her mind racing.

"Yes, but what if it is a trick to send the unworthy in the wrong direction, and maybe some of the clues the professor mentioned are also designed to throw seekers off the true path? Perhaps the rivers have their source *within* the garden? But I am more intrigued by the constellation of Adam and Eve - the stars touch the earth. I think it is all connected somehow and simpler than we think".

"So the rivers may be hidden do you think?" asked Tariq.

Evelyn took out the professor's journal and began flicking through the pages.

"Here it is...the Panjshir Valley...the Valley of Lost Rivers," she said, her finger tracing a sketch of an ancient map, "if the rivers are under the ground and once flowed into paradise, then surely this is where we must go?"

Evelyn thought for a moment then flicked through a few more pages of the journal.

"I recall something about a key...hang on...yes...here it is...*within the house of the rivers you will find the key that lights the way*".

They exchanged a glance.

"So there must be an underground river that houses some key or other...a torch maybe...a marker perhaps?" said Evelyn.

"It is worth a try," replied Tariq, "after all the answers we seek are hidden in the landscape that surrounds us".

Evelyn stood, brushing the dust from her hands.

"Let's keep going then. The stars and rivers won't wait for us to catch up".

Tariq gave a faint smile.

"You are beginning to sound like a real adventurer Miss Kane".

Evelyn grinned back.

"And I have the best guide in the mountains".

Tariq smiled a grateful smile.

"But first we must close up the entrance again to prevent prying eyes".

Evelyn nodded, although somewhat reluctantly as she thought of lifting the heavy rocks back in to place.

As they left the cave and returned to the Land Cruiser, they didn't know yet that they were being hunted, or that danger lurked closer than they imagined. But for now, their focus was on the path ahead, and the ancient secrets waiting to be uncovered.

The moonlight was still casting long shadows across the ancient site as Tariq looked toward the horizon, his instincts prickling.

"We should move and find somewhere safe to camp," he said, "if anyone saw us arrive, they might become curious. The Taliban destroyed this place for a reason - they would not want people poking around here".

Evelyn hesitated but nodded, as they climbed back into the truck, she cast one last look at the empty niche. Despite the destruction, the site still exuded a quiet strength, as if its secrets were waiting for the right moment to be revealed.

The vehicle roared to life, kicking up dust as it sped away from Bamiyan; but their journey had not gone unnoticed. Far in the distance, a lone figure on a motorbike watched their retreating silhouette before turning back toward the east.

The night sky gently hugged the rugged terrain of the Hindu Kush, its sharp peaks still crowned with a halo of silvery moonlight. Evelyn and Tariq stood at the edge of their makeshift camp, a small fire crackling between them, its warmth barely pushing back the encroaching chill of the mountain air. Above them, the heavens stretched wide, an infinite tapestry of stars shimmering against the velvety darkness.

Evelyn looked skyward, the glow of the firelight painting her features in gold and shadow.

"It's stunning isn't it?" she whispered, her voice soft, "I have never seen a night sky like this".

Tariq, sitting cross-legged beside the fire, followed her gaze.

"The mountains here have their own stories," he said, "the stars, too. They say if you look closely, they can guide you, not just in the physical sense, but in understanding your path".

She pulled her journal from her bag, flipping to the page where she had jotted a note from the professor's letter: *"Look to the heavens; the star that preserves and the moon that heals will light the way."*

Her eyes darted between the journal and the sky.

"The professor mentioned celestial markers...but I didn't realise how literal he might have been".

Tariq chuckled lightly.

"You mean the story of Soma and Vishnu?"

She looked at him, intrigued.

"You know it?"

He gestured toward the glowing crescent moon hanging low in the sky.

"Soma, the moon, is said to be the elixir of life. It guides the soul through its phases, like the moon itself, ever changing yet eternal".

He pointed higher, toward a cluster of stars forming a faint harp-like shape.

"And there...that could be Vishnu's constellation. Vishnu is the preserver, the balance. His light steadies even the most turbulent times".

Evelyn squinted, the harp-like shape coming into focus. She couldn't shake the feeling that the professor had intended this moment, that this sky was as much a part of the journey as the rugged terrain beneath her feet.

"The preserver and the elixir..." she murmured, "if this isn't a sign, I don't know what is".

Tariq's voice softened.

"Some believe Soma and Vishnu are more than celestial symbols. They say they are the ancient forms of Adam and Eve, their essences mirrored in the heavens. Soma, like Eve, is tied to the essence of life, and Vishnu, like Adam, embodies balance and creation".

"Adam and Eve!?" exclaimed Evelyn, almost in disbelief and questioning her own words, "that has to be it. I think we need to follow the stars".

"Just like the three wise men in your Bible?" replied Tariq.

"Exactly, and travellers and seafarers of old...maybe the key will be a marker to confirm Eden's location... perhaps even something through which starlight will shine".

A sudden gust of wind sent a chill through the air, making the fire flicker. Tariq's expression grew solemn.

"In this land, the old stories hold power. We follow them not just because they guide us, but because they remind us to tread carefully. Too much curiosity has a price".

Evelyn didn't reply. Instead, her gaze was drawn back to the moon, its light reflected on the icy ridges of the peaks.

"Maybe that's why it's Soma and Vishnu," she said quietly, "life and balance, guiding us through the unknown".

The Chinook roared through the darkness, its twin rotors slicing the thin mountain air with a rhythmic, pounding drone. Hugging the rugged slopes of the Hindu Kush, the massive helicopter seemed almost out of place in the narrow valleys, its dark silhouette a fleeting shadow against the tall mountain peaks. The pilots kept the aircraft low, weaving through the terrain with precision born of years of experience, using the mountains themselves as cover.

Inside, the cabin vibrated with the noise of the turning rotors. The soldiers sat in contemplative silence, their equipment strapped to their bodies, their faces striped with green and brown camouflage cream. Red lights bathed the interior, casting deep shadows that danced with the movement of the aircraft. Jake leaned forward, his voice cutting through the noise as he addressed his team.

"Listen fellas, as always we'll treat this like a hot LZ. The moment that ramp drops, we are out of here. No delays, no mistakes. Get into all round defence as soon as we hit the ground. All clear?"

A chorus of nods and murmured affirmatives followed, the men tightening the straps on their helmets and re-checking their weapons.

The Chinook banked sharply, the mountains seeming to close in on either side. Outside, the darkness was absolute, broken only by the faint glow of starlight reflecting off patches of snow on distant peaks. The crew chief gave a thumbs up from the rear, signalling that they were approaching the landing zone.

As the helicopter slowed, the downdraft from its rotors kicked up a storm of dust and loose gravel, as the six men clambered on to their ATVs. Hovering just above the uneven ground, the Chinook's ramp lowered with a mechanical whine. In a flash, the three ATVs roared to life, their engines a sharp counterpoint to the thunderous blades above. One by one, they sped down the ramp and leapt into the darkness, their headlights off to maintain stealth.

Once clear of the helicopter the soldiers dismounted and quickly formed a defensive perimeter, around their vehicles, their weapons trained on the shadows, searching for any sign of movement. The crew chief gave a final nod from the ramp as the Chinook's engines surged. The ramp rose, sealing the cabin, and the helicopter lifted off, disappearing into the night as swiftly as it had arrived.

Jake gave a hand signal for the team to regroup.

"LZ's clear, thank God" he whispered, "righto, mount up and let's make like a shepherd and get the flock out of here".

The ATVs purred quietly as the team manoeuvred them into the nearby countryside, searching for a defensible lying up position. They eventually found a narrow depression, about a mile away from the landing zone, shielded by boulders and sparse vegetation. Jake raised a hand to halt the convoy.

"This'll do," he said.

The team dismounted, working quickly and efficiently despite their lack of sleep. Camouflage netting and scrim were draped over the ATVs, breaking up their outlines against the rocky backdrop, and preventing any shine which may give them away. Within minutes, the vehicles were camouflaged, blending like a chameleon into their surroundings.

Lecky divided the men into shifts, assigning four to sleep while two acted as sentries, their eyes and ears attuned to the night. Wrapped snugly in their sleeping bags, the resting soldiers drifted into an uneasy sleep, the thoughts of the mission and the constant danger lurking in the night, prevailing on them even in slumber.

Above, the stars glimmered coldly, indifferent to the team below. The Hindu Kush loomed like an ancient sentinel, its peaks guarding secrets as old as time itself. Somewhere out there, in the labyrinth of valleys and passes, Tariq and Evelyn unknowingly waited. The team had no intention of leaving them behind.

CHAPTER 5

HUNTED

The soft hues of dawn painted the sky in shades of pink and orange as Evelyn stirred in her sleeping bag. The faint chirping of birds and the cold morning air greeted her as she blinked herself awake. The camp was quiet, save for the occasional rustle of dry heather in the breeze. She sat up, running a hand through her hair, and looked around. The vehicle was parked nearby, covered with a hastily draped tarp to blend into the rocky terrain.

Moments later, Tariq emerged from the shadows, his movements purposeful and quiet. He had been gone for nearly an hour, circling the area to ensure they hadn't been followed or stumbled upon in the night. His rifle was held at the ready, the butt firm against his shoulder, and his eyes searched the camp before meeting hers.

"Good morning Miss Kane," he said, as if it was just a normal day.

"You scared me," Evelyn said, pulling her jacket tighter against the morning chill, "do you always sneak up on people like that?"

Tariq smirked faintly, setting his weapon down and crouching near the remnants of last night's fire.

"Force of habit," he replied, "but everything is clear. No tracks, no signs that anyone has been near us".

Evelyn breathed a sigh of relief.

"Good. I don't think I could have handled another scare after that fellow in Kabul".

Tariq's expression softened slightly as he pulled a small pot and their modest supply of tea from his pack.

"You handled yourself well," he replied, "better than most".

Evelyn arched a brow, watching him as he worked to rekindle the fire.

"Was that a compliment?"

Tariq chuckled.

"It must not go to your head. Now, help me with breakfast. We have a long day ahead".

The two shared a quiet meal of flatbread, spicy lamb, and tea, their conversation light but touched with the unspoken urgency of their task. Evelyn asked about the route ahead, and Tariq described the terrain and potential challenges, his words painting a picture of steep mountain passes and narrow valleys.

As the sun rose higher, bathing the landscape in golden light, they packed up the camp. Tariq meticulously ensured no trace of their presence was left behind, while Evelyn checked the supplies in the vehicle.

"I still can't believe how you navigate all this without a GPS," she remarked as she closed the rear door of the hatchback.

"Experience," Tariq replied simply, climbing into the driver's seat, "and luck, sometimes".

Evelyn climbed into the passenger side, the seat now familiar yet no less uncomfortable.

"Well, let's hope your luck holds out," she said, half joking.

"It has to," Tariq replied, starting the engine, "we do not have another choice".

The truck rumbled to life, and they began their journey once more, the rocky landscape stretching endlessly ahead of them. The excitement of the previous day lingered, though neither spoke of it directly.

As they passed a narrow valley, Tariq suddenly braked hard. The truck skidded to a stop, and Evelyn's heart leaped into her throat. She grabbed the seat again, her knuckles white.

"What's wrong?" she whispered, her voice barely heard over the engine's roar.

Tariq's hand hovered over the gear stick, his eyes darting to the rear view mirror.

A small cloud of dust billowed from the road a few miles in the distance.

"We're being followed," he muttered under his breath.

Evelyn tensed and wound down her window. The hair on the back of her neck suddenly stood up as she strained to hear anything out of the ordinary. There was nothing but the sound of the wind howling against the truck's metal frame.

"Are you sure?" she asked.

Tariq didn't answer immediately. Instead, he reached into the glove compartment and pulled out a small, weathered map. He unfolded it slowly, his eyes flicking over the markings. Evelyn could see that he was tense, his fingers trembling ever so slightly as he traced the route they had planned.

"They know we are heading into the mountains," Tariq said, "no doubt the Taliban will have scouts up ahead, and they have likely already heard about the map. We have to move quickly".

"The map...but how?" Evelyn asked, for it had been safely tucked away in her back pack. Then she thought about their stop at the market and the man with the camera and knife.

"We may have his camera, but he obviously memorised a few words on the map".

It was now apparent that spying eyes had done some prying; but why didn't they just *steal* the map? Her journal had been in her trouser pocket. Perhaps they needed that?

Without another word, Tariq slammed the truck into gear and sped forward, the tyres flicking up dust in a cloud behind them. Evelyn held on, her heart palpitating as the truck rumbled over the rocky path.

The mountain pass ahead was the only route through the rough, uneven terrain, but it was also treacherous. Narrow roads wound through steep cliffs, and one wrong turn could send a vehicle tumbling down the side of the mountain.

As they approached the first series of bends, Evelyn's mind raced. She thought of the map, of the ancient garden, of what lay ahead. But the deeper they went into the mountains, the more her thoughts turned to the danger that was possibly closing in behind them. Every shadow, every moan and squeak of the truck's engine, seemed to signal their pursuers' arrival.

At the summit of the first ridge, they came to a halt. Tariq turned off the engine, his face imprinted with a look of purposefulness as he leaned forward, eyes narrowed, listening intently. Evelyn couldn't hear anything, but she knew what he was doing.

Tariq had grown up among these mountains, and his instincts were sharper than anyone else's.

"They're getting closer," he said softly, turning the key as the engine roared back in to life, "we cannot afford to stop now".

As the daylight was fading the driving became more treacherous, but, for their own safety, Tariq switched off the headlights and slowed down to a speed of 10 miles per hour. Although worrying, Evelyn understood his reasoning. Light travels far at night so without it their pursuers could no longer see them, or may even be lulled in to believing that they had halted for the night. Their speed too might be slow, but at least it prevented them falling foul of an unseen bend or long drop into the valley below.

Their snail like pace, however, was no help. As they rounded a blind corner, Tariq hit the brakes hard. A goat herder and his flock appeared suddenly, the animals spilling across the road like an avalanche. The Land Cruiser skidded, tyres struggling for grip on the loose road surface, and the vehicle veered sharply toward the edge of the road, the wheels catching on the uneven ground.

"Hold on!" Tariq yelled.

The Land Cruiser tipped, the world tilting wildly before slamming to a halt against a boulder. Dust filled the air as Evelyn coughed, her hands trembling as she unbuckled her seatbelt.

"Are you all right?" Tariq asked, his voice tight with concern.

"I think so," she replied, brushing dirt from her shirt, "it's a good job you were driving slowly as we'd surely have gone over".

Speed may have saved them from tumbling into the valley below, but the vehicle, however, was beyond saving - the axle was twisted, the front crumpled against the mammoth rock.

Evelyn glanced over to the goat herder who hastily gathered his flock and ushered them down the road without so much as a backward glance.

"Charming. Thanks for your help!" Evelyn shouted towards him.

Tariq shook his head.

"We walk from here," Tariq said, retrieving their packs from the wreckage, "but first we must make the Taliban think we have driven on...or worse".

Evelyn looked at the Land Cruiser then moved her gaze to Tariq.

"You don't mean?"

Tariq laughed quietly, peering over the edge.

"Yes I do. We must push the truck over the side".

As Tariq's words sank in, Evelyn blinked at him, incredulous.

"You want us to push a two ton vehicle off a cliff? Are you serious?"

Tariq gave her a flat look, dusting his hands on his trousers.

"Unless you want to stay and wait for the Taliban to catch up...yes. Now, help me".

Evelyn groaned, muttering something about ridiculous plans and insane guides as she walked around to the back of the Land Cruiser. Tariq had already positioned himself against the crumpled rear bumper, inspecting the precariously tilted vehicle. The front tyres were barely clinging to the stony edge, the whole truck balancing as though deciding whether to tumble or stay put.

"This thing weighs as much as a house," she grumbled, placing her hands hesitantly against the scratched metal, "do you think we'll even budge it?"

Tariq didn't answer. He just braced his feet and leaned into the truck, giving it a hefty shove. The Land Cruiser groaned like an old man being rudely awoken but didn't move an inch.

Evelyn huffed, joining him in pushing with all her might. The truck inched forward, the screech of metal on rock sending shivers down her spine. It teetered ominously, the rear wheels grinding against the dirt.

"Are you sure this is safe?" Evelyn asked, struggling against the weight, "what if it bounces back and crushes us?"

"It won't," Tariq replied through gritted teeth, though his expression suggested he wasn't entirely confident, "now, push harder".

Evelyn gave a sarcastic laugh.

"Sure, hang on while I just summon my superhuman strength! Maybe I'll throw it over by myself while I'm at it".

Tariq smirked.

"If you are going to talk, at least use your breath for pushing".

The truck suddenly shifted, the rear end rising slightly as the front tyres finally lost their grip. Evelyn yelped as she stumbled back, watching in both horror and pride as the Land Cruiser wobbled precariously on the edge.

"Almost there!" Tariq called, now pushing with all his weight.

Evelyn lunged back into position, adding her strength to his. With a final grinding groan, the truck tipped forward, teetering on the brink. For a split second, it seemed to hang in midair before gravity took over, the Land Cruiser plunging over the edge, tumbling in slow motion, cart wheeling down the rocky slope.

The crash was deafening as the vehicle slammed into the side of the cliff, flipping end over end. Dust and debris exploded into the air with every impact. Evelyn winced as the sound of shattering glass and twisting metal echoed through the range.

Finally, with a last, resounding thud, the Land Cruiser came to rest hundreds of feet below, crumpled like a discarded toy among the rocks.

"Well," Evelyn said after a moment, brushing dirt off her hands, "that was... dramatic".

Tariq straightened, his eyes scanning the wreckage below.

"If the Taliban see that they will assume we are dead," he said, looking up to the starry night sky and mouthing a prayer to himself.

"Fantastic," Evelyn exclaimed, "but perhaps next time, let's find a solution that doesn't involve nearly giving me a heart attack".

Tariq smirked, slinging his pack over his shoulder.

"We must get off this road. Come Miss Kane, the mountains won't wait".

As they started walking, Evelyn glanced back at the smashed vehicle, its ruined frame barely visible in the growing dusk.

"I hope that goat herder appreciated the show," she muttered.

Tariq chuckled quietly.

"If he is clever, he has already forgotten he ever saw us...I hope".

They abandoned the truck to its fate and made their way on foot, clambering off the road and on to the track made by the flocks of goats which grazed in the ranges, carrying only the essentials - water, food, and, most importantly, the map. The air was thin, and Evelyn's breath came in short gasps as they ascended the mountain trail. Tariq led the way, swift and sure, his knowledge of the terrain giving them an edge.

Hours passed, and the further they climbed, the more the landscape changed. The peaks of the Hindu Kush loomed above them in the dark, graced with snow at the higher elevations. Below, the valley was a maze of small villages, the lights from their simple brick houses dotting the landscape like scattered toys.

The ascent was brutal. The rocky path seemed to twist endlessly, the air growing thinner with every step. Evelyn focused on putting one foot in front of the other, her thoughts fluttering. How had the Taliban found them so quickly? If indeed it was the Taliban. Was it mere chance, or had someone in the last village betrayed them?

Behind her, Tariq moved easily, his steps silent despite the loose gravel on the track.

"We are not far," he said over his shoulder, "there is a cave ahead. We can hide there until morning".

The cave was little more than a shallow indentation in the rock face, but it provided both shelter and cover. Evelyn slumped against the wall, her chest heaving, whilst Tariq crouched at the entrance, his rifle resting across his knees.

"Why would they come all the way out here?" Evelyn asked, her voice hushed.

Tariq hesitated before answering.

"As I said before, the Taliban believe Eden is real, but they see it as a threat to their power. If the garden exists, it could prove that their teachings are flawed, that their version of faith is a tool for control".

Evelyn laughed.

"A tool for control? I think the world already knows how lying and controlling they are".

"Perhaps, but the people here do not. They fear the Taliban and their version of Islam," Tariq replied.

Evelyn frowned.

"So they want to destroy it?"

Tariq nodded.

"Yes. If they find it, they will burn it to the ground".

Evelyn's stomach churned at the thought. She had always believed the garden, if it existed, would be a place of peace, a sanctuary. The idea of it being reduced to ash was almost unbearable.

Evelyn began to shiver as she searched in the dark for her torch.

"What are you doing?" Tariq whispered.

"I'm looking for my torch and some matches to start a fire," she replied.

"No!" Tariq whispered gruffly, "from now on no light or fires at night".

Evelyn now had one of those light bulb moments.

"Yes...yes...I'm sorry," she replied, "I'm used to sitting in an office. I forgot about light giving away our location. Thank you Tariq. You are a good teacher".

Tariq nodded his appreciation.

"Get some sleep Miss Kane. I'll wake you in two hours for your stag".

"Stag?" asked a surprised Evelyn.

"Yes. It is what the British call being on sentry or on watch," relied Tariq.

"Oh, I see. Soldiers *do* have some strange terminologies don't they?" said Evelyn as she quietly unfurled her sleeping bag, "I'll see you in two hours then".

CHAPTER 6

BETRAYED

The young goat herder whistled and called to his nimble, shaggy flock as they followed him obediently down the winding mountain road. Their soft bleats and the occasional scrape of hooves on the road were the only sounds in the cool night air. He had thought long and hard about what he had seen - about the crash, the foreign woman, and the Afghan man. Curiosity gnawed at him, outweighing his usual caution.

The boy's young eyes spotted the glow of campfires ahead, and soon he reached the convoy. His flock slowed behind him as he cautiously approached the armed men clustered near the trucks. He hesitated at first, watching them from the shadows until one of the men noticed him.

"What's this?" the man called out, gripping his rifle but keeping it lowered.

The boy stepped into the firelight, his small frame illuminated.

"I saw a crash on the road above," he blurted out uncontrollably in Pashto, his voice trembling, "a truck nearly hit my goats. There was a man and a woman".

Rashid stepped forward from the group, his tall silhouette cutting an imposing figure. His dark eyes gleamed with interest as he studied the boy.

"A woman? Foreign?"

The boy nodded, rubbing his hands together in the cold night air.

"Yes. She was pale skinned. The man looked Afghan".

"Where was this?" Rashid asked, his tone calm but probing.

"Up the road, not far," the boy replied, pointing over his shoulder, "the truck stayed on the road after the crash. I left straight away".

Rashid raised an eyebrow, considering the boy's words. Finally, he pulled a small coin from his pocket and tossed it to the boy.

"Take this and go. Tell no one of what you've seen".

The boy caught the coin and hurried back to his flock, herding them quickly down the road as Rashid turned to his men.

"Get some rest," he ordered, "at dawn, we move".

The convoy rumbled up the steep and winding road, the morning sun spilling over the mountain peaks. Rashid sat in the lead truck, his eyes concentrated on the narrow road ahead. When the skid marks from the crash scene came into view, he motioned for the driver to stop.

The vehicles halted, and Rashid stepped out, his boots making a crunching sound on the stony ground. He surveyed the road. The faint arcs of tyre marks veered sharply to one side, and bits of shattered glass glinted faintly in the sunlight. Rashid strode to the edge and peered over. Far below, the crumpled remains of a truck lay wedged between rocks.

His second in command, Vakil, joined him.

"It looks like it did not stay on the road for long," Vakil said, shielding his eyes from the sun.

Rashid crossed his arms, his brow wrinkling in thought.

"The boy said it was still on the road when he left. If it fell later, where are the bodies?"

Vakil looked down toward the wreckage.

"Maybe animals got to them. Or they burned".

"No," Rashid said firmly, "they are alive. I want some men down there to check".

Three fighters volunteered, using lengths of rope to anchor themselves as they descended the steep slope. Rocks shifted and tumbled as they climbed down, gripping onto shrubs and jagged outcroppings to keep from falling. One man cursed under his breath as his boot slipped, sending a cascade of pebbles clattering into the gorge below.

When they reached the truck, they found it empty. The windscreen was shattered, the seats torn, and the cab bent out of shape, but there were no signs of blood - or its occupants. One of the men climbed inside and searched, but all he found was a dented jerry can and an empty crate.

"They're gone!" one of the fighters called up to Rashid, his voice echoing up the slope.

The men scrambled back up, their clothes dusty and damp with sweat. When they reported their findings, Rashid rubbed a hand over his face, his patience thinning.

"They must have gone on foot. But over land or on the road?" he muttered, "Vakil, take a vehicle ahead. If they are on the road, they could not have got far. Check for tracks or signs of them. We will wait here until you report back".

Unaware of the Taliban's discovery, Tariq and Evelyn were packing away their equipment further along the mountain trail. The early morning sunlight filtered into the shallow cave, casting long shadows on the rocky ground. Evelyn stretched, her back aching from the hard ground, while Tariq prayed after his return from his routine patrol.

"The area is clear," Tariq said, his expression calm but focussed.

Evelyn looked up from stuffing her sleeping bag in to its sack.

"Do you think they're still looking for us?"

"They will not stop. But hopefully they think we are on the road," Tariq replied, his tone resigned, "but at least we are ahead of them...for now".

Evelyn nodded, trying to push away the unease creeping into her thoughts.

"Then we'd better keep moving hadn't we?"

Tariq handed Evelyn her food silently, his eyes searching the horizon, as they shared a quick breakfast of tinned beans and dried dates, washing it down with water from their dwindling supply.

"We need to find more water," Evelyn said, breaking the silence.

"There is a stream a few miles ahead," Tariq said, "if we are lucky, we will reach it before midday".

"An underground one would be nice," Evelyn replied, hopefully.

She glanced at him, trying to gauge his mood.

"You always seem so sure of where we're going. How do you do it?"

He gave her a faint smile, the first she'd seen in days.

"I was raised in these mountains. They are my home".

Evelyn smirked, shaking her head.

"Well, let's hope your home keeps us alive".

As they packed up and resumed their journey on foot, the rising sun illuminated the irregular path ahead. Evelyn looked back once, the faint outline of the cave disappearing into the rocky hillside. She grasped the straps of her pack, leaned forward, and quickened her pace to keep up with Tariq.

They had no idea how close their pursuers were - or how much the wrecked truck had slowed them down.

Rashid stood by the remaining truck in his convoy, his arms folded as the sun climbed higher in the sky. The air was heavy with the heat of the day, the peaks of the mountains framing the narrow road where the vehicles were parked. A few of his men milled around, leaning against their trucks and staring across the valley, their eyes flicking to Rashid and back again. They knew better than to speak; he was not a patient man, and they feared him.

"How long does it take to drive along a road?" Rashid muttered under his breath, pacing back and forth.

Every so often, he stopped to peer up the road, following its winding path along the mountain side, shielding his eyes against the glare.

The men he had sent ahead to search for the fugitives had been gone for hours, and there was no sign of them. He scowled, kicking a loose stone that tumbled off the edge of the road and into the valley below.

Meanwhile, Vakil and the two men Rashid had dispatched drove their truck slowly along the winding mountain road. The landscape was dry and unyielding; steep cliffs dropped away to rocky gorges, and the occasional scrubby tree clung stubbornly to the crags. The heat was stifling, and dust swirled around the tyres as they drove on.

Hours passed, and the road twisted deeper into the mountains. The men exchanged few words, their eyes searching the edges of the road for any sign of travellers. Finally, as the sun began its descent, they spotted a cluster of houses clinging to the hillside. A small village.

As they rolled into the village, the air grew tense. The few villagers outside stopped what they were doing and stared, their expressions wary. A woman quickly ushered her children inside, and an old man froze, his hand gripping a walking stick.

The truck screeched to a halt, and the three men climbed out, rifles at the ready. Vakil shouted an order in Pashto.

"Gather here! Now!"

The villagers hesitated, their fear evident, but they obeyed. Soon, a small group stood before the armed men, their eyes wide with apprehension.

Vakil addressed them sharply.

"We are looking for a woman...a westerner. She's travelling with an Afghan man. Have they passed through here in the last day?"

The villagers looked warily at each other, their faces pale. Finally, the old man with the walking stick stepped forward, his voice trembling.

"No one has come this way. We would have seen them".

Vakil squinted at him, then looked around at the others.

"Is he telling the truth?"

A woman in the group nodded quickly.

"No one has come. We swear it".

Vakil stared them down for a long moment, then spat on the ground.

"If you are lying, we will be back," he said coldly, then signalled to his companions, and they climbed back into the truck.

As the vehicle roared away, the villagers breathed a collective sigh of relief.

By the time the searchers returned to the convoy, the sun was dipping low on the horizon. Rashid's expression darkened as he saw them pull up.

"You have taken your time," he snapped, stepping forward as they climbed out of the truck, "what did you find?"

Vakil shook his head.

"Nothing. We drove all the way to a village, but no one there has seen them".

Rashid's lips thinned, and his gaze turned toward the mountains looming above.

"Then they must have left the road. They are on foot now."

He shouted orders to his men.

"Two of you will take the vehicles higher into the mountains and wait for instructions. The rest of us are going on foot".

As his men scrambled to prepare, Rashid walked a few steps down the road, his eyes scanning the rocky landscape before him. The road was bordered by steep embankments and scattered boulders, but here and there, narrow goat tracks twisted up into the wilderness.

He knelt beside one of the tracks, brushing aside a layer of dust and debris. There, faint but visible, was the outline of a boot print. His eyes narrowed as he studied it. The size was small - likely a woman's.

"This way," he murmured to himself, rising to his feet.

He followed the track for about 20 metres, stopping to inspect the ground every so often. It was faint, but he could just make out a trail leading higher into the mountains.

Rashid turned his attention upward, his eyes narrowing as he traced the razor sharp peaks and ridges.

"They could not have gone far," he muttered to himself, his tone confident.

But in reality, Tariq and Evelyn were at least 15 hours ahead, their trek during the night and their early start, and knowledge of the terrain, giving them a significant advantage.

The sun was nearly gone now, the sky painted in hues of orange and purple. Rashid turned back to his men, his decision made.

"We stay here for the night," he announced, "tomorrow, we continue the chase".

As the men set up camp for the night, Rashid stood at the edge of the track, staring into the growing darkness. In his mind, the western woman was a liability - she wouldn't last long in these mountains. He allowed himself a small, confident smile.

"We will find them soon enough," he thought.

He had plans for Evelyn, to use her as a tool for propaganda. If captured alive, she would be paraded as evidence of foreign interference, then executed to warn others. Rashid and his Taliban masters hoped that this would strengthen the Taliban's grip and discourage further challenges to their rule.

Little did he know, Tariq and Evelyn were already well on their way. He had underestimated Tariq's knowledge of the mountains and Evelyn's resilience, setting the stage for a deadly game of cat and mouse in the harsh Afghan terrain.

As the Taliban's truck had been rumbling along distant roads in their search, Tariq and Evelyn had pushed onward, their journey through the mountains taking them closer to the Valley of the Lost Rivers. The path seemed never ending, winding through narrow trails that hugged the mountainsides. Loose dirt and stones shifted underfoot, and every step seemed to test their mettle.

Though Evelyn had never endured anything like this before, she kept up with Tariq, not wanting to let either of them down. Her muscles ached, her breathing came hard, but she matched his pace. Tariq glanced back occasionally, his eyes studying her. He had expected her to slow them down, but instead, he saw a strength that belied her appearance.

"You are stronger than I thought," he said at one point, his voice carrying a hint of admiration.

Evelyn managed a tired smile, wiping sweat from her brow.

"That's the nicest thing you've said to me all day".

The landscape changed subtly as they moved higher into the mountains. The air grew cooler, and sparse vegetation began to dot the rocky terrain - tufts of grass clinging to life against the odds. Occasionally, they came across narrow streams trickling down from unseen glaciers, the water ice cold and clear. Tariq paused at one such stream, motioning for Evelyn to refill her bottle and drink.

"We're making good time," he said as she knelt by the water, "if we can keep this pace, we'll reach the valley by tomorrow".

Evelyn nodded, splashing some water on her face before taking a long sip. The cold liquid was a welcome relief, but her body longed for rest. Despite her exhaustion, she scrambled uneasily to her feet and followed Tariq as he resumed their climb.

When they reached a small village nestled in a hollow between the peaks, Evelyn felt a flicker of hope. The sight of homes, no matter how modest, gave her a brief sense of normality. The villagers here seemed more open than the ones they had encountered before, but Evelyn could sense the unease in their eyes, their curiosity evident as they watched the pair approach.

While Tariq spoke with the elder in hushed tones, Evelyn noticed the children peeking out from behind their mothers' skirts, their wide eyes filled with curiosity and caution. But the whispers of "Taliban" that drifted through the air among the villagers quickly shattered any sense of peace, and she realised that her presence here wasn't entirely welcome.

After a few minutes, the elder gave a nod, indicating that they could rest.

"You cannot stay long," the elder said quietly, his voice hoarse, "the Taliban come through here every few days, searching for outsiders. You must move on".

There was no time to waste. They thanked the elder and departed quickly, continuing their trek through the mountains.

The journey grew harder as the sun dipped lower in the sky. The mountains cast long shadows, and the temperature plummeted, the wind biting at their exposed skin. When they finally found a rocky outcrop to shelter under, Evelyn dropped her pack with a sigh of relief.

It was not yet completely dark so Tariq unpacked his hexamine stove and lit a hexamine tablet which was heat enough, without the smoke or too much light to draw attention, to cook the boil in the bag rations that he had acquired during his time with the British. The tiny flame offered just enough heat, and Evelyn sat by its warmth, rubbing her hands together as she waited for the food to cook, the heat a welcome relief from the biting cold which was creeping in. The stars above began to appear one by one, twinkling in the clear sky. It was a beautiful sight, but Evelyn found little comfort in it.

"Do you think they're still looking for us?" she asked quietly, looking at Tariq.

He nodded.

"They will not stop. But we have the advantage now. They do not know where we are going".

Evelyn stared into the flickering flame, almost mesmerised, her thoughts jumping around in her head. She wasn't sure if it was courage or sheer exhaustion that kept her going, but as she sat under the vast expanse of stars, she promised herself she wouldn't give up.

For now, they had made progress - progress that might just buy them the time they desperately needed.

Arriving in the Panjshir Valley, the landscape before them was both tranquil and mysterious. Dry riverbeds meandered through the valley floor, their paths interrupted by patches of stubborn grass and smooth, pale rocks. Hidden streams whispered faintly from beneath the rocky terrain, the sound of water a gentle undercurrent in the otherwise still air. The valley walls loomed high, their surfaces weathered and carved out by time's careful hand.

Evelyn's eyes were drawn to a cluster of ancient petroglyphs cut into the stone, faint but distinctive. She ran her fingers lightly over the carvings, tracing shapes of animals, symbols, and human figures. Among them, a fragment of poetry caught her attention, its words written in an archaic dialect that seemed to shimmer with meaning:

"Rivers that quench the roots of eternity, Veiled beneath the earth's eternal weep".

"Tariq," Evelyn murmured, her voice tinged with excitement, "this...this is describing something beneath the surface".

Tariq stepped closer to take a look.

"Underground rivers?"

"Yes," she pointed to the last line, "this 'eternal weep', it's a waterfall. That has to be it".

Tariq nodded thoughtfully.

"This *is* the valley of lost rivers is it not?"

Evelyn's gaze turned upward, following the valley's contours until her eyes settled on a small, shimmering cascade spilling from a rocky outcrop in the distance. The waterfall was narrow, almost concealed by the surrounding stone, its waters catching the golden light of late afternoon.

"There," she said, as she pointed, "*that's* where we need to go".

The trek to the waterfall was slow, the terrain uneven and scattered with loose stones that threatened to slip beneath their boots. As they reached the base of the cascade, the sound of the rushing water grew louder, it's cool mist brushing their skin. Tariq knelt to examine the rocks near the edge, while Evelyn peered at the curtain of water, her heart beating fast with anticipation.

She stepped closer, reaching out to let the water flow over her fingers.

"There's something behind this," she said, her voice almost drowned by the roar of the falls.

Tariq stood and joined her as she pushed cautiously through the sheet of water, the cold spray soaking them both.

Behind the waterfall, the air was cool and damp, and a narrow opening revealed itself, partially obscured by moss and vines. Above the entrance there was a carving similar to the one at Bamiyan.

"Buddha is guiding us again," said Evelyn.

They squeezed through, and as their eyes adjusted to the dim light, the space beyond unfolded like a dream.

The cavern glimmered with faint reflections cast by the thin streams of water dripping from the ceiling. Crystalline formations stretched out like frozen rivers, their surfaces shimmering in hues of blue and white. A faint sound echoed through the chamber, the gentle murmur of flowing water beneath their feet.

Evelyn's breath caught as she spotted something etched into one of the crystal walls. Approaching carefully, she wiped a layer of condensation from the surface and revealed another series of carvings. These were unlike the ones in the valley; symbols arranged in a sequence that seemed almost mathematical. Among them, a single phrase stood out in a script she recognised from her research: *"The light of Nuristan awaits"*.

She turned to Tariq, her voice filled with wonder.

"This is it. This is leading us to the Crystal Caves of Nuristan".

Tariq glanced around the chamber, his expression wary but intrigued.

"I do not know of these caves, but I can take you to Nuristan," he said, "but we must move quickly, this valley will not stay safe for long".

Evelyn pondered.

"The light of Nuristan...I think we are looking for an object of some sort".

"I hope so Miss Kane. We seem to be travelling far for so little time at our destination," Tariq replied.

Evelyn laughed, then smiled.

"Patience dear Tariq. I'm sure all will be revealed soon enough".

Tariq and Evelyn resumed their journey through the hostile landscape, putting as much distance as possible between themselves and any potential pursuit. The terrain was tough - steep inclines, loose rock, and dry riverbeds that tested their stamina. Though exhausted, Evelyn still managed to keep pace with Tariq, her strength impressing him.

As twilight deepened, they found a sheltered spot nestled between two large boulders. Tariq gathered a few loose rocks to form a makeshift windbreak while Evelyn unrolled the sleeping bag from her pack. The night air carried a biting chill, and she pulled her jacket tighter around her shoulders.

Tariq lit a hexamine tablet, the small blue flame barely enough to cook their ration pack meal but enough to provide a sliver of warmth. Evelyn sat close, rubbing her hands together.

"You did well today," Tariq said, handing her a metal cup of tea.

Evelyn took it gratefully, blowing on the surface before taking a sip. The warmth spread through her, soothing her aching limbs.

"I won't lie, I'm exhausted. But I'm getting used to this".

Tariq gave a small nod, his gaze shifting to the darkened valley below.

"We shall rest for a few hours, then move at first light".

Evelyn nodded, then followed his gaze, her thoughts drifting to those who might be trailing them.

"Do you think they'll find the valley?"

Tariq's expression hardened slightly.

"If they do, they will not know where we have gone. But we should assume they are still searching".

They ate in silence, the crackling of the small flame the only sound between them. Then, as exhaustion finally won over, Evelyn curled up in her sleeping bag while Tariq took the first stag, listening for any movement in the darkness.

Rashid and his men had made steady progress, following any trace Tariq and Evelyn had left behind. They had questioned villagers along the way - most were reluctant to speak, but fear loosened tongues. Each account was the same, an Afghan man and a Western woman had passed through in a hurry, always moving towards the mountains.

By the time Rashid's group reached the valley, the sun had begun to dip behind the peaks. The dry riverbeds and craggy slopes offered no clear indication of which way their quarry had gone. Frustration flickered in Rashid's eyes as he searched the terrain with his eyes. Then, near the base of the waterfall, one of his men crouched, inspecting the ground.

"A footprint," the man muttered, "faint, but fresh".

Rashid stepped closer, studying the imprint. It was smaller than his own - a woman's, perhaps. His lips formed into a smile; unusual for him.

"They are close," he said, "but where would they go from here?"

The valley was vast, its dry riverbeds and rocky outcrops offering countless places to hide. His men fanned out, searching the ground for more signs of movement, but the fading light made it difficult.

One of his fighters gestured towards the waterfall.

"Could they have gone through there?"

Rashid turned to the waterfall, considering the possibility, the sound of rushing water filling the air, the fading daylight making it difficult to see clearly. It wasn't large, but the way the water cascaded down the rock face concealed whatever lay behind it. If they had hidden in the valley, this would be the perfect place. Without hesitation, he stepped forward, the cold mist dampening his clothes as he approached.

Drawing his rifle across his chest, and pointing the barrel downwards, he pushed through the curtain of water. The roar momentarily deafened him, and the chill sent a shudder through his frame. On the other side, the dim glow of twilight revealed a small cavern. Water trickled down the walls, pooling at his feet. He moved cautiously, sweeping the damp ground with his eyes for footprints.

Then he saw it.

Carved into the rock at the far end of the cavern were ancient markings. Petroglyphs, like the ones he had seen in other remote parts of the country. He stepped closer, running his fingers over the worn stone. Among the carvings, a few lines of text stood out. Though he could not fully decipher them, one word was jumping out at him; Nuristan.

He smirked to himself, a sense of satisfaction filling his mind. So that was their destination.

He turned and strode back through the waterfall, shaking the excess water from his sleeves. His men waited expectantly.

"They are heading to Nuristan," he said, his voice laced with confidence.

One of the fighters frowned.

"But that is a long way from here."

Rashid's smirk widened.

"On foot, it will take them days. But we will be ahead of them very soon".

He turned to two of his men.

"Go back to the trucks then travel into the mountains. Follow the main roads, see if they emerge anywhere along the way. The rest of us will track them on foot".

As the last of the light faded, Rashid cast one final glance toward the mountains. They were out there somewhere, exhausted, struggling across unfamiliar ground. He didn't believe for a second that a Western woman, or *any* woman for that matter, could keep pace for long.

"They will not get far," he muttered.

Then, signalling his men, he settled in for the night, confident that by sunrise, the hunt would truly begin.

Meanwhile, miles away, the special forces team were continuing their search. After investigating Bamiyan, they had discovered the wreckage of Tariq and Evelyn's truck. The vehicle lay grotesquely twisted at the bottom of the slope, but there was no sign of bodies; which suggested survival.

Determined to pick up the trail, they carried on to the nearest village, questioning the locals. What they found was unsettling - not reports of Tariq and Evelyn, but confirmation that the Taliban had passed through, asking about a Western woman and an Afghan man. The situation had escalated.

Realising they were falling behind, the team returned to the crash site, re-examining the surroundings. That was when one of the soldiers pointed to the ground.

"Here...look at this," he said.

In the dwindling light, a series of footprints were visible, leading away from the point where the truck had gone over the side. The tracks followed the narrow goat path, disappearing into the mountains.

Jake and Lecky crouched, and Jake traced the prints with his fingers.

"They're moving on foot," he murmured, "and judging from what those villagers said, they've got a good lead".

He straightened, glancing towards the mountains.

"We need to move fast though. If the Taliban are ahead of us, we may not get a second chance".

With that, the team set off along the narrow goat track, their three ATVs sending up a plume of dust as they weaved through the pitted country. The trail was rough but manageable at first, winding along the undulating track before climbing sharply into the mountains.

The further they went, the more treacherous the path became. Loose rocks tumbled away beneath their wheels, and sheer drops loomed on one side of the trail. Finally, after another mile of struggle, Jake signalled a halt. The track ahead was barely wide enough for a man to walk, let alone a vehicle.

"This is as far as we take the wheels I think boys," he said, "find cover for the ATVs and strip them of what we need".

The team sprang into action, hauling off their weapons, ammunition, and essential equipment. They pushed the ATVs off the trail, concealing them beneath a rocky overhang. Scrim, netting and scrub were thrown over them, the scrim weighted down by rocks and the camouflage nets pegged to the ground, blending them into the landscape. Satisfied with their work, Jake gave one final check before turning to his men.

"Time for a bit of a tab eh boys," he said.

Lecky scratched his chin.

"I thought you Brits said yomp when you were off on a hike?"

"No mate...that's the Royal Marines...us Toms tab," replied Mackie.

"Toms?" said Lecky, feeling more confused.

"Tommies...you know...Tommy Atkins?" Mackie tried to explain.

Lecky just shook his head.

"You Brits and your nicknames".

With a nod, the team shouldered their packs and set off up the track. More mountains emerged ahead, dark and imposing, as they pursued the only trail that would lead them to Tariq and Evelyn – hopefully before the Taliban found them first.

CHAPTER 7

SOME THINGS ARE NOT MEANT TO BE FOUND

The morning sun cast long shadows over the mountains as Evelyn and Tariq trudged forward along the slender path. The air was fresh, carrying the distant cry of an eagle circling high above the pointed peaks. The trail was nothing more than a footpath worn into the mountainside by centuries of animal and human foot traffic, with sheer drops plunging hundreds of feet into rocky ravines below.

Evelyn wiped her brow with the end of her scarf, peering down at the dizzying drop beside her. She was no stranger to hiking, but this was something else entirely.

"And I thought walking up Snowdon was scary," she thought to herself.

Every step required absolute focus. The loose soil and gravel made a noisy sound with every step, and the wind howled through the cliffs, tugging at her scarf.

Tariq moved ahead, his eyes scouring the path for any sign of danger. Evelyn followed closely behind, her legs burning from the almost endless climb. Then, without warning, her foot slid on a loose rock.

She gasped as she lost her balance, her arms flailing. Her boot scraped against the crumbling edge, sending a cascade of stones tumbling down into the abyss.

Tariq spun around just in time.

"Evelyn!"

She barely had time to react before his hand shot out, gripping her wrist in a vice-like hold. The muscles in his arm tensed as he anchored himself, pulling her away from the ledge. With one final heave, he yanked her up onto solid ground, and they both collapsed, breathing hard.

Evelyn's heart pounded as she stared at the spot where she had nearly fallen. Tariq released her hand but didn't move away.

"You must watch your footing," he said, his voice serious but not unkind.

She exhaled shakily and gave a half smile.

"Yeah, I figured that out," she replied as Tariq's words of alarm echoed through her mind, "did you know that you actually called me by my first name?"

Tariq studied her for a moment, then nodded, standing up.

"Did I? We *are* friends...no? Come...Evelyn...we still have far to go".

Evelyn smiled then took one last look at the drop, swallowing her fear, then clambered to her feet and followed.

Miles, and hours, behind them, Rashid and his men marched up the same treacherous path, their pace fast and almost unstoppable. The morning sun did little to warm the cold stone beneath their boots, and each turn in the trail revealed another sheer drop or a dangerous incline. Rashid's keen eyes searched the track, looking for any sign of Tariq and the woman.

Then he saw it; small scuffs in the dirt, barely noticeable. A slip? A disturbance in the dust? He smiled to himself.

"They came this way," he muttered, motioning for his men to carry on.

Further down the mountain, Jake and his team had already begun their own ascent. After leaving their ATVs behind, they moved in a diamond shaped formation, eyes constantly alert to any movement.

Jake took a sip from his canteen as he squinted up at the ridgeline ahead.

"This is going to be a long day".

The chase was far from over.

The late afternoon sun dipped low over the Afghan mountains, stretching shadows across the high peaks. The earth, a vast expanse of rock and dust, seemed to shift under Evelyn's boots, every step a battle against the loose dirt, gravel and sharp stones. She removed her wide brimmed hat for a moment and wiped her forehead with a scarf already damp with sweat. The heat was oppressive, seeping into her clothes, her skin - like an invisible weight she couldn't shake. Yet, despite the physical toll, she felt a sense of purpose she hadn't known in years.

Ahead, Tariq moved effortlessly, his long strides making easy work of the treacherous ground. His rifle rested against his back, more than just a precaution - it was a warning. Even in this vast emptiness, danger could be waiting just beyond the next ridge.

"Keep up, Miss Kane," he called over his shoulder, "we need to reach the rest point before dark".

Evelyn forced herself to quicken her pace, though her legs protested with every step, her calves burning with the effort. She took a sip from her canteen, the lukewarm water offering little relief.

"I thought you said this route was safer," she said, her breath coming in short gasps, "not faster".

Tariq looked back at her, a flicker of amusement crossing his otherwise stoic face.

"Safer does not mean easy. And you did not hire me for an easy journey".

"I think I did," she thought to herself.

But, he had her there. Tariq had come highly recommended - a man who knew these lands as well as any, with a reputation for discretion and for getting his clients, and soldiers, in and out of places others wouldn't dare set foot in. Finding someone willing to guide a foreign woman through the Afghan wilderness had been no small feat, especially with whispers of the Taliban reappearing in remote villages.

Evelyn held on to the strap of her pack tightly, its weight pushing against her shoulders, a constant reminder of why she was here. Inside were maps, a journal filled with meticulous notes, and a dog-eared copy of 'Guardians of Eden' - the book that had partly set her on this path. Written by her late mentor, Professor Richard Hallam, it explored the Garden of Eden as something more than myth, arguing that its origins lay in real geography, hidden somewhere in the ancient folds of the Middle East. Most of academia had dismissed Hallam's work as romantic speculation, but Evelyn had never cared for the opinions of armchair scholars.

For her, Hallam had been more than a mentor. He had been a lifeline - a father figure after she had lost her parents. His death two years ago had left her like a drifting boat, and no amount of work at the British Museum had managed to fill the void.

Then she had found the letter.

Tucked inside his personal copy of 'Guardians of Eden', it was addressed to her in Hallam's distinctive script. He had written of his growing certainty that Eden was real; not merely a story, but a place; a place hidden deep in the mountains of Afghanistan.

"You have the intellect, the courage, and the passion," the letter had said, *"do not let fear or convention hold you back".*

And so, she hadn't. She had left behind the comforts of her home in Kent, cashed in her savings, and boarded a flight to Kabul. That had been three weeks ago. Now, the weight of that decision felt heavier with every mile of barren landscape stretching before her.

She stared intently at Tariq, who remained focused on the path ahead.

"Why this route?" she asked, "it feels like we're doubling back on ourselves".

"Because the direct paths are watched," he said simply, "by Taliban, bandits...others. Did you not hire me as a guide?"

Evelyn could sense that Tariq was a little miffed.

"Yes, of course I did".

There was a moment of silence.

"Then let me *guide*, Miss Kane," Tariq replied.

She swallowed, pushing away the creeping doubt gnawing at her, whilst changing the subject.

"And you?" she asked. "What do *you* believe about Eden?"

Tariq halted in his tracks. His expression remained unchanged, but something shifted in his eyes; curiosity, or perhaps scepticism.

"My beliefs do not matter. But this land... it has secrets. Some holy, some cursed. The question is - what are *you* seeking?"

Evelyn pulled her scarf up over her mouth as the wind stirred up a fresh cloud of dust. Tariq walked a few paces ahead, keeping the conversation at bay, but the thoughts stirring in her head made the silence unbearable.

"Do you think it's real?" she asked, "The Garden of Eden?"

Tariq slowed, turning his head slightly as if trying to balance his answer.

"Maybe," he said, "but if it is, it should be left alone".

Evelyn raised an eyebrow.

"Why?"

"Because some things are not meant to be found," Tariq replied.

"But if Eden exists," she argued, "its discovery could change the world".

Tariq stopped. His brown eyes met hers.

"You believe Eden's goodness could free the world from evil. But what if that very goodness is corrupted the moment it is touched? Some things are meant to stay sacred; untouched by human ambition".

Evelyn considered his words.

"But isn't that the point of Eden?" she countered. "If it exists, its purity could inspire people to rise above their own failings. Maybe it's the key to something bigger; a way to unite humanity against greed and oppression".

Tariq exhaled, brushing sand from his jacket.

"You're thinking like an idealist," he said. "Did you know that in the Talmud and the Jewish Kabbalah, scholars describe two Gardens of Eden? One is terrestrial - a lush, fertile place on Earth. The other is celestial - the true paradise, where the righteous dwell with God. Even the rabbis said no mortal eye has seen the real Eden. Adam lived only in the garden, the lower Gan. Not Eden itself".

Evelyn's eyes lit up.

"That's fascinating. But how do you know all this?"

Tariq hesitated. Then, in a quiet voice, he said, "Like you, Miss Kane, I too have a university education. But what use is it here?"

Evelyn blinked.

"Really? What did you study?" Evelyn asked.

"History and Theology. I wanted to be a Teacher, but in these times..." Tariq paused, "education and knowledge bring only death".

Evelyn shook her head.

"I'm sorry to hear that," she said in an almost thoughtless manner, the subject of the garden still pressing on her mind, "so, you're saying even if we find it, we might not fully understand its nature?"

Tariq didn't respond. He simply turned and continued walking, the conversation left hanging between them like an unfinished thought.

The wind shifted, carrying the scent of pine from higher up in the mountains. Evelyn's mind buzzed with possibilities, but a sudden movement on the ridge above them snapped her attention back to the present. She froze, her heart pounding.

"Tariq," she whispered. "I saw something".

His hand moved instinctively to his rifle as his eyes searched the rocks above them. The world around them seemed to hold its breath. Only the wind moved, whispering through the valley.

Then, just as suddenly, the moment passed.

"It was probably nothing," she murmured, though the unease in her chest remained.

"Perhaps," Tariq said, his voice quiet, "but we should not linger."

They resumed their trek, the path growing steeper as it wound through a narrow gorge. The cliffs on either side rose like walls, their long shadows darkening the trail. Evelyn couldn't shake the feeling of unseen eyes tracking their every step, though she told herself it was just the isolation playing tricks on her mind.

As they climbed higher, the landscape began to change. The barren hills gave way to a plateau dotted with patches of scrub and the occasional twisted tree. The air grew cooler, the scent of heather and wild flowers engulfing their nostrils. It was beautiful in its desolation, but also deeply unnerving. But they had come too far to turn back now. Whatever lay ahead - whether it was the mythical Garden of Eden or simply another dead end - Evelyn was determined to see it through.

They stopped at a small plateau where the land flattened before the next climb. A gnarled juniper tree stood nearby, its branches barely shifting in the dry evening air. Tariq slid off his pack and knelt by the hexamine stove, striking a match to light the fuel tablets. The blue flame flickered to life.

Evelyn set down her own pack, stretching her shoulders.

"You were quiet on the way up," she said, watching him. "Thinking about Eden?"

Tariq focused on the flame for a moment before answering.

"Thinking about what happens if we find it".

She poured water into a small cooking pot and set it over the stove.

"And?"

"And if it should be found at all".

He took a sip from his canteen, glancing toward the darkening sky.

"According to the Jews, the higher Gan Eden is a 'Garden of Righteousness' that will only reveal itself at the end of time. The truly good - Jewish and non-Jewish - will walk with God there, in a dance of eternal joy. The rest? They'll be purified in places like Gehinnom or Sheol, far from heaven's reach".

Evelyn played with the boil in the bag meals as they floated in the pot, stirring it absently, watching the steam rise.

"It sounds like more than just a place," she said, "perhaps a symbol of hope, of redemption maybe. Imagine what that could mean for people suffering under oppressive regimes - like the Taliban".

Tariq's mouth tightened slightly.

"And that, Miss Kane, is exactly why it should be left alone. In Islamic tradition, Jannat 'Adn, the 'Gardens of Eden,' is also for the righteous - a destination in the afterlife. The Quran speaks of it as a reward for those who live justly. But there is a warning too".

He met her gaze.

"When Adam and Hawwa – Eve - were tempted by Iblis, the leader of the Devils, they were cast out. Some scholars believe this garden was not even in heaven but on Earth. Regardless, their disobedience was a lesson, not just a punishment".

Evelyn turned her head.

"What lesson?"

"That paradise is not just a gift," Tariq said, "it is a responsibility. In Islam, it is believed that God's wisdom destined humanity to leave the garden, to live on Earth, so we could experience the full range of His attributes - love, forgiveness, and power. Without struggle, people would not *long* for paradise or understand its value".

Evelyn frowned.

"But wasn't their exile caused by their own choice? They were tempted, sure, but they had free will".

Tariq nodded.

"Free will, yes. But their story is not just about choice. It is about trusting God over man-made interpretations. The guardians of Eden, if they exist, would say the same. That true belief comes from within, not from scriptures twisted by men to control others".

Evelyn inhaled sharply.

"You're saying it's not about religion but about faith".

"Yes," Tariq said, "in the end, the garden is a gateway. Not just to heaven, but to truth. And truth is dangerous. If the world knew Eden's power or treasures, greed would tear it apart. Imagine the chaos if people thought they could find eternal life or untold riches there. It would not be a sanctuary. It would be a battleground".

Evelyn stirred the pot again, though she wasn't really watching it.

"And yet," she said, "if it could bring peace..."

Tariq interrupted gently.

"Peace is not something you find Miss Kane. It is something you create. The Garden of Eden, if it exists, is not a shortcut. It is a test".

For a long moment, nothing was said. The flame in the stove hissed and crackled softly. The wind stirred the dust, carrying the scent of dry earth and juniper. Evelyn finally sighed, rubbing her arms against the chill creeping in.

"Maybe you're right," she admitted, "but if there's even a chance it could make a difference, isn't it worth trying?"

Tariq's expression shifted slightly; just enough for her to notice.

"That is what we are here to find out, is it not?"

She studied him for a second longer, then lifted the pot off the stove as the water reached a rolling boil.

"Tea?" she asked.

Tariq gave a small nod.

"Why not? If we are searching for paradise, we may as well enjoy the journey".

Evelyn huffed a quiet laugh.

"If paradise doesn't have tea, I don't want to go".

Tariq chuckled softly, and for the first time that evening, the conversation felt a little less heavy on his conscience.

CHAPTER 8

SUSPICION

The village rose from the barren land like a mirage against the harsh landscape, it's modest dwellings huddled together as though seeking protection from the vast emptiness surrounding them. Smoke curled from a few chimneys, and the sound of a bleating goat echoed faintly in the still air. Evelyn followed Tariq as he approached cautiously, his rifle slung across his back but his hand never far from it.

"This village is safe," Tariq murmured, sensing her unease, "for now at least...I hope".

As they entered, Evelyn felt dozens of eyes on her. Men sitting on low stools in the shade of the buildings watched her with suspicion. A few women, their hair covered by in colourful scarves, pulled their children closer and disappeared into doorways.

A wiry man in his fifties approached them, his beard streaked with grey. He and Tariq exchanged words in rapid-fire Pashto, their voices quiet but tense. Evelyn stood silently, her nerves jangling. Though she couldn't understand the words, the wary glances cast her way made their meaning clear.

Finally, the man gave a short nod and gestured for them to follow. He led them into a small courtyard, shaded by a patchwork canopy strung overhead. The scent of spices and wood smoke filled the air. Tariq motioned for Evelyn to sit on a woven mat.

"They are letting us rest," Tariq said quietly, "but they are suspicious of you".

"Because I'm foreign?" Evelyn asked, sinking onto the mat.

"Partly," Tariq replied, "but also because you are educated. An educated woman, especially one travelling without a husband, is an unusual sight here. Some will see it as a threat to their traditions, a challenge to their way of life".

Evelyn felt annoyed, a flicker of frustration sparking in her chest.

"I'm not here to challenge anyone, *or* their traditions".

"They do not know that," Tariq said, as he glanced toward the entrance, "but be careful what you say. And don't take offence if they test you".

Before she could ask what he meant, a young man entered the courtyard, his posture rigid, an old hunting rifle slung over his shoulder. He sat across from them, his stern gaze flicking to Evelyn. He spoke in Pashto, the challenge in his tone obvious.

Tariq answered him, his expression giving nothing away, but Evelyn caught a few familiar words "kitaab" and "madarasa" - book and school. She realised they were asking about her education.

The young man's glower deepened.

"He's asking why you are here," Tariq said under his breath, "he thinks outsiders only bring trouble."

Evelyn met the man's glare.

"I'm here to understand, not interfere."

The older man inclined forward, addressing Evelyn directly in broken English.

"You...teacher?"

"No," she said, forcing a polite smile, "I'm a historian; an archaeologist. I study the past".

The younger man frowned deeply, muttering something to his elder.

"They think you might be here to spread ideas," Tariq translated quietly, "they are wary of outsiders influencing their way of life".

Evelyn felt a flash of indignation but kept her tone measured.

"I'm here to learn about your history, not to change it".

The elder stared at her for a long moment, then nodded slowly.

The young man, however, was not convinced. He muttered something before standing abruptly and walking off.

Tariq breathed out sharply through his nose.

"We should leave soon".

The tense atmosphere eased slightly, and the elder motioned for a woman to bring tea. Evelyn sipped the bitter brew, relieved to have passed at least the scrutiny of the village elder, however narrowly.

As they rested, Evelyn observed the village with a historian's eye. The walls of the houses were sun-bleached, their surfaces marked with centuries of wear, baring the marks of generations. A group of children played with a makeshift ball in the dusty square, their laughter a rare note of joy in the sombre atmosphere.

But not all the villagers were at ease. A group of men loitering near the edge of the square cast furtive glances in Evelyn's direction. Their whispers carried an edge of hostility, and one of them spat on the ground when she met his gaze, a reaction which was becoming familiar to her.

"Not everyone welcomes foreigners," Tariq said quietly, following her gaze, "we should move on soon".

Evelyn nodded, though a part of her wanted to stay and ask questions - to learn more about the people and their stories. But the eyes watching her made it clear. Whatever stories this village held, they would not be shared today.

By the time they left the village, the sun hung low, stretching the mountains into deep shadows. The path grew steeper as they climbed, the air thinner and colder with every forward movement. Tariq led the way, his rifle once again in his hands.

They passed through another village just before sunset, but this one was eerily silent. The streets were empty, the windows of the houses dark. A lone dog barked somewhere in the distance, its mournful howl echoing through the stillness.

"What happened here?" Evelyn asked, her voice barely above a whisper.

Tariq knelt to examine the ground.

"They left in a hurry. See the tracks? Women, children. They took what they could carry and fled".

"Why?"

Tariq pointed to a faded symbol painted on the wall of one of the houses: a black flag with white script.

Evelyn's stomach turned.

"The Taliban?"

Tariq nodded.

"They were here recently. Maybe a day or two ago".

Evelyn looked around the village, her nerves on edge. The air felt stifling, heavy with the weight of unseen danger.

As they moved on, the signs of the Taliban's presence became more frequent. Burned-out vehicles, and old wooden carts, littered the side of the trail, their metal frames twisted and blackened. In one abandoned house, they found a pile of discarded ammunition crates scattered across the floor.

"Are they following us?" Evelyn asked

Tariq's expression darkened.

"Not yet. But they are not far".

The sound of gunfire in the distance shattered the silence, faint but undeniable. Tariq froze, his eyes narrowing to a squint as he listened.

"It is coming from the west," he said, "we need to move faster".

"The west? But isn't that the direction we just came from," replied Evelyn as she realised what was probably happening, "the village!"

Evelyn's legs ached, but she didn't argue. She kept pace with Tariq, her heart pounding as they disappeared into the growing shadows of the mountains.

The village was no longer silent. Fires burned in the courtyards, the flickering glow casting uneven shadows against the walls of the houses. Men gathered in clusters, voices muffled, their rifles slung across their backs or resting within arm's reach.

The scent of roasted meat and spiced tea drifted through the air, but beneath it lingered something darker - the sickly, metallic tang of blood.

The elder lay where they had left him, his body crumpled in the dirt outside his home, his sightless eyes fixed on the sky. Others who had stood with him were sprawled nearby, their lives taken in the same ruthless purge. No one moved the bodies. They were left as a warning.

Rashid sat in the largest courtyard, cross-legged, on the same woven rug on which Evelyn had sat only hours earlier, his rifle resting beside him. His men surrounded him, some tearing into flatbread, others gulping down tea as they laughed and spoke excitedly. Their hunt was nearly over, their prey driven into the mountains where escape would be impossible.

The younger man who had, the previous day, challenged Evelyn now sat close to Rashid, his posture rigid but his eyes burning with new purpose. He had pledged himself fully, and those who had once doubted him watched in silence, wary of what siding against him might now mean.

A woman, her face hidden beneath a scarf, moved carefully through the gathering, refilling cups and keeping her head bowed. Others like her remained in the shadows, speaking only when spoken to. They had seen what happened to those who resisted.

One of Rashid's lieutenants, a thick-set man with a beard streaked with grey, looked up from his meal.

"They will have no more places to run," he said, his voice full of certainty, "by tomorrow, it will be finished".

Rashid smiled a sinister smile, then nodded, his fingers idly tracing the carved grip of his pistol.

"They are already finished. They just do not know it yet".

Laughter rippled through the group. A few men cheered, slamming their fists against the wooden crates that they used as makeshift tables.

Yet not everyone joined in. A handful of villagers sat apart, watching the celebration with blank expressions. Their sons and brothers now fought under Rashid's banner, and their village belonged to the Taliban. But in the silence between bursts of laughter, their eyes flicked toward the bodies left to rot in the street.

Loyalty was not a choice. It was survival.

Evelyn stumbled, her boot catching on a rock protruding from the track, only just managing to catch herself before she fell. The narrow path twisted ahead of them, winding through the mountains, difficult to see in the dim starlight. Tariq moved ahead methodically, surefooted despite the uneven terrain, but even *he* was feeling the strain, breathing heavily now.

They had not stopped since leaving the village, carrying on through the night, the cold seeping into their bones as they climbed higher, driven by the knowledge that the Taliban would not rest. Every noise in the darkness sent a spike of fear through Evelyn's exhausted mind - the whisper of wind through dry grass, the distant howl of a wild dog, the occasional clatter of loose rocks tumbling down the slopes. Shadows shifted unpredictably, making every step treacherous. The darkness felt endless, swallowing everything beyond a few feet.

The air thinned even more as they climbed, forcing them to work harder for each breath. The mountains towered around them, their slopes treacherous, the loose soil and pebbles shifting unpredictably beneath their feet. More than once, Evelyn heard stones skitter off the edge into nothingness; the dark cavernous valley below. One wrong step could send them plunging into the unseen depths.

"We should stop," she gasped, her legs trembling from exhaustion.

"No," Tariq said, his voice hoarse, "not yet".

Evelyn bit back her frustration and forced herself to keep going. Her body ached, her lungs burned, but stopping wasn't an option. She knew Tariq was right. Even the shortest of halts meant giving their pursuers time to close the gap. They wouldn't rest, and if they did, it would only be to prepare for the kill. If she and Tariq were caught in the open, there would be no escape.

The stars wheeled slowly overhead, the night dragging on without end. Her thoughts blurred together, reduced to the rhythm of her own laboured breathing and the dull throb of exhaustion.

It wasn't until the first pale streaks of dawn lit the sky and began to creep over the peaks that Tariq finally slowed.

"There," he said, nodding to a craggy ledge jutting from the mountainside, "we rest there".

Evelyn could have wept with relief. They scrambled up the last stretch of the trail, using their hands to pull themselves up onto the high ground. From this vantage point, they had a clear view of the valley below, and the spiralling path stretching far into the distance.

Tariq dropped onto the cold stone, his rifle across his lap, surveying the horizon; sweeping every part of it as far as he could see. Evelyn collapsed beside him, her pulse still hammering. From here, they would see anyone who followed.

For now, they had a chance.

For a long moment, neither of them spoke.

Then, softly, Evelyn said, "The village".

Tariq didn't answer right away. His stare remaining fixed on the valley.

"They will be dead," he said finally, "the elder. Anyone who helped us".

Evelyn tried to swallow, her throat dry. She had known the answer before she asked, but hearing it spoken aloud made it real.

"The younger man?" she asked, "the one who challenged me?"

"He would have been given a choice," Tariq said, "join them, or die. But he, I believe, would have joined them willingly".

Evelyn puffed, staring out over the endless mountains.

"And the others?"

Tariq turned to her, his face shadowed in the morning light.

"Some will welcome them. Others will pretend to".

Evelyn closed her eyes. She could still see the wary faces of the villagers, and imagined the quiet glances exchanged behind the Taliban's back. Some had been afraid, she was sure of it. But fear wouldn't save them now.

She shivered, though the wind had nothing to do with it.

Tariq's voice was quiet when he spoke again.

"We need to sleep. A few hours, at least".

Evelyn nodded, though she knew sleep wouldn't come easily, despite her tiredness.

Rashid checked that the magazine on his rifle was securely fitted, then looked up at the rising sun, its golden light spilling over the mountaintops. It was time to move. The village had served its purpose - shelter, food, and a clear message to anyone who thought of resisting them. Now they would continue their hunt.

The young villager, the one who had challenged Evelyn, stepped forward. He no longer had the same hesitation in his eyes. Whether it was fear or conviction driving him, Rashid didn't care. What mattered was that the boy knew these mountains, and he had chosen the winning side.

"This way," the young man said, pointing toward the steep, winding pass that cut through the hills, "they will be tired. If we keep moving, we will close the distance".

Rashid smirked.

"Good. Then we make them suffer before they die".

His men fell in behind him, their boots stirring up the dust as they left the village behind. Some walked with the confidence of seasoned fighters, others with the nervous energy of those still proving themselves. Either way, they would follow him. They always did.

Behind them, the village lay still.

The moment the last of Rashid's men disappeared over the ridge, an old woman let out a long, shuddering breath. A child whimpered, quickly hushed by its mother. No one spoke. No one moved. It was as if they feared the sound of their own grief might call the killers back.

Then, finally, a man walked slowly towards the bodies, still lying where they had fallen, his face lined with sorrow. He knelt beside the elder's broken body and touched his forehead with trembling fingers. Others followed, some dropping to their knees, others pressing shaking hands to their mouths. Silent tears ran down weathered faces.

"They are gone," someone murmured.

But they all knew it wasn't over. Not really.

They moved quickly, dragging the fallen to the village square. The men who had sided with the Taliban had departed, and those who had feared them but remained, now struggled with guilt. Some muttered prayers under their breath, while others stood frozen, staring at the bloodied earth.

Then, in the distance, six armed figures approached in staggered file on both sides of the track.

Loose sand and soil swirled in the wake of the team as they moved cautiously into the village. The silence was unsettling, filled with something worse than fear - grief. Sergeant Allsop raised a hand, signalling the men to slow their approach. Weapons stayed ready, eyes searching every rooftop, every doorway, every shadow.

A few figures lurked at the edges of the village, peering out from doorways and behind crumbling walls. Women clutched their children, their dark eyes filled with terror. An old man hunched near the well, his lips moving in whispered prayer, hoping that death was not visiting yet again.

Then, suddenly, a sharp cry rang out.

The villagers had seen the weapons, the uniforms, and for a brief, terrible moment, they thought the Taliban had returned. A woman shrieked and turned to run. A child began sobbing. A few men grabbed what little they had - rusty farming tools, a knife, even a length of broken wood - as if they could fight off these armed intruders.

Jake immediately lifted his left hand, palm open, trying to calm them.

"We're not Taliban!" he called out in Pashto, "we're here to help!"

His words took a moment to sink in. Then, recognition flashed across some of the villagers' faces. These men were different - western soldiers.

The tension broke.

A wailing woman stumbled forward, her face streaked with dirt and tears. Before Lecky could react, she collapsed at his feet, her hands clinging to his leg. Her whole body trembled with uncontrollable sobs, her fingers gripping his trousers as if holding on to him could somehow undo the horror she had just lived through.

Lecky stiffened, momentarily stunned.

"Oh hell..." he mumbled under his breath, unsure of what to do. He glanced at Jake, who gave him a slight nod.

Lecky crouched down, trying to gently pry the woman's hands away, but she only clung tighter, her cries coming in heaving gasps.

"They killed my father!" she wailed, "they killed them all!"

Mackie, Parks, Carter and Taylor exchanged gloomy looks. They had seen this before; too many times.

Jake spoke softly.

"What happened here?"

An older man, his face lined with sorrow, spoke, his voice hoarse.

"The Taliban came...Rashid and his men. They were looking for a western woman. They murdered our elder, and anyone who stood with him. Then they left, taking some of our young men with them".

Mackie, standing nearby, was not impressed.

"How many?"

The old man sighed.

"Five...plus our four men. But one of them - he knew the mountains well. He led them".

"And the Western woman?" said Jake.

A murmur rippled through the villagers. A younger man, his face still blackened with soot, pointed toward the mountains.

"She and her guide left before the attack. Rashid is hunting them".

Jake turned to Lecky, who was already orientating his map. He jabbed a finger toward the ridgeline.

"So, if they're heading into the mountains, if we move now, we might catch them before Rashid does".

Jake nodded then looked back at the villagers.

"We'll help bury your dead, but then we have to go. We can't let them reach them first".

The old man nodded; his eyes a mixture of gratitude and sorrow.

As the soldiers got to work, Lecky gently pulled the grieving woman to her feet.

"I'm real sorry ma'am...for all of this," he said quietly.

Her tears didn't stop, but she clutched his hand for just a moment, a silent, desperate hope in her grip.

As Tariq and Evelyn neared Nuristan, the landscape grew wilder, the mountains steeper, and the forests denser. The barren slopes of the lower valleys gave way to towering cedar and pine, their dark green canopies stretching across the irregular terrain. Rivers carved deep gorges through the rock, their waters rushing down from the high peaks. The air was cooler here, carrying the scent of damp earth and tree resin, a strong contrast to the arid lands they had left behind.

Nuristan was a place of mystery and defiance, its people shaped by centuries of isolation. Once called Kafiristan - "Land of the Infidels" - it had resisted outside rule for generations, its inhabitants clinging to ancient beliefs and customs until their forced conversion to Islam in the late 19th century. Even after that, Nuristan remained a land apart, its villages hidden among the mountains, its traditions different from those of the rest of Afghanistan. Some Nuristanis claimed descent from Alexander the Great's soldiers, their fair features and distinct dialects setting them apart from their neighbours.

The topography itself was a fortress, its narrow paths and high ridges making travel slow and exhausting. But Tariq soldiered on, leading Evelyn along an old shepherd's trail that wound higher into the mountains. By midday, they came upon a strangely shaped pile of boulders, which had sat there as sentinels for centuries, where the wind howled through a narrow crevice in the stone. The sound was eerie, a hollow whisper that seemed to beckon them forward.

Tariq halted at the pile, running his hand along the rock face, then looked back at Evelyn.

"This might be worth a look," he said.

They squeezed through the gap, their footsteps echoing as they entered a hidden cavern. At first, it was nothing more than a shadowed hollow in the rock, but as their eyes adjusted, the walls began to shimmer. Embedded in the stone were veins of quartz and gemstones - raw rubies, sapphires, deep blue lapis lazuli, a metamorphic semi-precious stone that has been prized since antiquity for its intense colour, as well as glimmering topaz. The cave sparkled in the dim light, as if the very heart of the mountain had been cracked open to reveal its riches.

Evelyn stared in awe.

"This is incredible".

Tariq nodded.

"The mines of these mountains have been known for thousands of years. Alexander's men spoke of them. Kings and traders have fought over them. Even now, people risk their lives digging for gems like these".

She reached out to touch the cool surface of a spiky shaped ruby still half-buried in stone.

"And here we are, in the middle of it".

Tariq looked briefly back toward the cave entrance, his expression thoughtful.

"It could be a good place to rest. No one would think to look for us here".

Evelyn nodded then thought for a moment as she gazed at the precious gems scattered over the floor of the cave.

"Did you know that just a handful of these stones could see us rich beyond our wildest dreams?"

"I am not here to steal Miss Kane," Tariq replied.

"Steal? How is it stealing? By the look of this place no one has set foot in here before," she said, bending down to collect some of the gems, "I don't know about you but I would like to live a comfortable life and perhaps even have enough money to fund future expeditions. And you, think of your new life in Britain. Life there isn't cheap. Why not give yourself and your family a good start?"

Tariq pondered Evelyn's words.

"Yes. You are right. But only take enough for your future and do not increase the weight of your pack too much. We still have far to go".

Tariq felt as sense of guilt as the pair gathered up the precious stones, each filling the two side pockets of their packs, but for once he thought of himself and the life he could give his family.

Gem gathering done, Tariq and Evelyn were satisfied. It was time to rest.

For the first time in hours, they allowed themselves a moment of respite, hidden within the mountain's treasure trove, beneath the glittering gaze of ancient stones.

Elsewhere, their pursuers had also stopped for the night. The Taliban, now farther away than before, had spent the last several hours chasing shadows. Tariq's false trails had led them in circles, up dead-end gullies and over ridges that revealed nothing but empty wilderness. The realisation that they had been deceived gnawed at them, but fatigue dulled their anger. With no clear path forward, they huddled among the rocks, forced to rest and reconsider their next move.

Behind them, the soldiers moved swiftly, using the Taliban as their unwitting guides. They had no way of knowing exactly where Tariq and Evelyn were, but they didn't need to - not yet. The villagers had given them one crucial piece of information: the direction their targets had fled. Now, by tracking the Taliban, they would let their enemies do the hard work for them. If the militants found Tariq and Evelyn first, the soldiers would be right behind them, ready to strike.

Lecky crouched by the dirt track, tracing a gloved finger over the mess of footprints. He couldn't help but smile at the sheer absurdity of it.

Jake noticed his friend's expression.

"What's up with you mate...got wind or something?"

Lecky shook his head.

"Nope, but take a look at this circus act?"

Jake leaned over his shoulder, peering at the overlapping tracks.

"Mate, this fella's got 'em running in circles like a dog chasing its own tail".

Taylor let out a low whistle.

"You ever see anything like this before?"

Parks chuckled.

"Oh yeah, reminds me of when my kid brother tried to fake a sick day from school - went to all the trouble of heating up a thermometer on a light bulb, then forgot normal people don't run a 112 degree fever and live to tell the tale".

Jake gave Parks a cursory glance.

"Yeah mate, that's really relevant isn't it?"

Parks snorted.

"Well, this is even better. Look here...these prints go straight down the track, then double back on themselves, then veer off completely the other way".

He gave an exaggerated sigh.

"Classic let's see how dumb the bad guys really are manoeuvre".

Jake grinned.

"And by the looks of it, they fell for it".

He pointed to the deeper, more erratic prints.

"These are the Taliban's. See how they start bunching up? It means they stopped, argued about it, then probably picked the wrong trail".

Lecky couldn't help but laugh.

"A wild goose chase, but instead of a goose, it's a very pissed off bunch of terrorists wondering why they can't catch one guy and a blonde".

Lecky dusted off his knees as he stood.

"We keep this up, we'll be on 'em by nightfall. Hell, they might even do half the work for us".

Jake nodded, throwing one last amused glance at the chaotic footprints.

"Fingers crossed eh? Alright, boys, let's move. We'll let the Taliban keep chasing their own tails and use them to find the real prize".

As the first pale light of morning crept over the mountains, Tariq and Evelyn emerged from the hidden mine, squinting against the brightness. The valley stretched out before them, wild and untouched, the ancient landscape bathed in the golden glow of dawn. The air was fresh and clean, and for a brief moment, it felt as if they were the only two people in the world.

Evelyn's muscles ached from the strain of what had been, and still was, an arduous journey.

"So," she said, breathing out hard, "where do we even start?"

Tariq's eyes followed the contours of the valley, his gaze moving over the ridges, the boulder-strewn slopes, and the dense patches of trees clinging to the hillsides.

"If this Crystal Cave is real, it would not be in a place that people have passed through often. It would be somewhere untouched...undisturbed".

Evelyn began her own visual search.

"Somewhere hidden away by nature?"

Tariq nodded.

"A place no one has set foot in for centuries".

The two explorers moved cautiously, picking their way down into the valley, looking for anything that stood out - an unusual rock formation, an ancient landslide, a break in the cliffside that might hint at something beyond. Birds flitted between the trees, undisturbed by human presence, and the grass in some areas stood tall and untrampled, swaying gently in the morning breeze.

After nearly an hour of searching, Evelyn paused on a small rise, shielding her eyes with one hand.

The land ahead was different - untouched, undisturbed by the elements or man. Unlike the rest of the valley, which bore the scars of time and weather, this area seemed eerily pristine. The air itself too felt different, cooler, almost charged with something unseen.

"Over there," she said, pointing toward a cluster of boulders at the base of a sheer rock face, "see how everything around it looks...different? Like it hasn't been touched by time?"

Tariq followed her line of sight, his brow raised. The ground leading up to the boulders was uneven, but something about it seemed...wrong. No trails, no signs of grazing animals, not even weathered stones where rain and wind would have worn them down over time. It was as if that part of the valley had been frozen in place, untouched by the centuries.

His pulse quickened.

"That is it," he murmured, "it *has* to be".

Without another word, they set off toward the undisturbed ground, their hearts pounding with anticipation.

Evelyn paused.

"Do you feel that?"

A faint breeze whispered across her skin, yet there was no wind. It was coming from somewhere unseen. Tariq walked toward some large boulders, his outstretched hand hovering above the rock formation.

"There is air flowing from behind these stones," he said, glancing at her, "surely that means there is an opening".

The rocks in front of them weren't like the others in the valley. While most had been rounded and worn down over time, these had sharp, unnatural edges. Some looked as if they had been placed deliberately. At the base of the formation, patches of greenery thrived - ferns and moss, nourished by a hidden water source.

"There must be an underground spring," said Tariq.

"And where there is underground water there are usually crystals," replied a hopeful Evelyn.

She ran her fingers along the surface of one of the larger stones and stopped. Faint carvings, almost erased by time, marked the weathered surface.

"These aren't natural," she whispered, brushing away dirt and debris.

The symbols, though faded, bore a striking resemblance to those they had seen at Bamiyan and the Valley of the Lost Rivers. Tariq knelt beside her, his fingers tracing the ancient etchings.

"Someone was here...a long time ago".

Their excitement grew as they moved to the rear of the boulders. Evelyn pulled out the trowel that she used on archaeological digs. Beneath layers of compacted earth, they scraped away at the dirt and uncovered something astonishing - a larger, more intricate carving, partially buried beneath the soil. As they cleared more of the debris, the edges of a stone slab emerged. Tariq pressed his palm against it.

"It is not just a marking," he said, "it is a door".

They worked quickly, using broken branches as levers, wedging them beneath the heavy stone. With a final heave, the slab shifted and groaned, releasing a sudden gust of air. Then, as they pried it open, a blinding radiance erupted from the darkness below. A golden-white light, shimmering and otherworldly, spilled from the opening, as if the sun itself had been trapped beneath the earth.

Evelyn and Tariq stood in stunned silence as the glow slowly faded, revealing a cavern unlike anything they had ever seen. The walls, the ceiling, even the floor - everything was composed of immense, glittering crystals. They towered above them, some the size of trees, translucent and infused with shifting hues of blue, violet, and gold. A soft, ambient glow seemed to radiate from within the formations, casting the chamber in a perpetual twilight.

As they entered, the air seemed to be composed of something indescribable; an energy, almost spiritual in its presence. A gentle mist clung to the lower chambers, refracting light like a million tiny prisms. It was as if they had stepped into another realm, a sanctuary untouched by time, hidden away for millennia.

Tariq breathed out slowly, and whispered.

"This...this is not just a cave".

Evelyn nodded, breathless.

"It is a cathedral of the earth".

For the first time, it felt as though they weren't intruding, but rather, being welcomed into something sacred.

The winding path ahead shimmered with an ethereal glow, the very walls of the cavern pulsating with soft, shifting light. The crystals towered above them, some stretching high into the darkness like frozen lightning, others glistening in intricate clusters, their surfaces catching and refracting light into countless prismatic hues. The cave felt alive - not merely a hollow in the earth, but a sacred place, untouched by time.

As Evelyn and Tariq moved deeper, the air grew cooler, charged with an energy neither could explain, and the feint breeze made a sound like a choir of angels. The light guided them, flickering as though beckoning them onward, each step feeling less like a choice and more like an invitation. It was as if the cave itself was leading them on a journey, whispering secrets in the silent hum of shifting minerals and glistening stone.

Then, they saw it.

At the heart of the cavern, an island rose from a void of pure blackness, encircled by an abyss that seemed bottomless. At its centre, on a circular plinth, stood a crystal unlike any they had seen before - radiant and pure, its light forming the delicate shape of angelic wings. It pulsed gently, as though breathing, its presence commanding yet serene...The Angel's Tear.

Evelyn sighed in wonder.

"It's beautiful," she whispered.

But their awe was quickly overshadowed by a new challenge. Between them and the island, a ten-foot gap stretched over the darkness. What remained of a wooden bridge jutted from the edge - a single, narrow plank that had long since rotted in the damp air.

Tariq looked sullen.

"That is not a bridge. That is an accident waiting to happen".

Evelyn laughed out loud.

"Well, unless you've got wings, this is all we've got".

Before he could protest, she lowered herself onto the plank, sitting down and inching across on her backside.

Tariq stared.

"I thought you would just walk across".

She gave him a cheeky grin.

"Not a Hollywood moment, eh, the hero balancing like a tight rope walker and all that?"

The plank creaked under her weight, and Tariq held his breath as she edged further over the gap. She was nearly across when she turned back to flash him a triumphant smile - just as her balance shifted.

The smile vanished.

With a startled cry, Evelyn tipped sideways and disappeared into the darkness below.

Tariq's heart stopped.

"EVELYN!"

He scrambled forward, expecting to hear the sickening thud of her body hitting unseen rocks far below. Instead, a rustling sound came, followed by an unexpected voice.

"Huh? Would you look at that...coal".

Tariq blinked.

"What?"

A moment later, Evelyn stood up, brushing herself off, her boots crunching against solid ground.

"The walls of this thing are black as night. Looks like a cavernous drop, but..." she rapped her knuckles against the surface, "it's just coal. I didn't see *that* coming, did you?"

Tariq, his hands on his knees, couldn't believe what had just occurred.

"You are a mad woman Miss Kane," Tariq replied, checking his pulse, "and you are going to give me a heart attack".

She grinned, unfazed.

"This certainly doesn't happen in the movies, does it?"

Tariq shook his head and sighed, stepping down in to what was in effect a dry moat.

"No. In the movies, I would be the one falling, and you would make some dramatic last-minute grab to save me".

Evelyn laughed.

"Well, good luck. I'm fresh out of dramatic rescues today".

Still shaking his head, Tariq carefully made his way across. As he clambered up on to the island, Evelyn was already standing before the crystal, her expression softer now, almost reverent.

Together, they approached the Angel's Tear, its radiant light casting their shadows against the cavern walls. The journey had led them here, but somehow, it felt as though the true discovery was only just beginning.

The light of the crystal shimmered across the cavern, casting tall shadows as Evelyn and Tariq stood before it. The Angel's Tear pulsed gently, its glow seeming almost alive, as if aware of their presence. Around its plinth, the stone was smooth with age, worn by centuries of silence. But as they looked closer, they saw something else - an inscription, faint yet deliberate, cut into the rock.

Evelyn knelt, running her fingertips over the ancient words, their meaning hidden beneath layers of dust and time, and gently blowing away the dust. Tariq joined her, carefully tracing the unfamiliar script with his own hand.

"Hang on, I've seen this before," Evelyn announced excitedly as she reached in her pack to retrieve her journal. Quickly flicking through the pages she finally found it; a crude drawing by the professor of the crystal along with the same script, but the professor had deciphered it.

"Here we go...look," said Evelyn as she pointed out the page and the translation.

The symbols on the plinth were crude, yet their message was clear.

"When Adam and Eve see clearly, They, and they alone, must raise the Angel's Tear to the heavens. The Tree shall guide the worthy".

They exchanged a glance.

Evelyn read the words again, the importance of their meaning settling over her.

"It's a riddle," she murmured. "But *this*..." she reached out, fingers grazing the radiant stone "this *must* be the Angel's Tear".

Tariq agreed.

"And the tree...it must be a landmark".

Evelyn turned, scanning the chamber. Against the far wall, partially hidden by a fallen rock, was another carving, this one depicting a pointy mountain peak. She moved toward it, her fingers brushing the rough stone, tracing the ancient artist's worn lines.

"This is the key," she said, her eyes narrowing as she found a blank page in her journal and, with a pencil, began to sketch every detail, "we need to find this mountain".

She turned back to Tariq, but something caught her eye. A little further along the wall, her torch beam illuminated another carving - a gnarled and sprawling tree, its roots curling deep into the earth.

"The Tree," she whispered.

Tariq's expression changed and he stared at the carving, his expression altering as recognition dawned.

"I *know* this tree," he said, "it is the Tree of Eternity, in the Shibar Pass".

Evelyn looked at him sharply.

"You're sure?"

"I am sure." Tariq ran a hand over the carving, "it is sacred. People say it is older than time itself, grown from a seed from the Garden of Eden".

Evelyn let out a slow breath.

"Then that's where we need to go...but first, the crystal".

She turned back to the plinth, inhaling deeply before placing both hands on the stone. The glow brightened at her touch, warmth radiating through her fingertips. She hesitated, then, as gently as possible, lifted it free.

The moment the crystal left its resting place, the cavern seemed to sigh - a whisper of shifting air, of something ancient stirring. The light in the room dimmed slightly, as if the cave itself was reluctant to part with its treasure.

Cradling the Angel's Tear carefully, Evelyn wrapped it in her scarf, folding the fabric securely around it before slipping it into her pack. She then let out a quiet chuckle.

"This is where we run the gauntlet of poison darts and get chased by a huge spherical rock I believe".

Tariq seemed shocked by the remark and urgently looked towards their route out.

"Really?!"

Evelyn tutted and shook her head.

"Indiana Jones?"

Tariq shrugged his shoulders.

"You really *must* get out more Tariq," Evelyn said, "but, no matter what, I think some higher being wants us to find Eden. I can feel it in my bones".

"Let us hope that we are worthy".

Evelyn zipped up her pack and gave him a wry smile.

"Well, we're about to find out".

CHAPTER 9

PERFUME

The midday sun hung high, beating down on the rocky terrain as Evelyn and Tariq crested a ridge. Below them, nestled in the valley, lay a small village - a scattering of ancient houses, smoke curling lazily from a handful of chimneys. Fields of crops stretched out from its edges, and beyond them, a river cut through the land like a silver ribbon. It looked peaceful, untouched by the turmoil and hatred that lurked beyond the mountains.

Evelyn breathed out slowly, tugging her hat lower over her brow.

"We could rest there," she said, "maybe even get supplies".

Tariq shook his head.

"No, we cannot risk it. If the Taliban come through, the villagers might talk, whether willingly or not".

Evelyn didn't argue. He was right. The last thing they needed was to leave a trail.

Instead, she pulled out the map and traced a line with her finger.

"The Shibar Pass is still a few days away. We'll need to stick to the high ground, and stay out of sight".

Tariq laughed as he looked around, studying the landscape.

"So *you* are the guide now? We should move now while we still have light. If we follow the ridgeline, we can cover more ground before nightfall".

They turned away from the village, stepping carefully along the undulating path. Unbeknownst to them, a few hundred metres away, an old farmer tending his flock of goats lifted his head. His weathered eyes followed the distant figures as they moved across the rocky slopes.

He watched them for a long moment, his fingers idly stroking his beard. Then, with a quiet grunt, he turned back to his animals, guiding them down toward the village -where others would soon hear of the strangers who had passed by.

The Shibar Pass loomed ahead, its steep trails winding through the unforgiving mountain peaks. Not far from Bamiyan, it was a place of legend, where caravans once passed and armies had marched, centuries of travellers, from merchants and pilgrims to warriors and conquerors, their footprints lost to time. Now, it was just another brutal stretch of their journey leading them almost back to where they had first uncovered the mystery - one that seemed deliberately chosen to test them. Whoever had laid these clues had done so with purpose, ensuring that only those with stamina and determination in their quest would reach the end.

Evelyn took off her hat for a moment and shook her head.

"This is almost cruel. We've come all this way just to be sent more or less right back to where we started".

Tariq smiled.

"Perhaps *that* is the test. To see if we will keep going".

She ran her eyes over him, then back at the pass stretching ahead. The journey was designed to break the weak, to make the unworthy turn back. But *they* weren't turning back.

"Then let's prove that we're not quitters then shall we?" she said, taking a step forward.

Tariq followed without hesitation, the mountains watching in silent approval.

The Taliban fighters trudged into Nuristan, the dust along the narrow trail giving a tell tale warning of their approach. Rashid walked at the front, his scarred face impassive as he took in the village ahead. The journey had been long and punishing, but he continued on like a wolf hunting its prey. The woman and her companion were somewhere ahead, and *he* would not return empty handed.

A group of villagers stood waiting as they approached. The men were dressed in traditional tunics and pakols, their faces were lined with years of hardship, yet they bowed their heads, welcoming the Taliban with warm smiles and respectful nods. Rashid and Vakil exchanged a glance; such hospitality was rare, but not unheard of.

The villagers ushered them into the heart of the settlement, offering food, water, and a place to rest. Rashid accepted with cautious gratitude, lowering himself onto a worn carpet inside a simple stone dwelling. Opposite him, an elder sat, cross-legged, with an air of quiet authority, his hands steady despite his age, his beard, as white as the snow-capped peaks, resting against his chest.

"You have come far?" the old man asked, his voice as dry as rustling leaves.

"We seek two outsiders," Rashid replied, wasting no time, "a man and a foreign woman".

The elder ran a hand over his beard, nodding slowly, whilst pointing to the tall mountain peaks.

"Yes," he murmured, "they passed by some days ago. Heading west".

Vakil Khan pulled his weathered notebook from his coat and made a quick note. Rashid studied the old man's face, searching for any flicker of dishonesty, but the elder remained calm, his expression giving nothing away.

"You have been helpful," Rashid said, rising to his feet.

He turned to his men.

"We move".

The villagers gathered to see them off, offering words of blessing and waving, watching as the fighters disappeared into the mountains. The moment they were out of sight, the smiles faded and the warmth drained from their faces.

The elder spat into the dust where Rashid had stood. A younger man clenched his fists, his knuckles white with restrained fury. Others muttered darkly amongst themselves, their voices filled with contempt.

"They bring nothing but suffering and death," one said.

"They will find nothing but the graves they deserve," the elder replied.

As the last of the Taliban vanished beyond the crest, the villagers turned back to their homes, their outward politeness masking the hatred that burned beneath.

The mountains seemed to close in around them as the night deepened. The chill in the air caused their breath to cloud before them as they ascended a narrow, rocky trail. Evelyn's careful footsteps made a quiet patter on the track, each sound unnervingly loud in the stillness. Tariq moved ahead of her, *his* footsteps silent and deliberate, his rifle always at the ready.

Evelyn was acutely aware of the shadows stretching across the path, the sharp pointed silhouettes of the peaks cutting like a razor against the starry sky. Every rustle of wind through the sparse shrubs, every echo of falling stones from the cliffs above, set her nerves on edge.

Then she heard it. A low, hoarse voice carried faintly on the breeze. She froze, her hand gripping Tariq's sleeve.

"Do you hear that?" she whispered.

Tariq nodded, his expression more serious than usual. He gestured for her to crouch behind a large boulder as he crept forward. Evelyn obeyed, pressing herself against the cold rock and straining to hear.

The voices grew louder. More than one. Men, speaking in Pashto. They were laughing - an eerie, almost mocking sound in the oppressive silence of the mountains.

Tariq returned, his face tense.

"Taliban," he whispered, "three, maybe four. On the trail ahead. They have stopped to rest".

Evelyn's mouth went suddenly dry.

"What do we do?"

"We wait," Tariq said, "if they move on, we follow from a distance. If they stay..."

He didn't finish the sentence, but his hand tightened on the pistol grip of his rifle.

They waited in agonising silence, the minutes stretching into what felt like hours. Evelyn's heart thudded in her chest, each beat loud in her ears. The laughter ahead faded, replaced by the sound of footsteps on the rocky trail.

"They are coming this way," Tariq whispered, as he pulled her deeper into the shadows of the boulder, motioning for her to stay silent.

Evelyn waited with anticipation, her mind racing.

The first man appeared around the bend, his silhouette tall and menacing in the faint starlight. He carried an AK-47, his finger resting casually on the trigger guard. Three others followed; their weapons similarly at the ready.

Evelyn held her breath, willing herself to become invisible. The men passed within a few metres, their voices low but their demeanour relaxed. One of them paused, glancing around as if sensing something amiss. The man appeared to be sniffing.

"Atar," he said as he clenched his rifle and looked quickly at his friends.

Atar is the Pashto word for perfume.

Evelyn's pulse raced as his gaze swept over their hiding spot.

But Tariq didn't wait. In a sudden motion, he stepped out from behind the boulder, his rifle raised.

"Drop your weapons!" he shouted in Pashto.

The Taliban fighters reacted instantly, shouting and raising their rifles. Tariq fired first, the crack of his rifle echoing through the mountains. The lead fighter crumpled to the ground, his AK-47 clattering against the rocks.

Evelyn pressed herself against the boulder, her hands over her ears as the gunfire erupted around her. Tariq moved with speed, taking cover behind another rock and firing in quick bursts.

One of the fighters shouted an order, and the others fanned out, their movements quick and coordinated. Evelyn peeked around the boulder and saw the muzzle flash of an AK-47, the rounds kicking up dirt dangerously close to Tariq.

Evelyn thought about her pistol, which was only useful at short range, then her eyes darted to the fallen fighter's weapon. It lay just a few metres away, glinting faintly in the starlight. Summoning every ounce of courage, she crawled slowly towards it.

Her fingers closed around the cold metal of the rifle, and she dragged it back to the boulder. Although she had used similar weapons in the past, this one was different, and she strained her eyes to find the safety catch and the lever which switched the rifle from automatic to single shots. As she fumbled around in the darkness the rifle's weight in her hands gave her a fragile sense of security.

"Tariq!" she shouted, her voice trembling.

He glanced over his shoulder, a serious look on his face.

"Stay down!"

Evelyn's fingers found the switch, and with a satisfying click, she flicked the rifle onto single shot. Her breath was steady now, her hands sure. She was ready.

Her eyes locked onto the three remaining Taliban as they moved in an attempt to encircle Tariq. He was pinned down, his cover shrinking with every second.

A sudden calmness settled over her. Instinct took over.

In one swift motion, she rose from behind the boulder, bringing the rifle up to her shoulder in a smooth arc. The first man saw her too late.

Her shot punched through his throat, a wet gurgle replacing his battle cry. He clutched at his shattered windpipe, eyes bulging as he collapsed to his knees, drowning in his own blood.

The second fighter whirled, eyes wide at the sight of a woman with a rifle. Evelyn squeezed the trigger again.

The round slammed into his cheekbone, smashing it and sending a spray of bone and brain matter across the rocks. He crumpled backwards, his body convulsing as his nerves fired one last time.

The third man tried to dive for cover, but Evelyn tracked him smoothly. She took a fraction of a second to aim - then fired.

The bullet tore through his spine, just below the neck. His body stiffened violently, then collapsed like a rag doll, his limbs twitching as he gasped his last breath in the dirt.

Then - silence.

Tariq inhaled deeply and slowly rose from cover, surveying the carnage. He turned to Evelyn, a hint of approval in his eyes.

"Not bad".

Evelyn lowered the rifle, her adrenaline beginning to fade. A small, exhilarated smile played at her lips.

"Yes...I was taught well".

Tariq stepped closer, then sniffed the air. His expression changed to one of mild irritation.

"Next time," he muttered, wiping sweat from his forehead, "do not wear perfume".

Evelyn blinked, then let out a breathless laugh.

"What?"

"You were easy to smell. They knew you were here before they even saw you".

She shook her head in disbelief, then grinned.

"A girl must always look and smell her best, Tariq".

He just sighed.

"Not if she wants to stay alive."

She rolled her eyes but nodded.

"Fine. No more perfume".

Tariq gave her a final look, then turned away, reloading his weapon.

"Good. Now let us move before more of them show up".

Before departing, they searched the bodies, relieving them of ammo, food, water and rifle cleaning kits.

Evelyn followed, stepping carefully over the bodies of the men she had just killed. The night felt colder now, but she pushed the thought aside.

She was still alive. And she wasn't going down without a fight.

The wind sighed through the narrow pass, threading between the mountains which towered over them on all sides. The chill of dawn still lingered in the air. The sun had begun its slow climb, casting long, broken shadows across the desolate landscape.

Ahead, the steep slopes levelled out into a plateau, scattered with weather-worn boulders and tufts of dry grass. And there, standing alone like a relic of another time, was the tree.

The wind stirred the branches, making them creak like an old door on rusted hinges. The tree stood alone, its trunk was thick and knotted, scarred by centuries of wind and time. Its bare branches twisted skyward, their skeletal limbs swaying gently as if whispering to the mountains. Beneath it, the ground was cracked and dry, yet the tree stood firm, defying the elements. Twisted roots clawed at the earth, as though refusing to be swallowed by the land that had long since dried around them.

Tariq slowed his pace, his expression one of awe. He moved toward it as if drawn by some unseen force, his fingers brushing the rough bark.

"If any tree grew from Eden's seed, it is this one," he murmured.

Evelyn stopped beside him, catching her breath from the long trek. The wind stirred around them, ruffling her hair, and for a moment, she had the strange feeling that the tree had been waiting for them.

Then, something caught her eye.

She took a step closer, her fingertips trailing over faded carvings in the bark. The marks were rough but deliberate - lines and angles forming a pattern.

Her heart gave a small jolt, then she reached into her breast pocket and pulled out the worn map she had been following. She unfolded it, smoothing it against her knee as she compared it to the rough carvings etched into the bark. The lines, though crude, held a familiar shape.

She stood for a moment just contemplating.

"It's a map," she said, running her fingers over the faint grooves, "but something doesn't quite match up".

Tariq studied both the tree's carvings and the map in her hands. After a moment, he tapped a section with his finger.

"Here. *This* is the Ghorband Valley".

Evelyn looked up.

"Are you sure?"

He nodded.

"I have been there before. The valley runs west, toward the old caravan routes. If whoever left this map wanted someone to follow it, then that is where they would be going".

For a long moment, neither of them spoke. The distant cry of a vulture echoed through the pass, and the wind carried the scent of dust and dry earth. Then the wind picked up, rustling through the branches, sending dry leaves tumbling across the ground, as if a heavenly being was willing them on.

Evelyn folded her map and tucked it away.

"Then that's where we're going," she said.

Tariq nodded, stepping back from the tree, giving it a last pat.

Evelyn's fingers lingered on the carvings before she finally let go. The tree stood silent once more as they turned away, leaving behind its whispered secrets and stepping toward the unknown.

Tariq gave a small nod, his gaze temporarily fixed on the tree for a final moment, continuing their journey, their path set, the valley waiting ahead.

The afternoon sun hung low in the sky, casting black shadows across the barren slopes. A vulture circled overhead, its dark silhouette gliding silently as Rashid and his men trudged through the dry earth. The smell hit them first - blood, gunpowder, and the sickly stench of bodies left in the sun too long.

The corpses lay where they had fallen, twisted and broken. One man had been shot clean through the head, the exit wound leaving a mess of blood and bone sprayed across the rocks. Another lay crumpled against a boulder, his fingers still curled around his rifle as if clinging to life even in death. The last had taken a single shot to the neck, dark stains spreading across his shirt like ink spilled onto cloth.

Vakil Khan crouched beside the bodies, studying them intently.

"Clean shots," he muttered, brushing dust from one man's still-warm skin, "these were no ordinary kills."

Rashid's face was like stone, but his fury simmered beneath the surface.

"This was no desperate fight for survival," he said coldly, "this was skill".

His gaze hardened.

"We underestimated them".

Vakil stood, rubbing his beard thoughtfully.

"The man, Tariq...we thought he was a traitor, running like a coward. But he fights like a soldier".

Rashid spat into the dirt.

"And the woman?"

Vakil gestured to the bullet wounds.

"She is not just running either. She is killing".

For a moment, the men stood in silence. Then Rashid smiled grimly.

"Good. Let them think they have won. Let them think they are safe".

His voice dropped to a growl.

"When we catch them, I will show them what it means to challenge us".

He turned on his heel, giving a cursory glance to the stale corpses.

"We must go".

Later that evening, as the sun dipped below the mountain tops, another group arrived at the scene. Jake and his men moved in cautiously, looking for any lingering threats. Mackie crouched by the nearest corpse, nudging it with the barrel of his rifle.

"Well, shit," Lecky murmured, looking over the carnage, "someone had a good time".

Jake nodded.

"Yes mate, and I don't think it was *these* blokes".

Carter whistled low as he kicked over a rifle.

"These aren't just dead men. They were dropped fast .Controlled shots. No panic. No wasted ammo".

Lecky shook his head in amusement.

"Looks like we're following a two man army, boys".

Jake smirked, feeling quite impressed.

"Not bad for an interpreter and a woman eh? And I'd say they're just getting started".

"Tut, tut...not very PC Jake," Lecky joked, referring to his "woman" comment.

"Bollocks to all of that shit mate...have you *seen* where we are?" replied Jake.

CHAPTER 10

THE WATCH TOWER

The Ghorband Valley stretched before them like a vast, untamed wilderness, its golden grasslands rippling in the afternoon breeze. Low shrubs clung precariously to the hillsides like limpets, their roots twisting into the dry earth, while beyond them, the towering ridges of the Hindu Kush rose against the sky, their peaks capped in snow that never melted. The wind carried the scent of distant cedar forests, mingled with the earthy musk of the land. A river snaked through the valley floor, its waters gleaming silver in the dying light.

Evelyn and Tariq walked silently on, following the remnants of an old long-forgotten caravan road that wound its way toward the crumbling silhouette of the watchtower in the distance. It stood alone, weathered and beaten by centuries of wind and war. Its walls, once mighty, were now broken and scarred, ivy and moss clawing at the ancient stones. A single arched entrance yawned open, dark and foreboding, as if it had been waiting for their arrival.

They stepped inside cautiously. Inside, dust hung in the air like a fog, disturbed by their movements. The floor was uneven, strewn with debris - chunks of fallen stone, shattered pottery, and the brittle remains of long-dead fires. High above, a fractured ceiling let in slivers of light, illuminating the ruined chamber in a ghostly glow.

Evelyn's foot caught on something, and she stumbled. Looking down, she drew in a sharp breath, stifling a scream.

A skeleton lay slumped against the wall, its bony fingers curled around a weathered leather book. The skull, tilted slightly forward, seemed to stare at her, as if it had been waiting for someone to hear its final words.

She crouched and gently pried the book loose, her fingers trembling as she opened the fragile pages. Faded ink stained the brittle parchment, the words carefully scribed by a steady hand. And then she saw it - a complete rubbing of the mountain carving they had found in Nuristan. Unlike the damaged version they had seen before, this one revealed every missing detail.

Her pulse quickened.

"Tariq, look at this".

He knelt beside her, his dark eyes taking in the ancient symbols written in a now faded ink, his lips moving silently as he read. Then, at the bottom of the page, they found the riddle:

"The origins of mankind must raise the angel tear to the heavens, at the place where shadows fall at dusk".

Evelyn thought for a moment then began flipping through her own map, her eyes darting between the markings.

"It's not a map," she exclaimed, "its a picture of a real mountain. We need to find it".

Tariq pulled out his own map, spreading it out beside hers. They studied the contours, comparing the shape of the peak to the terrain around them.

"There," Tariq said, tapping a point near the northern ridges, "this could be it".

Evelyn took a closer look, as she thought intently for a moment. Then it came to her and she cursed silently to herself as she studied the map again, running a finger over the contour lines. The mountain in the rubbing had a distinct shape, one she felt she *should* recognise, but with so many peaks in the region, pinpointing the right one was proving difficult.

Then, a memory from her school days surfaced. Contour profiling.

"Wait," she murmured, pulling out her notebook.

She tore a blank page from the back of the book and laid it carefully over the map, aligning the edge with a section of the contour lines. With a pencil, she placed small dots at each point where the contours intersected the edge of the paper, carefully noting their elevation beside each mark.

Tariq watched with curiosity.

"What are you doing?"

She looked up briefly.

"Creating a cross-section; if we can compare the mountain's profile to the rubbing, we'll know if we're in the right place".

Using a ruler from her pencil case, she drew a vertical axis on another blank page, marking the elevation in ten metre intervals. Then, she placed the first marked sheet along the horizontal axis and carefully transferred each contour point to the corresponding height on her graph. Once all the dots were in place, she connected them with smooth, sweeping strokes, revealing the mountain's silhouette.

She held it up beside the rubbing. The outline was a perfect match.

A thrill of excitement shot through her.

"Eureka...what do you reckon Tariq?"

She turned the notebook so he could see.

"It's the same mountain".

He leaned in, nodding with approval.

"You are certain?"

"As certain as I *can* be. This isn't just *any* peak, it's the one from the rubbing, and now we know exactly where to go".

Tariq compared their maps again and smiled.

"If we are right, it is at least another day's journey from here," said an excited Evelyn as she glanced at the skeleton, "and who-ever this was... never made it".

Tariq folded his map.

"Then we will need to be careful".

Outside, the wind howled through the ruins, whispering se-crets long forgotten. The journey was nearing its end - but the real danger had only just begun.

"We should camp here tonight," said Tariq, "it is solid shelter and we have a good view of the valley from here".

"Great. I'll pop the kettle on shall I?" Evelyn responded.

Tariq laughed.

"You English and your tea, you are almost as bad as the Amer-icans with their coffee".

Evelyn smirked as she pulled out her canteen.

"Well, if we had a kettle, I'd be using it".

She took a sip of water instead, feeling the chill of the night creeping in.

The light was fading fast, staining the mountains in deep hues of crimson and violet. Evelyn and Tariq sat against the base of the ruined watchtower, the air cooling rapidly as night settled over the valley. They had been moving hard all day, and exhaustion was taking a heavy toll on their limbs.

Tariq reached into his pack and pulled out a ration pack and handed Evelyn a tin labelled 'rich fruit cake'.

"No flames tonight so we shall eat our food cold".

Evelyn flicked out the can opener attachment on her pen knife and quickly opened the tin.

"Mmmmm...this smells like Christmas cake," she said as she inserted a spoon full of cake into her mouth. "Oh my goodness...it *is* Christmas cake".

Tariq smiled as Evelyn consumed the cake like a ravenous dog, while he worked on a tin of beans.

"Not exactly a feast," she murmured, "but it is better than starving".

Tariq smirked.

"I have shared worse meals in worse places".

He passed her an open can of cold beans.

"Eat. You will need your strength".

They ate in relative quiet, sharing what little they had, chewing in silence as the wind moaned through the ruins, the sounds of the wilderness filling the gaps - owls calling from the far off treetops, the occasional rustling of unseen creatures in the undergrowth. Somewhere far below, a stream trickled over rocks, its quiet babble almost soothing. The cold stone beneath them was a bit of a discomfort, but at least they had solid walls for shelter.

Once their meal was finished, they focused on their weapons. Tariq gently and slowly pulled the cocking handle back on his rifle, then removed all the working parts, checking for dirt and ensuring the mechanism moved smoothly, lightly oiling the breach block. Evelyn did the same, stripping her AK down as best as she could in the dim light, her fingers working by memory. She had never been an expert in stripping down a weapon, but under Tariq's watchful eye, she was learning fast.

"A jammed weapon is a dead man's weapon," he muttered, "so clean it and oil it well".

"Not exactly reassuring," Evelyn replied, but she followed his lead, checking and reassembling her AK.

"Clean rifle, working rifle," Tariq reminded her as he wiped down his own weapon with a cloth.

She nodded, then set the rifle beside her.

"How many rounds do you have left?"

Tariq counted his spare magazines, checking each one before slotting them securely into his webbing.

"Three full magazines...you?"

She pulled out her spare magazines, thumbing a few rounds to ensure they were seated properly before sliding them back into place.

"About two and a half".

"We'll have to make them count," said Tariq.

"I'm hoping that we won't have to," replied Evelyn.

Once satisfied, she attached a fresh magazine into place, ensuring that the safety catch was on, then chambered a round.

Tariq cast his eyes toward the valley.

"We'll take turns keeping watch. You sleep first".

Evelyn didn't argue as she lay back against her pack, tucking her jacket around her, exhaustion claiming her almost instantly. The last thing she saw before drifting off was Tariq crouched by the ruined wall, rifle in hand, eyes staring in to the darkness; before he too succumbed to fatigue, unable to fight his heavy eyelids..

But down in the valley, shadows moved.

Rashid and his men crouched among the rocks, their breath misting in the cold air. The footprints they had found were fresh. The two fugitives were close - so close that Rashid could almost hear their breathing carried by the wind.

He turned to his men, his expression cold and full of purpose.

"They are close, but we shall wait until just before sunrise to see where they might be".

The hunt was almost over. The Taliban were closing in, and they would stop at nothing to find the map and prevent Evelyn Kane from reaching Eden.

The first shots shattered the silence of the cold mountain dawn. Tariq and Evelyn jolted awake as bullets ripped into the exterior of the watch tower, sending shards of stone slicing through the air. The Taliban had found them.

Tariq grabbed his AK-47, rolling into position behind a boulder, while Evelyn snatched up her weapon; her breath coming fast. Shadows moved through the morning mist, advancing fast – at least a dozen of them. Rashid was leading them, his scarred face set with an expression of pure evil.

"Evelyn, right side, stay low!" Tariq shouted, firing off three quick rounds.

The nearest Taliban fighter jerked backward, his rifle falling to the ground as he clutched at his chest, blood spraying between his fingers.

Evelyn took a deep breath, raised her rifle, aimed fast, and squeezed the trigger. The 7.62mm round punched into a man's thigh, knocking him violently off his feet. He dropped like a sack of grain, twitching in the dust, bleating like a terrified goat.

Vakil snarled and threw up a hand.

"Flank them! Move!"

Two fighters sprinted to the side, their weapons raised. Tariq saw their movement, swung his weapon around, and let off three rounds in quick succession. The first man crumpled mid-step, as he tumbled backwards down the rocky slope his body hitting the rocks with a sickening crack. The second threw himself to the ground hoping to evade the keen eyes of their prey to the front of them. Tariq had other ideas as he trained his sights in the area he had seen the fighter land, and within seconds the man lifted his head to have a look around. There was no hesitation from Tariq as he squeezed off a round, hitting the man square in the face, his head exploding from the force of the bullet pushing through his skull.

They were holding their own - for now. But the Taliban kept coming.

Evelyn was already re-loading; hands steady despite the terror clawing at her chest.

Then came Rashid's voice, cold and sure.

"Push forward. They are finished".

He was right. Tariq and Evelyn had done well - but they were outnumbered. The Taliban were closing in, circling like wolves, ready to finish them off.

Then - hell itself erupted.

A deep, thump rolled through the valley and a boom shook the pass as a grenade exploded behind Rashid's men. Shrapnel tore through flesh, sending limbs and dust flying, the screams of two fighters lost in the concussion.

Gunfire burst from the ridge. Controlled. Precise. Deadly.

Jake and his team had arrived.

It was shock and awe on a small scale as Jake, Lecky, and Mackie moved first, sprinting forward while Carter, Parks, and Taylor dropped to their bellies, rifles up, laying down a storm of suppressive automatic fire.

A Taliban fighter tried to return fire but Taylor's round caught him in the sternum, the force lifting him off his feet before he hit the ground, dead.

Carter shouted, "Go!" and the three prone men jumped up, sprinting past their comrades, taking their turn to move while Jake's group dropped to cover them.

It was textbook. Lethal, precise and unstoppable.

The Taliban had no time to react before the next volley tore through them.

A fighter lunged for cover - Mackie caught him with a burst to the spine, his body folding in on itself before he hit the dirt.

Rashid fired back, eyes wild, shouting orders - until Parks's bullet punched through his ribs, knocking him sideways into the dust, where he lay still.

Vakil Khan turned to run, but Taylor lobbed a 40mm grenade from his Underslung Grenade Launcher, otherwise known as a UGL. The explosion swallowed him, leaving nothing but blood-streaked rock.

The last few Taliban fighters tried to retreat, but Lecky, Mackie, and Carter surged forward, rifles kicking. A man was blown off his feet, another collapsed clutching his throat, choking on his own blood.

And then - silence.

Just the crackle of burning cloth and the slow drip of blood on to stone.

But one man still lived.

Faheem.

Faheem - young, nervous Faheem - pressed himself against the rocks, clutching his rifle, breath coming in ragged gasps. His hands shook, his heart slammed against his ribs, his ears rang. From the shadows, he watched, terrified, as the Western soldiers moved through the carnage, checking the bodies, kicking each man between the legs to test that they were not feigning death, removing papers, weapons and ammunition.

He would wait, because now, he was the last one left, and the only one who could still take revenge.

Mackie moved through the rocks, rifle up, his eyes scouring the wreckage of the ambush site. The stench of blood and burned flesh hung in the morning air. A few feet away, a body twitched - one of the Taliban fighters not quite dead yet. Mackie put a round in his head without breaking stride.

Then he saw the movement.

A shadow wedged tight between two boulders, trembling. He moved quietly closer, rifle trained. A pair of wide, darting eyes stared back at him.

"Got one!" Mackie called out.

He reached in, grabbed a fistful of filthy shirt, and yanked the man to his feet.

Faheem's legs buckled. His rifle fell from his grip.

Then came the sharp stink of urine.

Mackie wrinkled his nose.

"Bloody hell, he's pissed himself!"

He gave the boy a shake, making him whimper.

"Not so brave now you little shit. Can't fight real soldiers can you, but innocent unarmed people are easy for gutless pricks like you aren't they? Jake!" Mackie called over his shoulder, "you want me to off this one?"

Jake glanced over, saw Faheem, and gave a shrug.

"Fill yer boots, mate".

Evelyn stepped forward fast.

"No!"

Her voice snapped through the morning air.

"Look at him - he's terrified!"

Mackie sneered.

"Yeah? So were half the poor bastards these pricks killed".

He tightened his grip on Faheem's collar, pistol sliding from its holster.

"Wait," Tariq said, stepping in, "let me speak to him first".

Jake rolled his eyes but gave a nod.

"Make it quick".

Tariq turned to Faheem, eyes narrowing.

"What is your name?"

"Faheem," the boy whispered. His knees were still shaking.

"Why are you with *them*?"

Faheem hesitated. Then replied, in a whisper: "They...made me".

Tariq studied him for a long moment.

"But you still fought?"

Faheem's fingers twitched, his eyes darting between them all. He knew what Tariq wanted to hear. What might keep him alive.

"I...I didn't want to!"

He swallowed.

"They would have killed me if I refused!"

Tariq watched him carefully, then said in Pashto, "But if you had the chance, you would kill us now, wouldn't you?"

Faheem said nothing.

But his silence was enough.

Tariq turned to Jake.

"I do not know what to think. He is scared and tells me he was forced to fight, but I do not know..."

"Sit him down and I'll have a think about it," Jake replied, as he held out his right hand to Tariq, "any way mate, long time no see eh?"

His grip tightened on Jake's hand for a moment, as if making sure he was real.

"Yes, it *has* been a long time dear friend".

"Your family is safe, by the way, probably in England by now, so we're just out to liberate you and Miss Kane here," Jake announced.

Relief flooded Tariq's face.

"That is good news. You do not know how much that means to me".

"No mate...I think we do," replied Jake.

Evelyn looked at the two men, surprised.

"You two know each other?"

Jake chuckled, giving Tariq a knowing look, holding out his hand in greeting to Evelyn.

"Pleased to meet you Miss Kane...yes we go way back. Tariq worked with us as a translator for years. Accompanied plenty of our patrols - sometimes in places even *we* didn't want to go".

Tariq nodded, his expression turning nostalgic.

"I learned more than just language from you soldiers. You taught me how to fight, how to track. Even how to drink that terrible black coffee you all love".

Jake laughed.

"That's these Yanks. We British drink tea, and other stuff or course...*and* you still never bought a round, you tight bastard".

Tariq placed a hand on his chest in mock indignation.

"My coca cola is much cheaper than your beer. I was on an interpreter's salary! You, on the other hand, were being paid far too much, my friend".

Evelyn smirked at the banter between the two men.

"So, let me get this straight - you were part of the SAS before?"

Tariq shrugged and shook his head.

"I was never part of them, but I was trusted. And I trusted them".

He turned to Jake.

"Though I did not expect to see you again like this".

Jake's grin faded slightly.

"Yeah, well. The world's gone to shit, hasn't it? But when we heard you were in trouble, we weren't going to sit back and do nothing".

Tariq's expression was solemn but grateful.

"Then I owe you again, all of you, my friends".

Jake patted him on the shoulder.

"You don't owe us a bloody thing. Let's just get through this in one piece, yeah?"

There was a silent pause.

"What is the plan for him?" said Tariq, nodding toward the captured Taliban fighter.

Jake's gaze shifted to the prisoner.

"We can't afford to let him live".

Evelyn froze.

"What?" she exclaimed.

Jake turned to her, his expression serious.

"We're deep in hostile territory, Miss Kane. If he escapes or gets word out about our presence, this whole mission goes to hell. I won't risk *my* team *or* you for the sake of one fanatic; and besides, do you think he'd do the same for you?"

Evelyn's stomach churned. She wanted to argue, to protest, but the steely resolve in Jake's voice silenced her.

The SAS and the US special forces had been formed during the Second World War in order to fight an unconventional war against their foes. They struck silently, fast and hard, leaving no trace for the enemy. Their mission always came first and they rarely took prisoners...much like their enemies.

Tariq, too, seemed uneasy.

"I understand your reasoning, Jake, but there must be another way..."

"There isn't," Jake interrupted, his tone leaving no room for debate, "we can't take him with us, and we can't leave him behind. You're here because of the risks we take. Those risks have limits".

Evelyn looked away as the sergeant gave a curt nod to Taylor. The soldier stepped forward, his weapon ready, and grabbed Faheem by the collar. Jake moved towards Taylor and whispered something to him, before he dragged Faheem behind a cluster of rocks. The young fighter whimpered, his body trembling, his feet dragging in the dirt, and Evelyn closed her eyes momentarily and swallowed hard, forcing herself to stare straight ahead. She didn't want to hear it. Didn't want to see it.

A minute passed.

Then another.

The sharp crack of a pistol shot never came. Instead, Taylor returned, his expression stern, sheathing his knife as he walked.

"All clear," he said simply.

Evelyn's eyes flicked to Jake, who gave a barely perceptible nod. She wasn't sure whether she was relieved or just disturbed by what had happened.

Tariq let out a breath he hadn't realised he was holding.

Amongst the group there was silence.

The six soldiers exchanged looks before suddenly shaking their heads in silent laughter.

"Take a look, Miss Kane," Mackie said, jerking his chin toward the valley.

Confused, Evelyn turned - and her eyes widened.

In the distance, a small figure was scrambling over the rocky terrain as fast as his legs could carry him. Faheem.

"We are soldiers, Miss Kane," Jake said, smirking, "not murderers".

Evelyn's tense shoulders loosened slightly.

"He's been given a choice," Jake continued, "stay gone, or die next time".

Evelyn watched Faheem disappear over a ridge. She hoped they wouldn't see him again.

But for now, they had bigger concerns.

Jake clapped his hands once, then turned to the group.

"Right kids once it starts to get dark we'll make tracks. Double time and we won't be stopping for shit".

Evelyn hesitated, glancing toward the ruins of the watch tower behind them.

"What about...?"

"The Garden of Eden?" Jake cut in, "yeah, I know about that".

His voice was all business.

"But as amazing as it would be to find, we don't have time".

Evelyn couldn't contain her disappointment, especially after what she and Tariq had gone through.

"But..."

Jake turned, fixing her with a look that silenced any protest.

"But nothing Miss Kane. Even if we did have time, it wouldn't matter. Our orders are clear - if the Taliban get anywhere near it, we destroy it".

Evelyn inhaled sharply.

"Destroy it?"

Tariq's face darkened, but he said nothing.

Jake sighed.

"Look, I don't like it either, but we can't let them turn it into some propaganda piece, or worse - an operations base. If we confirm it exists, we level it".

Evelyn clenched her fists. The thought of wiping away something so ancient, so untouched by war, made her stomach twist. But she understood the cold logic behind the decision. The Taliban would twist its existence into something monstrous.

Tariq placed a reassuring hand on her shoulder.

"Survival first. The rest can wait".

She nodded reluctantly. The conversation was over, though her determination to continue to search was not.

CHAPTER 11

WE NEED A MIRACLE

As darkness fell, the team pressed on, moving in a tight formation through the valley, the only sounds the whisper of the wind and the occasional hoot of an owl.

Every so often, one of the soldiers would halt, scanning the ridgelines with night vision goggles before giving the signal to move on. Their objective was clear - get back to their vehicles and then radio in for a rendezvous point for extraction. But between them and that goal lay miles of open ground, enemy patrols, and the ever present threat of an ambush.

Jake led the way, his rifle butt firmly in his shoulder, weapon at the ready, every step calculated.

"We stick to cover," he had said before their departure, "stay low, stay quiet. If we're spotted, we go loud and we go fast".

They weaved through dry riverbeds and uneven gullies, keeping to the shadows. The night was alive with distant sounds - a lone dog barking somewhere in the hills, the rustling of wind through the sparse trees, and, far away, the faint murmur of voices.

Lecky gestured ahead, speaking in a whisper.

"There's a ridgeline up ahead. Once we clear it, we'll have a straight one day run to the ATVs".

Jake nodded then waved the group onwards, their senses heightened.

The wind shifted, carrying a faint scent of wood smoke. It was a small detail, but enough to put everyone on edge. Somewhere in the darkness danger lurked.

The next day, the group managed a brief rest before continuing on their journey. The tension grew even more obvious as they moved through the mountains, closer to the point where their transport was hidden. Each step seemed heavier, laden with the weight of the risks they were taking. They knew the Taliban were out there, hunting them. The soldiers were on high alert, their eyes constantly searching for danger, their fingers always ready on the triggers of their rifles.

As they made their way through a narrow pass, they came upon the remains of a village - abandoned, gutted. The signs of the Taliban were unmistakable: burned buildings, broken roads, and bodies left behind in the dust. The village had been a symbol of defiance, a symbol of the struggle the people here faced every day. Now, it was just another casualty of war.

Jake stood and observed the ruins of the village and shook his head.

"Another piece of senseless destruction by our Taliban mates".

"What do you mean?" Evelyn asked.

"Two years ago we were at this very spot guarding what was then a construction site," he replied, pointing at several wrecked buildings, "that there was a school, and over there a medical centre, but look at it now...bloody bastards. They just don't want to be in the new century at all, or have women, or anyone educated. Makes no sense does it?"

Evelyn couldn't look away. This was the reality of her mission, the truth she had hoped to avoid. But she knew that this was why she had come - to witness it, to understand it. The destruction, the bloodshed, it wasn't just a part of the story - it *was* the story. And in this country, it had been the story for far too long.

Her resolve suddenly strengthened, the guilt, the fear, the doubt - it all melted away. She had a job to do. She had a mission, and it wasn't over yet. Somehow she would find the Garden.

The mountains ahead emerged large and overbearing, but Evelyn took a deep breath and continued forward. No matter what lay ahead, she would face it. She had no choice, and she would do it with the strength of those who had come before her, those who had fought and died for a future that was still so far out of reach.

Despite her determination, Evelyn struggled to keep up, her mind racing. She had known the risks of coming to Afghanistan, had prepared herself for the dangers, but the shocking reality of war was far more brutal than she had anticipated.

Tariq's voice broke her thoughts.

"Are you alright Miss Kane?"

She looked up at him, his concern evident despite his usual stoicism.

"I'm fine," she lied.

Tariq didn't believe her, but left it at that.

The terrain was becoming steeper as the daylight was becoming more intense, the trail narrowing as they ascended higher into the mountains. Evelyn's muscles burned, but she forced herself to keep moving, knowing that stopping was not an option.

Jake was soon walking beside her, concerned that she might not be able to keep up.

"How are you doing mate?" he asked.

"Tired, but I'll get there," Evelyn replied.

Jake nodded his approval.

"You'll be fine. It's all in the mind. Just lean forward and look at the ground and not where you're going. We'll keep you safe".

The special forces soldiers were masters of stealth, and even in the middle of enemy territory, they moved with an eerie calmness that Evelyn couldn't quite replicate. She had always prided herself on her strength and staying power, but the brutality of what they had just encountered, what they were still encountering, was a level of violence she had never imagined.

By the time the mid day sun had crept high in the sky, they had reached a narrow ridge that offered some degree of protection from the surrounding mountains. They set up a temporary rest point, huddled beneath a rocky overhang where the wind could not reach them. Tariq, exhausted, but always watchful, sat beside Evelyn, his eyes constantly flicking back and forth to what lay ahead.

"Do you think they'll find us?" Evelyn asked in a low voice.

"Maybe," Tariq replied, his face sombre, "they know we're close. They'll send more patrols".

His gaze shifted to Jake, who was overseeing the setup of their position.

"But with the soldiers here, they're not going to find us easily. These men know how to disappear".

Evelyn nodded, though she felt no real sense of relief. The Taliban were ruthless, and their thirst for power had led them to become unstoppable in their pursuit of anyone who opposed them, whether that opposition came in the form of foreign soldiers or local collaborators. There were no lines between right and wrong in their world. There was only victory and death.

Their break, although for half an hour, seemed to last for only a few minutes; at least to the uninitiated few. Then the group continued on their hike, crossing undulating terrain as if it was a Sunday stroll, the hours passing quickly by.

Jake slowed as they approached a crest, signalling for the group to halt again. The daylight was beginning to fade as he motioned for Tariq and Evelyn to stay low while he and Lecky crawled forward to scout the area.

Evelyn crouched in a dip in the ground, her heart pounding. She could see the faint glow of a campfire in the distance, its flickering light illuminating the silhouettes of several men.

Tariq sat beside her.

"Another Taliban group," he murmured.

Evelyn nodded, her throat dry.

"How many?"

"Five, maybe six," Tariq said, "too many for us to avoid without being seen".

Jake returned, his expression serious.

"They're blocking the trail. We'll have to take them out".

Evelyn's stomach tightened.

"Is there no way around?"

"Not without losing hours," Jake replied, "and the longer we're out here, the more likely we'll run into another patrol - or worse".

The soldiers prepared to strike, their movements quick and efficient. Carter set up a sniper rifle, complete with silencer; his telescopic sight trained on the campfire. Jake briefed the group, his voice a whisper, detailing the plan of attack.

Evelyn watched, feeling both awe and unease at how ordered and organised they were. These men were professionals, trained to operate in the most hostile environments. But their efficiency was a stark reminder of the stakes they faced.

Carter fired first, the suppressed shots a faint whisper, as two Taliban fighters dropped before they even knew what hit them. The others scrambled for their weapons, shouting in panic, but the team moved in with lethal speed.

Evelyn stayed behind with Tariq, her breath caught in her throat as the battle unfolded. The crack of gunfire echoed through the mountains, mingling with the shouts of the Taliban fighters. The encounter was over in minutes.

Jake returned, changing magazines on his rifle as he walked. His tense expression told Evelyn everything she needed to know.

"It's done," he muttered.

Behind him, the rest of the team emerged from the darkness - but something was wrong. Lecky, Taylor and Carter were carrying Mackie between them, Taylor gripping the laces of his boots as the other two held onto his webbing straps, trying to keep his body stable. Blood soaked through his uniform, dark and wet, spilling onto the rocky ground with every step.

Jake's eyes swept over him.

"Shit!"

Mackie let out a low groan, his head lolling against Carter's thigh. His breathing was shallow, his face pale and glistening with sweat.

"Looks bad, Jake. Real bad," Taylor said through gritted teeth.

Jake knelt beside Mackie, gently opening his shirt. The wound was in the stomach, a deep, ugly gash. Blood oozed between Jake's fingers as he pressed down, trying to slow the bleeding. Mackie gave a weak grunt but barely reacted.

"Get the medical kit," Jake ordered.

Lecky was already ahead of him, yanking out bandages and gauze. He and Taylor worked fast, packing the wound, trying to stop the bleeding. But the look they shared told Jake the truth - this was beyond anything they could fix out here.

"We need a casevac," Carter said urgently, pulling out the radio.

He tried the frequency twice. Only static.

"Nothing," he said, adjusting the antenna, "still nothing. Bloody mountains!"

Jake exhaled sharply, pressing his knuckles against his forehead.

"Bloody hell!"

They were trapped. Taliban forces were everywhere, the radio was useless, and Mackie was dying.

A soft voice broke the silence.

"We have to find the Garden".

Everyone turned to Evelyn.

She met their stares, with a determined defiance.

"I know it sounds mad, but if there's even a chance that some-one...something...that can help him, we have to take it".

Taylor let out a dry laugh.

"You think Eden has a field hospital waiting for us?"

"It might have *something*," she shot back, "people, medi-cine...the hand of God...I don't know...anything is better than sitting here waiting for him to bleed to death".

The soldiers exchanged uncertain glances.

Tariq spoke calmly.

"I do not know if the legends are true, but I do know one thing - we have nowhere else to go".

Jake thought for a moment, looked at Mackie, barely clinging to consciousness, then at his men. They needed a miracle.

"Alright," he said finally, "we find the bloody Garden".

Jake stood, turning to Tariq.

"So mate, what's the move?"

Tariq looked over to Evelyn and, after a quick nod of ap-proval, reached in to her pack for her notebook and flipped it open to a page from the watchtower. There, drawn in careful de-tail, was the cross-section they had sketched days ago - a perfect match to the mountain carving they had found in Nuristan. He tapped the drawing.

"We already know where we need to go," he said, "we worked it out back at the watchtower".

Evelyn pulled out her map, her fingers quickly finding the marked location.

"Right here," she said, pointing to the mountain they had identified before, "this is our destination".

Jake turned his attention to the surrounding terrain.

"How far?"

"Twenty, maybe twenty five kilometres from the tower," Tariq estimated, "rough ground, but we can make it".

Jake exhaled sharply, glancing at Mackie.

"So more than two days away? Not with him in this state. We'll need to carry him. What do you reckon Mac?"

Mackie said nothing but just smiled and nodded his approval through the pain.

Taylor frowned.

"We're exposed if we get caught carrying him, but I suppose we're damned if we do and damned if we don't".

"We don't have a choice," Jake said, looking at his team "he's our mate and I don't know about you lot, but I'm not going to let him die in this shit hole".

All present grunted their agreement.

Jake smiled.

"Right then...good...let's sort old Mac out here, then check your weapons and kit, get some rest, and we'll head off at first light. Let's see if we can get there in a day".

They worked quickly, going through Mackie's pack for anything useful, then, using the pack as a pillow made Mackie as comfortable as possible. Lecky and Carter spread out a poncho and rigged up a crude stretcher using the poncho and two sturdy branches which they hacked to size with a machete. Taylor, meanwhile pressed more gauze into his wound. Blood still seeped through, but at least it had slowed.

Jake crouched beside him, gently placing a hand on his shoulder.

"Are you still with us, mate?"

Mackie's eyelids fluttered, his breath shallow.

"Yeah," he whispered through blood stained teeth, "but I feel like I've been kicked by a flaming donkey or something".

"You look like one too," Taylor quipped, forcing a smirk.

Mackie gave a weak chuckle that quickly turned into a grimace.

"Cheers mate".

Evelyn knelt next to him, adjusting the makeshift pillow under his head.

"You'll be fine," she said gently, "we're taking you to heavenly help".

"Hopefully not *too* close to heaven Miss," Mackie replied as he coughed and spluttered more blood.

Faheem had fled into the night like the coward that he was, stumbling through the harsh wilderness, gasping for air, his heart pulsating from the terror of his near execution. But by the time he reached Bamiyan, something inside him had shifted. Shame curdled into rage, fear into burning hatred. He had been spared, not out of mercy, or so he thought, but as an insult, a humiliation he could not bear. Now, he would prove himself. He would return, not as a defeated man, but as the one who would deliver vengeance.

The remnants of Rashid's men, who had remained with the vehicles, gathered around the trucks, their expressions mixed as they listened to Faheem's breathless tale. He painted himself as a survivor of a ruthless ambush, describing in vivid detail how he had outwitted the foreign soldiers, escaping death by sheer will. He spoke of the infidel woman and the traitor Tariq, how they travelled with a handful of Godless soldiers, remnants of a larger force that he and his brethren had killed. Lies to fuel the already festering hatred.

"They are weak," Faheem insisted, his voice rising with conviction, "and I know where they are going. They cannot move fast, not with a *woman*. If we move now, we can catch up with them and kill them all".

In reality he had no idea of where they were going, but would take them back to the watch tower in the hopes of finding a trail.

A grizzled fighter, his face marked with old battle scars, leaned forward.

"And you are sure of this?"

Faheem nodded, eyes gleaming.

"I swear it. I live because I am a lion, and I shall have my revenge".

The men talked amongst themselves. They had lost Rashid and the others in the attack, but revenge was a powerful motivator. Faheem had given them something they desperately needed - a target, a chance to strike back.

Finally, the scarred man stood.

"Then we move when the sun rises".

Faheem grinned, feeling a rush of pride. He had done more than survive. He had taken control of his own fate, or so he thought. Now, he would lead the hunt, and this time, there would be no mercy.

At first light, they moved out, the sun cresting the mountain peaks as they shouldered their packs and began the gruelling march. The terrain was uncompromising - loose, shifting shale, steep inclines that tested their endurance, and narrow ridges where a single misstep could mean a fatal fall.

Mackie lay strapped to the makeshift stretcher, pale and sweating as his comrades took turns carrying him. Taylor and Carter started off, gripping the wooden poles as they navigated the uneven ground. After an hour, they changed over, Lecky and Tariq taking over, Tariq, gritting his teeth against the weight, and Jake moving with a quiet strength of will born from years of physical endurance. Even Evelyn took her turn, struggling as she helped shoulder the burden alongside Jake. The strain burned in her muscles, but she refused to complain.

Every few miles, they stopped to adjust the stretcher, drink from their canteens, and catch their breath before pressing on. The heat bore down on them, the dry wind whipping dust into their faces, but they didn't falter. They had planned to reach the tower by midday, and by the time they spotted its silhouette against the horizon, the sun hung high, casting harsh shadows across the landscape.

"You beauty," Carter muttered, rolling his shoulders as they crested the last ridge.

They had arrived at the watchtower as planned, the crumbling structure standing like a lone sentinel over the barren landscape. As the others set Mackie down and checked their gear, Evelyn found herself standing slightly apart, rolling the tension from her shoulders. Her body ached from the march, her throat raw from the dry air, but her mind was restless.

She looked briefly at Jake, watching as he crouched beside the stretcher, checking Mackie's pulse.

"How are you mate?" he asked.

He groaned, his breath shallow, but gave Jake a weak thumbs-up.

The sun cast sharp angles on Jake's face - strong jaw, tanned skin, a slight shadow of stubble across his cheek. His dark hair was damp with sweat, pushed back from his forehead, and despite the dust and exhaustion, there was something steady about him. Something solid.

He caught her looking.

"Are you alright, Miss Kane?"

She straightened, suddenly aware that she'd been staring. Her expression like that of a naughty child who had been caught out, but was trying unsuccessfully to hide her guilt.

"I...er...yeah. Just...catching my breath".

Jake smirked, standing up and adjusting the sling of his rifle over his shoulder.

"Long march. You did well, though. Not bad for a civvie".

"High praise," she said dryly, but she couldn't ignore the flicker of warmth at his words.

Her gaze dropped briefly to his left hand - no ring. But that didn't necessarily mean anything. Soldiers rarely wore them in the field.

She hesitated, then asked casually,

"Do you have a family back home?"

Jake studied her for a moment, his green eyes giving nothing away. Then he breathed out, almost sighing, shifting his weight slightly.

"I'm married to the regiment, Miss Kane. These fellas are my family...well until someone special comes along anyway".

Something about the way he said it, light hearted on the surface, but with an edge of truth underneath, made butterflies flutter in her stomach.

She nodded, looking away toward the horizon.

"Shame," she murmured, barely loud enough for him to hear.

If he did, he gave no sign. Instead, he turned back to Mackie, and his team.

"How's he looking?" Jake asked as Taylor knelt beside him, checking the wound.

"Still with us," Taylor replied, "but he will need proper care soon".

"Then we can't afford to waste time".

Jake turned to the others.

"Five minute breather, then we're off".

No one argued. They gulped down water, ate what little rations they could stomach, and "cracked on", as Jake put it.

Evelyn let out a breath, shaking her head at herself. Now was not the time for distractions. But as she followed the others, she couldn't quite shake the feeling that, against all logic, Jake had just become one.

The landscape changed as they descended toward the valley. The steep slopes of the Salang Pass loomed ahead, its peaks dusted with snow, even in the brutal heat.

It was Tariq who first spotted the glade, a patch of green hidden in the otherwise barren terrain.

"There," he said, pointing, "water".

They followed him down a narrow track until they stepped into an oasis of shade. A small spring bubbled gently between the rocks, its water so clear it seemed almost unreal. The air was cooler here, the aroma of wild herbs filling their lungs.

Evelyn crouched beside the stream, running her fingers through the water. A strange sensation prickled at her skin; not just the cold, but something else. A hum, a whisper, just at the edge of hearing.

"These springs," she murmured, staring into the depths, "could be what's left of Eden's rivers. The tales of immortality might not just be legend".

Jake knelt beside her, scooping a handful of water and letting it trickle through his fingers.

"Immortality sounds good, but right now, I just care if it's drinkable".

"It is," Tariq assured him, "and it is the best we are going to find out here".

They took the chance to refill their canteens, splashing water on their faces to cool down. Meanwhile, Taylor checked Mackie's wounds.

"He's burning up," Taylor muttered, reaching in to his medical kit for another ampoule, "we need to keep the morphine going, or he won't last the next stretch."

"Then give it to him," Jake replied.

Mackie exhaled shakily as the drug took hold, his body relaxing despite the heat and pain. Taylor unscrewed his canteen, pouring a small measure of the spring water into the cap before lifting it to Mackie's cracked lips. The wounded soldier swallowed weakly, a slight wrinkling appearing on his sweat coated brow.

"Easy, buddy," Taylor whispered.

He then dabbed his fingers into the cool water and smeared it across Mackie's forehead. At first, nothing happened. Then, almost imperceptibly, the tension in Mackie's features eased. His ragged breathing grew steadier, his skin losing some of its ghastly pallor. It wasn't a miracle, but there was a change - subtle, yet undeniable.

"Hey everyone look at Mac. Does he look a little better to you?" Taylor asked.

"Still looks his usual ugly self to me," Lecky joked as he crouched next to Mackie, "seriously though bud, how are you?"

Mackie managed a small cough.

"A little better thanks".

Jake glanced at the others.

"Must be the morphine".

Taylor shook his head.

"No, I think it's the water Jake".

"A miracle eh?" Jake laughed, "whatever it is, this place is a gift, but we need to keep moving".

Evelyn nodded, but as she stood, she swore she still heard those whispers - faint, ancient, calling, like a heavenly choir.

CHAPTER 12

THE TREE SHALL GUIDE THE WORTHY

Long shadows spilled across the mountains and valleys as the team continued their journey. It was harsh country – razor sharp ridges, deep ravines, and steep inclines that tested their every step. Sweat streaked their dust-covered faces, muscles ached, and exhaustion gnawed at them, but none of them slowed. There was too much at risk.

Mackie, though still pale and weak, looked noticeably better since drinking from the Whispering Springs. His breathing was steadier, and his eyes, once glazed with fever, now held a spark of awareness. He hadn't spoken much, but he clung to consciousness, his fingers gripping the sides of the stretcher as they carried him in shifts.

The sky turned amber, streaked with deep purples and fiery reds, as they reach the top of, what they hoped was, the final ridge, and looked down into a vast valley. The air felt different here - cooler, fresher, as though untouched by the war torn world beyond; lost in time. At its heart, rising like an ancient custodian, stood the mountain.

It was unlike anything they had seen before. Not the tallest peak, nor the most imposing, yet it commanded attention in a way none of them could explain. The summit seemed to glow in the fading sunlight, an exquisite gold hue reflecting off its rocky face. A hush fell over the group as they took it in, an unspoken sense of reverence passing between them.

Evelyn felt it most keenly - a stirring in her chest, a pull deep in her soul. Hope. Her attention moved to Tariq, who was staring at the mountain with wide eyes, lips mouthing a silent prayer. Even the hardened soldiers seemed affected, their usual banter and grumbling replaced by quiet awe.

Jake exhaled, hands on his hips as he surveyed their destination.

"Well, I'll be buggered".

Taylor nodded.

"It feels...different here".

"It does," Evelyn agreed softly, "this place... its special".

They all felt it. Something about this mountain, this valley, whispered of forgotten truths, of mysteries waiting to be uncovered.

Jake gave a final glance at the darkening sky.

As the light of the sun began to slowly dim, the team gathered around Evelyn as she unrolled the map, placing it carefully on a flat rock. Jake crouched beside her, inquisitive, as he compared their earlier cross-section sketch to the mountain before them.

"Bloody hell," he muttered, running a hand through his dust-caked hair, "it's a perfect match. Every ridge, every peak - it's exactly the same".

He sighed, shaking his head slightly.

"Alright, Miss Kane. We're here. Now what?"

Evelyn turned to the sergeant with a smile.

"Oh for goodness sake, you *can* call me Eve you know".

Evelyn flicked through the pages of her journal, her fingers tracing the inked lines of an old passage. She read aloud:

"When Adam and Eve see clearly, They, and they alone, must raise the Angel's Tear to the heavens, The Tree shall guide the worthy".

Jake glanced at the others.

"And that means...?"

Evelyn tapped the words, excitement creeping into her voice.

"It suggests that Adam and Eve - meaning two people - need to see clearly. That could mean finding the right vantage point".

She looked up at the mountain.

"And 'raising the Angel's Tear' - that might mean holding something up to the sky. But the last line - 'The Tree shall guide the worthy' - that's the key".

Tariq, who had been listening intently, pointed toward the valley floor.

"It could mean we need to look for where the mountain's shadow falls. If this place is as old as the legend claims, then the clue might be referring to something that only reveals itself at the right time of day".

Jake let out a relieved breath.

"So we don't have to climb the bloody thing".

Taylor smirked.

"That's a win in my book".

"Yeah, mine too," replied Jake, "I think I'm getting too old for this malarkey".

Evelyn nodded.

"We watch where the shadow lands at sunset. That might lead us to the next step".

The group made camp in the valley, the air was crisp, and the last golden rays of the sun bathed the peaks in a warm glow. They took turns eating rations, checking their weapons, and setting up a rotating watch. Taylor volunteered for the first shift, taking position near a boulder with a clear line of sight across the valley.

Evelyn sat near Jake, wrapping her arms around her knees.

"You said you were getting too old for this," she said with a small smile, "how long have you been doing this kind of work?"

Jake exhaled and leaned back on his pack.

"Nearly twenty-two years," he admitted. "My time in the army is almost up. One more tour, then I'm done".

She studied him in the flickering firelight. The strong lines of his face, the faint scars, the streaks of grey at his temples - he had the hardened look of a man who had seen too much, but there was still something steady and reliable about him.

"What will you do when it's over?" she asked.

He shrugged.

"Dunno. I could go private, do security work. Plenty of companies would take me on".

Evelyn hesitated, then took a chance.

"Or...you could come on expeditions with me".

Jake turned to look at her, his brow raised in surprise.

"Expeditions?"

She smiled.

"Yes. There are plenty of mysteries yet to be solved. You seem handy in a crisis. And this life...it suits you".

Jake huffed a laugh.

"And there I was, thinking you were propositioning me or something".

"Maybe I was," replied Evelyn, with a cheeky grin.

Jake felt relieved and embarrassed at the same time.

"Well, let's survive this one first, Miss Kane...er Eve".

Before Evelyn could respond, Tariq called out, his voice urgent but not alarmed.

"It's happening."

They turned their heads to the valley. The sun had finally dipped below the horizon, and as the mountain's shadow stretched across the valley floor, something shimmered into existence.

A tree.

But not just any tree.

It stood alone in the valley, massive and ancient, its branches reaching toward the heavens. Its bark gleamed like polished gold, and its leaves shimmered with an ethereal glow, each one shifting between vibrant greens, silvers, and deep blues, as though capturing the essence of life itself. A gentle breeze rustled through its branches, and with it came a whisper - not of the wind, but of something older, something sentient...being able to see or feel things.

Evelyn gasped suddenly.

"The Tree of Life," she whispered.

Jake's eyes scanned the valley as if struggling to believe what he was seeing.

"Bloody hell…"

The whisper came again, curling through the air like an ancient melody.

"Raise the key to the heavens".

Tariq gasped and pointed to the sky.

"Look!"

Above them, the Adam and Eve constellation had appeared, its twin figures outlined in countless stars.

Evelyn's hands trembled as she reached into her pack, carefully unwrapping the Angel's Tear that they had retrieved from the cave at Nuristan. The crystal - clear as water yet holding an inner glow - felt warm in her palm.

"*This* is the key," she said softly.

Tariq nodded.

"Hold it up to the sky".

Evelyn did as he instructed, raising the crystal toward the constellation. They waited.

Nothing happened.

The whisper came again, more insistent this time.

"Only Adam and Eve must raise it".

Tariq was confused and turned to Evelyn.

"Evelyn…*you* are Eve…but we have no Adam".

Jake gave a short, incredulous laugh.

"That's ridiculous".

Tariq shook his head.

"No. It is written. Adam and Eve must be here together. That has to be the answer".

Jake rubbed a hand over his face.

"This might sound strange, but...*my* first name is Adam."

Evelyn blinked at him.

"I thought you were Jake?"

"Jake...well, Black Jake, is just a nickname," he admitted, "I'll explain later".

Tariq exhaled sharply and praised God.

"It is fate. You two were meant to be here".

The importance of the moment settled over them like a warm embrace. Evelyn looked at Jake, her heart pounding. He met her gaze, something undiscernible in his eyes.

"Alright," Jake muttered, "I'm game. Let's see where this goes".

Together, their hands wrapped around the crystal, they lifted it toward the heavens, and as they did so, a sudden hush fell over the valley. Anticipation filled the air, the very fabric of reality seeming to hold its breath. The crystal, cold and solid in their hands moments before, now pulsed with a warmth that spread up their arms and into their chests.

Then, the heavens answered.

A great beam of golden light descended from the Adam and Eve constellation, a shaft of pure radiance splitting the darkness like the dawn of creation itself. It struck the crystal, refracting through its flawless surface, and for an instant, Evelyn swore she could see entire worlds swirling within its depths - galaxies spinning, rivers flowing, life in its purest form.

The crystal magnified the celestial glow, bending it, focusing it, until a single ray shot down into the valley below.

The earth trembled.

From the point where the light touched, the barren ground cracked, and from its depths, something impossibly ancient began to stir. Like mist burning away at sunrise, the desolate valley gave way to something new - no, something restored.

Lush greenery spread outward in all directions, unfurling like the first day of spring after an eternal winter. Flowers of unimaginable colours burst into bloom, their petals opening as if awakening from a long slumber; their scent intoxicating, pure, untouched by the decay of time. Towering trees with golden leaves swayed in a wind that touched nothing beyond the garden's borders, their trunks thick and gnarled with wisdom, reaching toward the sky, their leaves shimmering with an unnatural vibrance. A river, clear as crystal, more radiant than any water they had ever seen, flowed through the heart of it all, its surface reflecting the light of the unseen sun, catching the golden light as if cradling the very essence of the heavens.

Eden had returned.

The beautiful scent of jasmine and myrrh filled the air, mingling with something indefinable - a fragrance that carried the memory of the first breath, the first sunrise, the first moment of pure existence. The wind, gentle and warm, carried a whispering melody, a song of life itself; as though the garden itself was welcoming them home.

Tariq fell to his knees, tears shining in his eyes.

"Subhan Allah..." he breathed. "This... this is paradise".

Evelyn's heart pounded in her chest, her breath stolen by the sheer wonder before her. She turned to Jake, who stood in stunned silence, the golden light dancing across his chiselled face.

"*You're* seeing this, right?" Jake murmured.

Evelyn could only nod.

Before them, at the heart of the Garden, stood the Tree of Life in its fullest glory. Its trunk gleamed with a golden hue, its branches stretching wide as if to embrace the world, its leaves whispering secrets carried from the dawn of time.

The whisper came again, but this time, it was no longer faint. It was clear, powerful, yet gentle - like the voice of something beyond mortal comprehension.

"The worthy have come. The path shall be revealed".

The light dimmed, but the Garden remained. Eden, lost for millennia, had once more found its place in the world.

Then it happened. The very ground beneath their feet trembled once more, and, as if the earth itself was responding to the will of the heavens, a pathway began to form. It was not made of mere stone or dust, but of something far greater - polished, luminous, glowing faintly with the same golden radiance as the Tree of Life. The path stretched forward, winding through the newly formed paradise, leading them downward toward the heart of the valley.

At the end of the path stood the Gates of Eden.

They were immense, crafted from celestial gold, etched with symbols and patterns too intricate for the human mind to fully comprehend. Vines of emerald green curled around their base, their leaves shimmering as if woven from light itself. The gates seemed both ancient and untouched by time, radiating power and peace in equal measure.

And before them stood the Angels; the Guardians of Eden. Their presence was overwhelming, not in form but in essence, as they shimmered like heat mirages against the golden horizon.

They were humanoid, but not of this world, tall, draped in flowing robes of white fire, their faces obscured by radiant light, yet their gaze was unmistakable - piercing, knowing - their features ageless, their eyes glowing with celestial fire. Great wings, vast and shimmering, flickered between both the physical and supernatural, as if they existed in more than one realm at once. Their very presence was overwhelming, filling the valley with an authority that was beyond mere men. Their robes, woven from light itself, shimmered and shifted like the surface of a great river under the sun.

Jake, Evelyn, and Tariq halted at the sight, awestruck. Even Lecky, hardened by war and loss, found himself gripping his rifle as though instinct alone could anchor him to reality.

A groan snapped them from their trance.

Mackie.

He had been carried all this way, held aloft on a rough and ready stretcher, his body weak but his spirit still intact. His wounds still marred his flesh, but since drinking the spring water, something about him had changed - his breathing was stronger, his eyes more focused. There was hope now, a flicker of something unspoken.

"We need to get him to the gate," Evelyn said, turning to Jake.

He nodded, and together, the other four soldiers lifted Mackie, carrying him forward with reverence and urgency. As they walked, the golden path pulsed beneath their feet as if guiding them, as if welcoming them.

As they approached the gate, Evelyn's heart felt like it was going to explode. Would the angels let them pass? Would this place - the garden of life itself - be Mackie's salvation?

Beyond the gates they could see the Garden of Eden. It was more than a paradise; it was perfection made manifest. The desert world they had left behind felt like a distant memory, an illusion compared to the breathtaking expanse before them.

Evelyn felt it deep in her soul - a peace beyond reason, a warmth and love that pressed into her very spirit. It was as if every burden she had ever carried was lifted, every sorrow eased, every doubt quieted.

"This isn't possible," Carter whispered, his voice hushed with reverence.

"It's not just possible," Evelyn whispered, "it's real".

Yet as they approached the gates, the air shifted. The serenity of the garden was replaced by something else - something vast, something watching. A low hum vibrated through the earth beneath their feet, a silent force acknowledging their presence. The very air laced with unseen power.

One of Guardians raised a hand.

"*You have entered sacred ground,*" the voice spoke - not aloud, but within them, echoing in their minds as though the words carried the weight of eternity.

Tariq, breathless, murmured yet another prayer under his breath. Jake, however, took a slow pace forward and motioned for the others halt.

"We're not here to harm anyone," he said cautiously, his voice steady despite the awe he felt.

The Guardian's gaze swept over them, piercing, knowing. And then their eyes settled on Evelyn, studying her for a long moment.

"*You seek the truth,*" the Guardian said, "*but the truth is not for all to know*".

Evelyn gulped, then stood next to Jake. Her heart was still pounding, but she refused to falter.

"We mean no harm," she said, her voice firm yet pleading.

"Please - we need shelter. Our friend needs your help, and the Taliban are pursuing us".

At the mention of the Taliban, the Guardians' expressions darkened. The golden glow in their eyes burned hotter, and an unseen force rippled through the valley. The very air around them hissed, charged with an energy too great for words.

"*Those who bring hatred and violence will not be allowed to defile this place*".

Mackie groaned from where he lay, weak but still breathing.

Evelyn took a slow breath and dared to hope.

If this was truly the Garden of Eden... if this was the land of eternal life...then maybe ...just maybe...Mackie still had a chance.

The Guardians conferred silently, their forms flickering like flames in the wind.

Finally, one of them spoke.

"*You may stay. But know this; the Garden is a gateway to the eternal. It cannot be destroyed, but it can be corrupted. Only those whose hearts are pure may pass fully into its embrace*".

"That's you out then mate," Jake quickly whispered to Lecky.

"What does that mean?" Evelyn asked.

"*It means,*" the Guardian replied, "*that the garden is not just a sanctuary. It is a test*".

Meanwhile, on the heights above, eyes watched from the shadows. Although only a small party, re-enforcements had been sent for and, no doubt, would soon arrive.

Faheem crouched low, his dark eyes narrowing as he took in the impossible sight below. Beside him, the other men murmured in disbelief, their gazes flickering between wonder and greed.

"This...is Eden," one of them whispered.

Faheem barely heard him. His mind was racing, filled with both fury and hunger. He had told Rashid's remaining men a story - a lie woven with enough truth to ignite their hatred. He had spoken of betrayal, of infidels desecrating something sacred, of a destiny that belonged to them and them alone. Now, as he watched the gates of paradise stand before them, guarded by beings of unfathomable power, he knew only one thing.

This was not meant for *them*. This was meant for *him*.

He clenched his hands tightly and with a new found confidence spoke to the men.

"Let them pass. Let them unlock it. And when they do..."

A cruel smile spread across his face.

"...Eden will be ours".

CHAPTER 13

PARADISE FOUND

The golden light of the Garden of Eden shimmered around them, its radiance not harsh like the sun, but warm and soothing, as if the very air carried a song of peace. After days of peril and uncertainty, the Garden was like a dream; green and vibrant, untouched by the chaos that had ravaged the world outside. The scent of citrus, herbs, and fresh earth filled the air. Birds flitted through the trees, their calls a soft melody that seemed to echo the peace that reigned here, and as the golden gates of the garden swung open, a towering figure stepped forward to greet them. He was massive, standing well over seven feet tall, with broad shoulders and a presence that exuded both power and wisdom. His long silver hair flowed past his shoulders, and his beard, just as thick and white, framed a weathered yet noble face. His eyes, impossibly deep and knowing, shimmered with the light of the heavens. His robes, woven from a fabric that seemed to shift like liquid gold, hung from his strong frame.

The group instinctively halted, overwhelmed by his sheer presence, the weight of ancient history forcing itself upon them.

Taylor, still in disbelief, muttered under his breath, "It can't be...Noah?"

The giant figure nodded, his expression kind yet firm, for it was indeed Noah who stood before them, his height imposing yet welcoming, his eyes filled with an ancient knowing.

"We have been waiting for you for a long time," Noah said, his voice resonating through the air like a song carried on the wind.

Jake was cautious, his soldier's instincts telling him this was no illusion.

"You *knew* we were coming?"

Noah smiled.

"Since before you were born".

Parks, still trying to take in what was happening, swallowed hard and blurted out his thoughts.

"Was the story true? The Ark - was it real? Where is it now?"

Noah chuckled, a deep, rich sound filled with both mirth and patience.

"The truth is always real, but it is rarely what men believe. Yes, the Ark was built, and it *did* sail the great flood. But men have distorted the story to fit their own wants and desires. It was never about punishing the wicked, nor was it about divine wrath. It was about preservation - about giving life a second chance".

Jake butted in, still confused about Noah's statement.

"Why?"

Noah smiled.

"Because you were *always* meant to come," he answered, turning to Evelyn, "as was she".

Evelyn, still holding onto Mackie, her voice tight with urgency, spoke.

"Please. Our friend Mackie...he's dying".

Noah turned his gaze toward Mackie, who was barely conscious, his breath coming in ragged gasps. A flicker of concern crossed Noah's features.

"Not this day, he won't," he said firmly.

He gestured for them to follow.

"Come. The waters will heal him".

They carried Mackie through the lush, endless expanse of the Garden until they reached a fountain unlike any they had ever seen. It wasn't made of stone or marble, but something else - something alive. The water glowed faintly, shifting in colour like a reflection of the cosmos itself.

Noah gestured.

"Place him in the water".

Jake and Taylor hesitated.

"Are you sure about this?"

Noah's smile did not fade.

"Trust".

With that, they lowered Mackie into the water.

The moment his skin touched the surface, the air itself seemed to tremble. A soft sound, like the voices of a choir, rose from the fountain, and the water shone brighter, wrapping around him like a living light.

Mackie's body arched, a gasp tearing from his throat as his wounds vanished, his pallor replaced with vibrant life. His eyes sprang open, filled with a clarity and strength beyond the physical.

He sat up abruptly, blinking.

"Bloody hell..."

He flexed his fingers, his voice tinged with wonder.

"I feel...I feel like I could run for miles".

Evelyn knelt beside him, touching his arm in surprise.

"You were dying".

Mackie let out a breathless laugh as he acknowledged Noah with a grateful nod.

"Yeah, well, not anymore".

As he pushed himself to his feet, he expected the familiar ache in his bones, the dull throb of his injuries - but there was nothing. Not even a trace of pain. He stretched his arms, rolling his shoulders, his movements almost effortless.

Jake let out a low whistle.

"Mate, you look like you could take on the world".

Mackie grinned, shaking his head, then glanced down at his hands, turning them over as if they belonged to someone else.

"This is...I don't even know how to describe it".

Tariq, who had been standing back in quiet awe, spoke.

"It is as if you were remade".

He met Noah's gaze.

"This water... what is it?"

Noah placed a hand on Mackie's shoulder, his touch warm.

"It is life in its purest form. It restores what was lost, not just the body, but the spirit".

Jake laughed.

"Someone should bottle that".

Mackie's smile faded slightly, his brows drawing together.

"I...I remember the pain. I remember thinking - this is it. I was done".

His voice wavered.

"But now…"

He breathed out heavily, shaking his head.

"I don't even feel like the same man".

Noah studied him with quiet understanding.

"You are not."

The words lingered in the air, leaden with meaning. Mackie stared at him, then at the others, a strange feeling fluttering in his chest - not a burden, but something profound.

Evelyn squeezed his hand, her eyes shining.

"You got a second chance".

Mackie met her gaze and nodded.

"Yeah".

He looked around at the Garden, at the glorious beauty surrounding them, and let out a slow breath.

"And I don't plan on wasting it".

Noah smiled.

"Then come. There is more to see".

The Garden was impossibly vast, yet every step they took seemed guided by an unseen force, leading them exactly where they needed to go. As they walked Evelyn could hold her curiosity no longer.

Turning to Noah she asked the question that every person surely wanted to know.

"Is there a heaven?"

"This garden is the gateway *to* paradise," "Noah replied, "but it is not meant for the wicked".

Evelyn hesitated.

"Why reveal it to us?"

"Because the world has forgotten the truth," Noah said, "and to answer your question, yes, this is the cradle of creation, a place of eternal life and infinite wisdom. But it must remain hidden, for if humanity knew of its existence, they would seek to exploit it".

Evelyn nodded slowly, the heaviness of the revelation settling over her.

"And what of faith?" she asked, "what does this place mean to those who believe?"

Noah smiled faintly.

"True faith resides in the heart, not in the words of men or inside a house of religion. Scriptures have been twisted to serve the ambitions of the powerful. But here, the truth endures".

And then, in a clearing bathed in golden light, four figures awaited them.

The first was Adam, the original and beginning of all mankind, his presence commanding yet gentle, his features carved with wisdom. Beside him stood Eve, her beauty unlike anything earthly, not in perfection but in an overwhelming sense of warmth, of peace.

Then there were the brothers - Cain and Abel.

Cain, the one whose name had been cursed in every tongue, stood beside his brother; no longer burdened by sin. His face held sorrow, but also acceptance. Abel, reborn, had his hand on his brother's shoulder, not in condemnation, but in love.

Cain was the first to speak.

"The world has turned me into a monster," he said, his voice steady, "but I was never beyond redemption".

Abel nodded.

"Forgiveness is real. It always was".

Mackie frowned.

"But...you killed him".

Cain's eyes darkened.

"Yes. And I bore that sin for ages. But tell me - how many have killed in war? In anger? In desperation?"

He turned to them, his gaze piercing.

"And how many have been taught that there is no path back?"

Evelyn's breath caught.

"But you were forgiven".

Cain nodded.

"Because God's love is greater than our worst sins".

There was silence, the kind of silence that demanded a deeper thought.

And then Noah spoke again.

"This is why you are here."

Before them, a pedestal rose from the very earth, as if the Garden itself had willed it into being. Upon it lay a book, unlike any they had ever seen. Its cover was made of a material not of this world, shifting between stone and light, as if reality itself could not contain its truth.

"This is the Book of Truth, the true history of mankind. The truth of what was...and what must be," Noah announced.

Evelyn reached out, hesitant.

"What do you mean?"

Noah's eyes burned with certainty.

"The Bible, the Quran, the Vedas, the Talmud, all of the sacred texts of your world... they were written by men. Not by the hand of God".

Jake thought for a brief moment.

"So you're saying...they're lies?"

"No," Noah said, "they are history. They are pieces of the past, written with human hands, shaped by human fear, by human greed".

He looked at each of them in turn.

"They were written to control, to divide, to preach hatred, to keep the poor in their place; to make the powerful richer".

Evelyn's hands trembled.

"But they were meant to guide us...surely?"

Noah nodded.

"And they did...but not always toward the light".

Mackie shook his head.

"Then what's the truth?"

Noah lifted the book.

"That God does not preach hatred. He does not call men 'infidels' or 'heathens'. He does not treat women as inferior beings and dictate how they should dress, and He does not demand war in His name".

He held the book toward them.

"God's only law is love, just as Jesus preached".

"And this book," said Evelyn, "this book is meant to replace them all?"

Noah nodded.

"It must".

Jake ran a hand through his hair.

"And we're just supposed to...what? Hand it over to the Pope? The Dalai Lama? The Ayatollah? The Arch Bishop of Canterbury?"

He let out a short laugh.

"*They* won't listen".

Noah smiled.

"Some will. Some will fear it. But the truth has a way of reaching where it must".

Cain added to the conversation.

"There are other keys, scattered throughout the world and in the great darkness that surrounds it. If you had not come, another would have, one day. Like those from other galaxies who visit so often. The truth was always meant to be found".

Tariq, quiet until now, finally spoke.

"But why is it that across all cultures, all lands, there is always a chief God? From the Romans, the Greeks, the Norse, the Egyptians, the Hindus - there are many Gods, but always one above the others".

Noah's eyes softened.

"The answer is simple...because they were *never* different Gods, only different names for the same".

"And the *many* Gods?" asked Tariq.

"They are Angels. Messengers of the Lord, my son," replied Noah.

A hush fell over them.

Evelyn turned and whispered to Jake.

"This changes everything".

Jake gasped, looking at the book in Noah's hands.

"So this is why we're here. Not for gold or power?"

Noah moved towards Evelyn, placing the book in her hands. The moment her fingers touched it, a pulse of light spread through the Garden.

"This is your task," Noah said. "Deliver this book to the world. Let it be read. Let it spread. When mankind understands, when they finally see that they were never divided, that they were always meant to be one people under one God...the wars will end. *This* is the gold and the power".

Evelyn held the book close.

"And the world will be the paradise it was meant to be?"

Noah nodded.

"Yes".

"Are we the first to do this sir?" Jake asked.

Noah shook his head.

"There have been others," he said.

"But the powers that be just ignored it," Jake replied, not expecting an answer.

Noah nodded.

"Well, hopefully, this time they won't," Evelyn added.

Mackie looked around at the Garden, at the light, at the beauty surrounding them, and let out a sigh.

"Well," he said, a slow grin forming, "no pressure then. While we're at it though mate...er...sir...er...Noah, I think we will need more than one book. You haven't got a heavenly photocopier here have you by any chance?"

Noah laughed.

"It will be done".

"On earth as it is in heaven," Jake thought to himself.

That evening, beneath the celestial glow of the stars, the group was led to a vast pavilion set within the heart of the Garden. Golden lanterns hung from trees, their soft light shimmering like captured starlight. A long table, carved from the very wood of the garden, stood laden with food - fruit of every kind, meats, bread warm and fragrant. The air in the Garden held an otherworldly stillness, a deep and profound peace that settled over them like a warm embrace. The scent of jasmine and citrus blossoms drifted in the soft night breeze, and the stars above seemed impossibly bright, casting a silver glow over the gathering, whilst the distant murmur of a stream blended with a faint, melodic song that seemed to rise from the Garden itself.

Mackie, still marvelling at his restored body, let out a low whistle.

"This makes a change from army rations eh?"

Jake chuckled.

"No boil in the bag tonight".

Evelyn, though awed by the abundance, was more taken by something else - the undeniable sense of peace in the air. Even the soldiers, usually wary and tense, sat with ease, their weapons resting beside them, forgotten for the first time in a long while.

As they ate, figures began to join them. Not just Adam and Eve, Cain and Abel, but others - figures from history, faces that had long since passed into myth and legend.

And then He came.

At first, there was no grand entrance - no blinding light, no fanfare. He simply *appeared* among them, tall, clad in robes of purest white, his presence as natural as the air they breathed. A faint glow surrounded him, not harsh or overwhelming, but a quiet radiance that softened the shadows and made the night feel warmer, safer. His hair fell past his shoulders, his beard neatly kept, but it was his eyes that held them - deep, endless, filled with a kindness that seemed to see into the very depths of the soul.

Silence fell over the table.

Tariq immediately dropped to his knees, bowing his head, overcome by the sheer holiness of the moment. His wanted to pray, but no words would come.

The soldiers, hardened men who had spent years facing death, now found themselves breathless, motionless, as if they were in the presence of something, *someone*, beyond comprehension.

Evelyn's hand trembled as she placed her goblet down.

"It's you," she whispered.

Jesus smiled.

"I have always been here, just as you were always meant to come".

Lecky let out a shaky laugh.

"You know, I always figured if I met you, it'd be at the Pearly Gates. Not at dinner".

A ripple of laughter, light but filled with understanding, passed through the table.

"So...you *are* real," said Jake.

Jesus turned to him, his expression gentle.

"You have always believed in something greater, even when you denied it. Your heart has known me longer than your mind will admit".

Jake breathed out slowly, looking away, unable to hold the gaze for long.

"Yeah, well...I suppose that's a fair point".

There was a muffled cough as Taylor cleared his throat awkwardly.

"Uh...what should we call you? Lord? Sir? Just...Jesus?"

Jesus laughed.

"My name is Jesus of Nazareth. I am but a poor carpenter. Call me whatever you feel comfortable with - there is no etiquette here; or anything to fear".

The nervous feeling in the air eased just slightly, though none could shake the weight of His presence.

Jake, although he had spoken already, felt agitated, shifting in his seat, a question burning in his head.

"Can I ask you something?"

Jesus met his gaze.

"Of course".

Jake swallowed.

"Can I...be blessed...please?"

Jesus stood in front of Jake and rested a hand on his shoulder. A warmth spread through Jake's entire body, like standing in the morning sun after a bitterly cold night. It was something beyond physical - something deeper, something that touched his very core.

The others, seeing the change in Jake's face, hesitated only a moment before stepping forward one by one, each asking for the same. As Jesus laid his hands upon them, each felt something unexplainable - a lightness in their chests, a peace that settled their racing thoughts, an unshakable certainty that, for the first time in a long time, they were exactly where they were meant to be.

Jake breathed out slowly, his voice a mere whisper.

"I don't know what that was...but I feel like I could do just about anything...the impossible maybe".

Jesus smiled.

"And you will".

Evelyn, still overcome, found her voice.

"We were given The Book of Truth," she said. "It says that the Bible, and all the other books, were just history. That they weren't written by God".

She hesitated, as if fearful of the answer.

"Is that true?"

Jesus nodded.

"They were written by men seeking power, seeking control. They took my words, my Father's words, and formed them into shackles. They built temples of stone when I told them to build temples in their hearts".

Tariq, his faith shaken to its core, found the courage to speak.

"But the Quran..."

Jesus turned to him, his expression filled with understanding.

"All faiths seek me, though they know me by different names," Jesus said, turning to him, "and all faiths have been corrupted by men who crave power".

Tariq's head dropped.

"Then everything I believed..."

"Not everything," Jesus reassured him, "faith is not found in books. It is found in love. In kindness. In the way you treat those who can do nothing for you".

A deafening silence followed, the weight of truth settling over them all.

Then, Noah appeared, his face solemn.

"But now, my friends, you must listen carefully".

Jesus's expression grew more serious as well.

"There are those who seek to destroy you," Noah said, "one who you gave pity to. They know you are here. They know you carry the truth".

Jake couldn't believe what he was hearing. He felt annoyed...betrayed even.

"That young lad...what was his name? Faheem".

Noah nodded.

"They wait beyond the Garden's veil. They do not understand what they seek to destroy, only that they fear it".

Jesus placed a hand on Jake's shoulder.

"You must leave at dawn. Take the book. Take the truth. And deliver it to the world".

Evelyn's heart pounded with worry.

"But the Garden...if they attack...?"

"They cannot harm what they cannot reach," Noah said, "the Garden will endure. But you...you must go".

The group exchanged glances. The peace of the Garden had lulled them into a sense of safety, of belonging. But now, reality was rearing its ugly head once more.

"Well then...looks like we've got work to do," said Mackie.

Jesus smiled.

"And you will not be alone".

As the night deepened, the Garden seemed to vibrate with a quiet, unseen energy. The group had been given a mission - one that would change the world. But first, they would rest.

They were led through winding pathways to a series of stone-built dwellings nestled within the Garden. The buildings were simple yet elegant, their walls smooth and cool to the touch, illuminated by flickering oil lamps. Inside, soft cushions lined the floors, and woven blankets lay folded neatly at the edges of low wooden beds. The scent of incense and myrrh hung in the air, soothing and warm.

Noah's family greeted them with kindness and familiarity, as though they had always known them. Among them were two figures who needed no introduction - Mary and Joseph.

Evelyn's held her breath at the sight of the holy virgin.

Mary took her hands in hers, her touch warm and reassuring.

"Rest, my child. The world will still be there in the morning."

Joseph, standing beside her, nodded at Jake, his voice steady but kind.

"Strength alone does not make a man. The burden you carry will only grow heavier, but you do not have to carry it alone".

Jake, for once, was lost for words, and for the first time in what felt like forever, Evelyn believed it.

That night, they were offered comfort beyond anything they had known in weeks, but before sleep came another gift.

Water.

Real, fresh, abundant water.

Scattered throughout the garden were fountains and pools, their surfaces shimmering under the glow of the torches. Water cascaded from carved stone mouths into crystal-clear basins, flowing into narrow channels that wound through the marble courtyards. The air was filled with the scent of blooming jasmine and the cool, crisp purity of running streams.

Jake ran a hand through his tangled, sweat-caked hair and grinned.

"I think we just found paradise".

Lecky was already pulling off his boots.

"Last one in is a dirty name".

The men wasted no time, stripping down and stepping into the cool embrace of the pools, letting weeks of dust, blood, and exhaustion melt away. Some leaned back against the stone edges, eyes closed in bliss, while others scrubbed the grime from their bodies with soap made from fragrant herbs, left for them in small clay pots.

Evelyn, of course, had no intention of joining them. She had been led to her own secluded bath, a shaded alcove where vines draped over a smooth stone tub filled by a gentle stream. The water was perfect, neither too cold nor too warm, wrapping around her like silk as she sank in.

Yet, curiosity got the better of her.

She had seen Jake in battle, watched him move with expertise and power, but here... here was something else entirely. Keeping to the shadows, she risked a glance toward the men's pool.

Jake stood under one of the cascading falls, water sluicing over the hard planes of his body. Scars from past battles marred his skin, but they only seemed to add to the sheer, raw strength of him. His muscles shifted as he ran a hand over his face, slicking his dark hair back, droplets clinging to his jaw, his chest...

Evelyn swallowed.

"Bloody hell".

She had never been one to swoon over a man, but this was different. There was something rugged yet calm about him, something real. She knew the discipline, the sharp edge of his mind, the humour he used to mask things he never spoke of. But here, beneath the water, stripped of weapons, of rank, of war - he was just Jake.

And she liked what she saw.

A little too much.

Realising she had been staring longer than she should, Evelyn turned quickly, her cheeks hot despite the cool night air.

By morning, they would be back in the real world. Back to danger, uncertainty, and a battle that might cost them everything. But tonight, under the watchful stars, in the sanctuary of Eden, they were simply alive.

The night passed in peace, engulfed in warmth and safety and the Garden continued to hum a heavenly song.

At dawn, they would leave, and the world would never be the same again.

CHAPTER 14

SHADOWS OF RETRIBUTION

The Taliban fighters, many of them unaware of the true significance of the valley, came charging into the lush paradise with their weapons raised. They were like locusts, intent on plundering anything they could find, unaware that they had entered the very birthplace of humanity's greatest truths. They came in numbers, more than expected, their determination fuelled by fear and ignorance.

Jake crouched beside Lecky and the others, keeping a watchful eye on the approaching force through his rifle's sight.

"They're coming in hot," he said, "we hit them fast and hard. Make every shot count".

Lecky flexed his fingers.

"Sounds like a darn good plan to me".

The team moved like ghosts, slipping into position. Silencers whispered in the dawn's half light, dropping the first wave of attackers before they even realised they were under fire. The enemy faltered but continued on, fanning out in a loose formation, weapons raised.

Then the Garden's defenders struck.

Noah led them, moving with an agility no mortal man should possess. His blade shimmered in the dim light, cutting through the enemy ranks with terrifying precision. Other guardians followed, their ancient weapons cleaving the air, arrows finding targets with unerring accuracy.

The Taliban fighters hesitated. This was no ordinary battle. Their bullets seemed to slow, their aim wavering as if the very air resisted their violence. Yet, they did not stop, driven by the belief that they fought against heresy, against something unholy.

And then Faheem appeared, apparently fearless; not the scared boy that the team had released just a few short days earlier. He strode forward, unshaken by the battle unfolding around him.

"You dare to defy the will of God?" he called out, his voice carrying over the chaos.

Jake felt a sense of uncontrollable anger. This wasn't just another enemy. This was personal.

Faheem raised his weapon, taking aim at Evelyn, but before he could fire, Jake was already moving.

He emerged from cover, firing two quick shots. Faheem dodged with unnatural speed, his body twisting as if guided by something beyond human instinct, rather than pure luck.

Jake snarled to himself.

"Alright, mate. Let's see what you've got".

They clashed, like warriors of old, bullets whizzing past. Faheem, the timid young man, was fast - too fast - but Jake had fought monsters before. He sidestepped a knife thrust, slammed his rifle stock into Faheem's ribs, punched him hard in the face, and followed through with a savage kick to the knee.

Faheem stumbled but recovered instantly. His eyes burned with something unnatural, something wrong. He smiled, blood staining his teeth.

"You fight well infidel," he admitted, "but you fight for a lost cause".

Jake snorted.

"Yeah? Tell that to your mates, face down in the dirt you bastard".

Faheem lunged. Jake barely dodged, the blade grazing his side. Pain flared, but he ignored it. He grabbed Faheem's wrist, twisted hard, and drove his knee into the man's gut.

Faheem coughed, staggering back - but not far enough.

Jake lunged forward, slamming a fist into his jaw. Faheem reeled, and in that moment, Jake drew his knife.

"You're done," Jake growled.

Faheem sneered.

"You think killing me will stop this? Others will come. More than you can imagine".

Jake didn't hesitate.

"No, but it will make me feel bloody good".

With one swift motion, he buried the knife into Faheem's chest.

Faheem gasped, his arrogance vanishing in an instant. His body sagged, he tried to speak, but only a choked gurgle escaped.

Jake yanked the blade free, watching as Faheem crumpled to the ground. There was no redemption. No last words. Just the silence of a man who thought himself invincible, meeting his end.

But the battle wasn't over.

The Taliban had regrouped, rallying for a final push. The soldiers fought fiercely, but they were outnumbered. For every enemy they cut down, two more seemed to take their place.

Then the earth trembled.

The air itself thickened, charged with an energy beyond comprehension. The very trees of the garden seemed to shift, their leaves whispering in an ancient tongue. A deep, bone-chilling cold slithered through the battlefield, cutting through the dry heat. The wind howled unnaturally, whispering with voices long dead. The Taliban faltered as an oppressive force pressed down upon them, unseen but undeniable.

Something ancient had awakened.

The Taliban faltered; terror overwhelming them. They had come to destroy the Garden, but now they saw the truth - they had never stood a chance.

From the shadows, a great army of guardians emerged in full force. They did not run. They did not charge. They simply appeared.

Shadows twisted and solidified, stepping out from the very air itself; tall, spectral figures wreathed in swirling darkness and eerie, golden light. Their faces were obscured by shifting veils of shadow, their eyes empty voids, deeper than the abyss.

They were no longer restrained, no longer holding back. They moved like living legends, their weapons glowing with ethereal light. Arrows streaked through the air like falling stars, cutting down enemies with deadly accuracy. Swords sliced through flesh and steel alike, wielded by hands guided by something far beyond mortal skill.

The first Taliban soldier raised his rifle, only for his arm to wither and rot in an instant. The flesh shrivelled away, his bones blackening and crumbling to dust. His scream was cut short as his body disintegrated, vanishing into the night.

Another fighter lunged forward, slashing wildly with his knife, only to freeze mid-strike. His eyes widened as invisible hands gripped his throat, lifting him high into the air. His mouth gaped open in a silent scream as his skin blackened, cracks of burning red splitting across his body. Flames erupted from within, consuming him from the inside out before his charred remains crumbled to ash.

Panic spread through the enemy ranks.

The Taliban fired wildly, their bullets passing harmlessly through the guardians, swallowed by the darkness surrounding them. The very ground rebelled against them. The earth beneath their feet turned to shifting black sludge, sucking them down like quicksand. Hands - pale, skeletal hands - erupted from the earth, clawing at their legs, dragging them into the abyss.

One Taliban turned to flee. He barely made it three steps before a guardian glided in front of him, moving faster than the eye could follow. A long, spindly hand reached out, resting gently on his chest.

For a heartbeat, nothing happened.

Then - his body convulsed violently.

His eyes rolled back, his veins bulged, and he let out an unearthly wail as his soul was ripped from his body - a ghostly, screaming form torn free and devoured by the darkness. His body collapsed, empty and lifeless.

The battlefield became a slaughterhouse.

Some of the Taliban dropped their weapons, falling to their knees, whispering desperate prayers. But there was no mercy here. The guardians did not pause, did not hesitate. They did not grant surrender.

A voice, deep and resonant, thundered through the Garden, though no lips moved.

"Leave this place, for you have no place here. This garden is not for your hatred.
It is a sanctuary for the pure of heart, not for those who seek to dominate or destroy".

A final, gut wrenching scream rose as the last of the invaders who had remained on the battlefield were torn apart, their bodies dissolving into the darkness, their souls snatched away by unseen hands.

The last of those who valued their own lives fled into the mountains, their screams swallowed by the wind.

The expanse of land before the Garden was silent, save for the crackling of burning scrub and the distant howl of desert winds. The metallic scent of blood and gunpowder engulfed the air. Many of the Taliban lay where they had fallen; their lifeless bodies sprawled across the sacred ground, weapons still clutched in dead hands.

Jake wiped the sweat from his brow, his knife, still caked with Faheem's blood, hung loosely in his grip. He glanced at the carnage around him, shaking his head.

"So much for their seat in heaven and their virgins," he muttered.

Mackie let out a tired chuckle, nudging a fallen fighter with his boot.

"Yeah, I reckon paradise is fresh out of rooms for these bastards".

But then - a sound.

A deep groan rippled through the air.

The bodies were moving.

One by one, the dead Taliban stirred, their limbs jerking unnaturally. Their eyes - once vacant and lifeless - flashed open, burning with an eerie, golden light. Bones cracked as they rose to their feet, their mouths moving in silent horror.

"Jesus Christ," Mackie whispered to himself, taking a step back.

"Yeah, mate. But I don't think He's the one who did that," Jake replied.

The team instinctively raised their weapons. It didn't make sense. These men were dead. Jake had felt Faheem's last breath, had seen the life drain from his eyes.

Yet now they stood.

A tremor rumbled beneath their feet. The ground cracked open, deep fissures snaking outward from the corpses. A foul stench filled the air - sulphur, smoke, something ancient and rotten.

Then came the screams.

Not from the living, but from the dead themselves.

Their golden eyes widened in terror as the ground split apart, gaping chasms forming beneath them. From the depths, fire erupted, scorching the night sky with an unholy glow. Shadows moved within the flames; twisted figures, clawed hands reaching upward.

The dead Taliban screamed as the darkness wrapped around them, dragging them downward. Their hands clawed at the earth, at each other, at nothing, desperate to escape.

Jake and the others could only watch.

Faheem, his face contorted in sheer horror, was the last to be pulled in. His lips moved, forming a prayer; but no God was listening.

With one final, bloodcurdling wail, the ground slammed shut.

Silence.

The battlefield was still once more, as if nothing had happened.

The team stood frozen, their weapons still raised, their minds struggling to comprehend what they had just witnessed.

Taylor let out a feint whistle of relief.

"Well...that ain't in the bloody handbook".

Noah appeared, staring at where the chasm had been. His voice was quiet as he spoke.

"*They* were never meant for paradise".

Jake let out a slow breath, sheathing his knife.

"I suppose that answers that".

The wind picked up, carrying away the last traces of smoke. The Taliban...the dead...were gone. Not buried. Not left behind. Not just dead. Just...gone...erased.

And the Garden remained.

Noah spoke again.

"This was only the beginning," he said, "more will come one day, so we must ensure that Eden remains undiscovered".

The atmosphere still reverberated with the echoes of battle as the team stepped through the great stone archway, re-entering the Garden. The moment they crossed the threshold, the tension in their muscles seemed to ease. The air was warmer here, fresher, carrying the scent of blooming flowers and ancient earth.

The destruction and death they had just witnessed felt like a dream, a nightmare that did not belong to this place. Inside Eden, all was as it had always been. The rivers still shimmered, the trees stood tall and undisturbed, and the eternal sun above cast golden light across the valley.

Noah stood calmly before them, as he gestured for them to follow him back to the great stone table in the garden's centre. Upon it lay several identical books, bound in thick, weathered leather.

"The Book of Truth," Noah said, his voice like rolling thunder softened by age, "a copy for each of you".

Jake stared at the books and felt slightly relieved.

"Thank goodness for that," he whispered to Lecky.

"For what?" Lecky replied.

"I thought they were going to be some bloody huge and heavy thing, but look...they're about the size of a decent novel," said Jake.

One by one, the team stepped forward. They picked up the books reverently, feeling the weight of history in their hands. The pages were thick, the ink dark and clear. Though none of them could yet read some of the strange symbols, the books were actually in English, and they each understood its significance.

Evelyn pressed her palm against the book's cover, a shiver running down her spine.

"You said others would come. People like the ones we just fought. How do we stop that?"

Noah turned his deep, knowing eyes to her.

"As long as the Angel's Tear is in your possession, the Garden remains visible. It's location known. Its gates open".

Evelyn, without hesitation, retrieved the crystal from her pack. A fragment of pure, celestial light, trapped in a solid form. It pulsed softly in her hand, as if alive, shifting colours between brilliant blue, silver, and gold.

"If I give it back to you...?" she asked, holding it out to Noah.

Noah smiled.

"Then Eden will disappear once more. Hidden. Safe. It will not cease to exist, but no army, no explorer, no man driven by greed or conquest will find it. Not until the world is ready...if it *needs* to be ready".

The team exchanged glances. None of them spoke.

Evelyn's heart fluttered.

She had dreamed of discoveries like this her entire life, devoting herself to unearthing lost truths, rewriting history; and now, she had the key to one of the greatest mysteries of all time.

But she had also seen what knowledge like this could bring. The death. The war. The corruption of truth into something monstrous.

She exhaled slowly, looking up at Noah.

"You said before that there are other keys?" she asked hesitantly.

A small smile touched the ancient man's lips.

"There are," he said simply, "scattered across the earth. Hidden in the ruins of what once was. They can be found, if one knows where to look".

Evelyn nodded, gripping the crystal tightly. Then, with a deep breath, she held it out to Noah.

He took it gently, closing his fingers around it.

The moment the crystal left her grasp, the world around them shifted.

The trees shimmered, the sky darkened, and a great hush fell over the valley. A wind howled through the trees, twisting the air itself, bending reality.

Then...

The Garden was gone.

Or rather, it was still there, but no longer a part of the world they knew. The archway behind them now led only to rock and desert once more, as if Eden had never existed at all.

Jake unzipped up his pack, glancing back over his shoulder at the empty space where paradise had once been.

"Well," he muttered, slipping his copy of the 'Book of Truth' inside, "that's one hell of a magic trick".

Noah smiled knowingly, speaking softly, as his form faded away.

"The greatest wonders are not those that can be seen...but those that are protected".

Evelyn turned back to face the barren landscape ahead.

They had what they came for.

Now, it was time to leave Eden behind.

CHAPTER 15

THE ESCAPE

The group stood in awe for a moment, and then Jake instinctively reached for the radio. No one expected it to work - not here, not after everything. The last time they'd checked, the signal had been dead, swallowed by the oppressive silence of the mountains.

But as Jake switched it on, a soft vibration filled the air. Clear. Strong. Almost as if the Garden had worked its magic on more than just them.

He exchanged glances with the others before depressing the pressel switch on the handset.

"Hello Zero, this is Alpha Two One, we have the package. On route to our means. Over".

There was a brief pause, then a crackle of static as the response came.

"Alpha Two One, this is Zero. Roger. Out".

Jake breathed a sigh of relief.

"Well, well...I did not expect that...cheers Noah, me old mate," he said, as he looked back to where Eden had stood only minutes ago.

They didn't wait. The Garden was gone, lost behind them, and ahead lay the difficult terrain which they would have to traverse in order to reach the ATVs...their "means". With books secured in their packs and the knowledge of the task ahead, they moved out, aware that somewhere out there the Taliban still lurked

Reaching the high ground above the valley they could see that, for now, their route seemed clear of enemy, thus allowing them some quiet chatter as they walked.

Jake glanced around the group.

"Do any of you ever think about it? You know...what happens when we go?"

"All the time," Taylor responded.

Jake laughed to himself.

"Yeah, but I mean, after what we've seen? Noah. The Garden. Doesn't it change things?"

"Don't forget Jesus, we *did* meet him after all," said Evelyn.

Jake rolled his eyes.

"Yeah, well, that goes without saying doesn't it?"

Taylor was quiet, still ruminating about Jake's question, his eyes scanning the ridgeline ahead before answering.

"Yeah. It does. Before this, I figured death was just...lights out. Game over. But now?"

He shook his head.

"Now I feel invincible".

Jake raised an eyebrow.

"Invincible?"

Taylor nodded.

"Because there *is* no death. Not really. There's just...the next step. And after seeing what's waiting on the other side...I'm not afraid anymore".

Jake let the words settle. He'd been in enough close calls to know fear intimately - had felt its cold grip more times than he could count. But now? Now, it was gone. Taylor was right.

"Yeah, I think I feel the same, and it's good to know that the Taliban won't be getting *that* version of paradise," Jake muttered.

Taylor smirked.

"No. But I reckon that's what happens when you fight for hate instead of something pure".

"Hey, look at you, we'll be ordaining you as a preacher when we get back with all that talk," laughed Lecky.

The conversation faded, but the feeling remained. They were still in enemy territory. They were still hunted. But fear? That was something they had left behind.

The next few hours passed in a blur of tense silence and constant movement. The only sounds, apart from their own footsteps, were the whistle of wind through the ravines, and the occasional low murmur of a command.

The mountains loomed, both a sanctuary and a prison - isolated, rugged, but offering enough cover to keep them hidden from watchful eyes. Every peak, every shadow held the potential for danger. The Taliban were still out there. They all knew it.

Evelyn kept pace with the team, her body screaming with exhaustion, but her mind appeared more focussed than ever. She had spent so long chasing myths and legends, believing in grand discoveries, but reality was far harsher. The truth she had unearthed about the location of the Garden, wasn't for the world to see. Not yet. Maybe not ever. But the books were.

She watched the soldiers, their movements careful and exact, their silence almost unnatural. They didn't waste energy on words or uncertainty. Survival wasn't just instinct to them - it was an art. They made the impossible seem inevitable, every step calculated, every look a silent language.

As the daylight was beginning to fade, it was time to rest. But not for the soldiers, as they diligently set up defensive positions, before settling in for the night. Again they had cleverly selected a rocky outcrop at the highest point, a position with good views and all round arcs of fire, which any enemy would have to climb in order to reach them.

As they all tucked in to their cold rations they managed a few whispered conversations.

"Do you ever think about what happens when this is over?" Tariq asked in a low and thoughtful voice, "What comes next? For us? For Afghanistan?"

Jake was quick to respond.

"I wish I knew mate, I really do. But at least you and your family, and many others, will be safe to lead a quiet life somewhere else".

Evelyn looked up; the starlight flickering in her eyes.

"I don't know," she admitted, "it sometimes feels like we're all just surviving until something changes. But will it ever?"

Tariq let out a deep sigh and shook his head.

"There are those who believe it can. But it is hard to hold on to that belief when the world is so broken".

Jake butted in before Evelyn could reply.

"I blame this current generation and all the bloody do good-ers who support these hateful people. They don't see the evil, or want to believe it, but are happy to send disgusting messages to the families of our dead soldiers...bastards!"

Evelyn listened to both Jake and Tariq, then hesitated, her fingers absently brushing against the worn leather of the 'Book of Truth' in her pack.

"I used to think I could change things," she murmured, "I thought that revealing the truth - finding proof of an ancient myth - would make a difference. But now..." she paused, staring at the starry sky above, "now it feels like the world has gone too far. So much destruction. And for what? Power? Control? I can't even see a way out anymore".

Tariq met her gaze.

"The way out is not always clear Miss Kane. But we keep moving. We fight, we resist, and we keep believing that something better is possible. It is all that we can do".

The others were quiet, listening but saying nothing.

Evelyn nodded slowly. The dreams she once clung to felt further away than ever, slipping like sand through her fingers. This wasn't the world she had hoped to change. This was a world soaked in blood, ruled by fear.

Hope was a rare thing here.

But maybe that's what made it worth holding on to.

Even when it felt impossible.

"Well," added Lecky, "I reckon once we get these books to the heads of each religion, things *will* change".

"I bloody hope so mate...I really do," said Jake.

The next day was much like the last, but with every step their transport was getting closer. One more night of rest under the stars and their feet would finally feel some welcome relief.

The first gunshot cracked through the still evening air like a whip, followed by the harsh, stuttering chatter of automatic fire. The team froze instantly, instinct taking over. No one moved. No one breathed.

Evelyn's heart pounded in her chest as she dropped into a crouch, feeling the earth beneath her palms. Lecky had already raised his binoculars, sweeping the ground to their front. The sun was dipping toward the horizon, casting long shadows over the mountains, but even in the fading light, it wasn't hard to see.

A large force of Taliban - too many to count - was moving across the valley below, their weapons bristling, their movements deliberate. But what were they shooting at? The team exchanged brief glances, unspoken questions hanging between them. It didn't matter. What mattered was that the enemy was heading in their direction.

Lecky lowered his binoculars.

"Too big," he murmured.

Jake gave a single nod, gesturing to the group.

"Off the path, down the slope," he whispered.

There was no argument. The soldiers signalled for Evelyn and Tariq to move - slow, measured steps, careful not to send loose rocks tumbling. They descended into the brush, slipping between the protruding boulders, until they were nothing more than shadows against the landscape. Then they waited.

The minutes dragged like hours. The darkness crept in, wrapping around them, turning the world into a murky void where sound was sharper than sight. The Taliban force moved closer, their footsteps crunching on the dirt path above, their voices low but still carrying through the darkness.

Evelyn lay still, her breathing shallow. A single mistake, one misplaced movement, one uncontrolled sound, could mean death. Today she was not wearing perfume, much to the relief of Tariq, but she silently sniffed the air around her just in case, not really knowing why.

Then, the footsteps stopped. Someone above them muttered something in Pashto. A reply came, questioning. Then silence...a long, suffocating silence.

She could hear them shifting, boots scuffing against loose gravel. Did they sense something?

The soldiers slowly raised their weapons to their shoulders...waiting.

A rock rolled from above. A boot scraped. A torch clicked on, its narrow beam cutting through the darkness, as each soldier instinctively closed one eye to protect their night vision. The light swept left, then right - slow, deliberate.

Evelyn's fingers curled into the dirt. If that beam landed on them...

Then, as suddenly as it had turned on, the light clicked off. Someone grunted, dissatisfied. Another voice spoke, dismissive. The footsteps resumed.

The Taliban moved past, their march steady, their presence lingering in the night air long after the last man had gone. They remained motionless for a long time after the Taliban had passed, listening to the night. Only when the last sound faded into the distance did anyone dare to move.

A slow, careful exhale. A glance exchanged in the dark.

They were still alive. For now.

Evelyn felt her muscles protest as she carefully uncurled from the ground. Every instinct screamed at her to stay down, but they had no choice. The Taliban were too close. Staying here until daylight would be suicide.

Jake was already checking his compass.

"We're going to have to move through the night and put as much distance between us and them as we can," he whispered.

All were in agreement. They all knew the risk of staying where they were.

Still crouched, Evelyn reached into her pack and pulled out a protein bar. The soldiers did the same, wolfing down rations in quick, silent bites. A few sips from their canteens, just enough to wet their throats, and then they were moving again - slow at first, careful to avoid making noise, then picking up the pace as the terrain allowed.

The night stretched on, seemingly never ending. They navigated by moonlight and shadow, keeping to the rough ground where their footprints wouldn't be easily tracked. The air was cold, biting at their exposed skin, but no one complained. The only sound was the silent brush of their feet on the vegetation that covered the hillsides.

Hours passed. They were all tired, even the soldiers, but adrenaline kept them moving.

Then, as the first pale hints of dawn began creeping over the horizon, Taylor, who was lead scout, raised a fist to signal a halt.

There, just ahead, camouflaged and partially hidden by the rocks and vegetation, sat the ATVs, exactly where they had left them.

Relief flooded through Evelyn. They had made it...well, to this point at least. Surely now their journey could only get better.

Jake moved in first, sweeping the area with his weapon before giving the all clear. One by one, they approached, checking the vehicles. No signs of tampering. Everything was still intact.

Taylor patted his ATV.

"Right where we left you, buddy," he uttered as he looked across to the others.

"Huh!" said Parks, "I half expected them to be stripped and balancing on bricks or something".

"Talking about being stripped," said Jake, "let's get them topped up with fuel and discard anything, like empty jerry cans, that we don't need".

Without hesitation, the team set to work, stripping the ATVs of anything unnecessary and ensuring every inch of their equipment was secured. They worked quickly, their movements precise and methodical. This wasn't just about efficiency, it was about survival.

The soldiers checked the Minimi machine guns mounted on each vehicle, whilst Tariq and Evelyn acted as sentries. Their 7.62mm version of the weapon was magazine fed, reliable, and deadly accurate up to a thousand metres - perfect for keeping heads down if they ran into trouble. The men quickly dusted the working parts, pulled the barrel through and oiled the breach blocks; not a full clean, but good enough considering where they were. Taylor ran a final function check on his gun, the cocking handle clicking smoothly into place as he nodded in satisfaction.

"Good to go".

Jake glanced at Evelyn and Tariq.

"You two ever used one of these?"

Tariq shook his head. Evelyn hesitated before answering, a cheeky look on her face.

"No...they are somewhat frowned upon in the museum. Not good for the displays *or* the public for that matter".

Jake let out a quiet laugh.

"Right...crash course, then".

Jake gestured for them to step closer.

"It's simple. Safety is here...red means dead. It only fires on automatic, but you'll mostly be laying down suppressing fire anyway, so no worries there. Feed it right, keep it clean, and don't ride the trigger, try and keep to bursts only or you'll burn through a mag in seconds".

Taylor handed Tariq an empty magazine.

"Stick this on and get the feel of it".

Tariq slotted it in, pulled back the cocking handle, and nodded.

"Good," Jake said, "if it jams, don't panic. Clear the chamber like so, swap mags if you have to, and if we're moving, don't just spray and pray - short bursts, keep it controlled; this isn't bloody Hollywood with never ending rounds".

Evelyn ran through the same drill, her fingers surprisingly steady. She wasn't a soldier, but she was quick, learning fast.

"Now, for obvious reasons, we aren't going to let you fire off any rounds and have a practice shoot, but what do you reckon?"

Both students nodded, with some trepidation, but felt reasonably sure of the weapon.

Satisfied, Jake slapped them both on the shoulder.

"You'll do fine, just don't freeze up".

Meanwhile, the others worked on making space. As well as stripping the vehicles they had to make room on the rear luggage rack for their two additional passengers, clearing the racks to accommodate Evelyn and Tariq, the extra gear being shifted or strapped to the sides. Every ounce of weight had to be balanced carefully - they'd be moving fast.

Next came food and water. Everyone took a few moments to eat whatever they could stomach - ration packs, energy bars, a handful of dried fruit. Water was rationed carefully; they didn't know how long until the next refill.

Whilst the others were digging holes to bury the discarded equipment, Lecky was on the radio, static crackling, requesting a grid reference for a Landing Zone.

There was a pause, then a voice came through, dictating the details in Batco, or Battle Code, something which the British Army had used since the 1980s. Simple and effective, and no technology required. Also in the message came a warning of increased enemy activity and of the Taliban takeover over the country since they had set out on their mission.

Lecky looked to the others.

"Looks like the country has gone to shit, so I reckon we should get the hell out of here boys...and lady".

The soldiers huddled together, exchanging information, and plotting their route and destination on their individual maps;

then they mounted their vehicles, and engines fired up, rumbling softly in the dawn light .

Their rendezvous point, or RV, with the helicopter was a landing zone on a high plateau about a day's ride from their current position.

Jake patted the seat beside him with an easy grin.

"Here, Miss Kane...Eve...you sit in the front next to me. Don't want you tumbling off the luggage rack like a sack of spuds, now do we?"

Evelyn raised an eyebrow, but the corner of her lips twitched in amusement.

"Oh? And here I thought you just wanted the pleasure of my company".

Jake's grin widened.

"Well now, I won't deny a bit of charm makes the ride more enjoyable".

He gestured grandly to the seat.

"Your chariot awaits".

With an exaggerated sigh, Evelyn climbed in to the passenger seat beside him, settling in as Jake gave the Minimi, which was mounted in front of her, a quick check.

"Happy with the gun? It's loaded and ready to go; you just need to flick the safety catch off and Bob's your uncle".

She ran her fingers over the cool metal, feeling the weight of responsibility settle on her shoulders.

"I'm as happy as I *can* be, all things considered," said Evelyn.

Jake smirked.

"That's the spirit. A bit of faith, a steady hand, and you'll be just fine".

As Carter clambered onto their luggage rack and made himself comfortable, Taylor revved his engine, calling back.

"Quit the flirting, lover boy. We're burning daylight".

Jake chuckled and tipped an imaginary hat to Evelyn, whilst flicking a two fingered salute towards Taylor.

"Righto, let's be off then".

As the engines of the ATVs fired up, rumbling softly in the dawn light, Evelyn couldn't help but steal a quick glance at Jake. There was something reassuring about his confidence - not just bravado, but a steady, unshakable presence; and "damn it all if that wasn't just a little bit swoon-worthy," she thought to herself.

The ATVs tore through the arid landscape, engines growling as they navigated the uneven ground, kicking up dust as they wound their way through the hostile landscape, weaving between boulders and dry riverbeds. It wasn't ideal - the dust trail could give them away - but there was no way around it. The harsh midday sun bore down on them, turning the surrounding countryside into a shimmering furnace. Heat waves danced off the rocky ground, distorting the horizon and making every distant movement suspicious.

No one spoke. Their focus was on the ground ahead, every dip, every rise in the earth, every potential ambush point. The terrain was a mess of dry ravines, sharp outcroppings, and crumbling rock faces. One wrong turn, one misjudged slope, and they could flip a vehicle or snap an axle.

Every so often, Jake or Lecky would raise a hand to signal a change in formation, keeping their movements controlled and deliberate. Tariq, riding with Taylor, kept his rifle across his lap, his eyes constantly scanning the ridgelines. Evelyn, gripping the Minimi mounted on Jake's ATV, felt her heart beating in time with the vehicle's engine.

It was hard to shake the feeling that something, or someone, was out there.

The mountains in the distance seemed both a promise and a threat - a sanctuary if they could reach them, but also a labyrinth of danger if they were forced to fight within its unforgiving depths.

Several miles behind, the Taliban force from the previous night had doubled back. The fighters had retraced their steps at dawn, scouring the dry riverbeds and rocky passes, searching for any sign of the foreigners.

It hadn't taken long.

The faint tyre tracks, the disturbed gravel - subtle markers to an untrained eye but obvious to the hunters. But now they had a myriad of motor vehicles with them, which they had brought along the highways and out on to the dusty tracks.

A warlord in a dark turban crouched at the edge of a ravine, running his fingers through the dust. His men stood behind him, weapons in hands, awaiting his command. A satisfied gleam flashed in his eyes as he examined the tracks, then rose to his feet.

"They are not far," he murmured.

But how could he know? In the end they were far enough, that's all that mattered.

A fighter beside him, gripping a rusted RPG, nodded.

"They will not escape. Soon we will have our vengeance".

With that, the warlord signalled forward. Engines sputtered to life. Motorbikes and battered pickup trucks, their beds loaded with men and weapons, surged across the desert. The hunt was back on; whilst, half a day ahead, the team pressed forward, unaware of the now mobile force tracking their every move.

The extraction point was a desolate plateau, a stretch of rock and dust surrounded by snow capped peaks. The air was cooling fast now, the last light of the sun bleeding out over the mountains. Evelyn felt nervous as she searched the high ground. They had made it to the rendezvous, the Landing Zone, but the silence felt deafening.

Then - gunfire. Sharp cracks echoed off the cliffs.

They all knew the sound all too well.

"We've got company," Jake shouted.

The special forces team was already moving, dropping low, weapons up. The fragile peace of the mountains was shattered as rounds whined past, thudding into the dirt and stone around them.

Evelyn and Tariq remained with the ATVs, instincts overriding fear. The Minimis sat there almost beckoning Tariq and Evelyn to use them. No time to hesitate. Tariq took control of one, Evelyn another, her body shaking with fear as she flicked off the safety catch.

"Suppressing fire - NOW!" yelled Jake.

Evelyn squeezed the trigger, and the Minimi roared to life. Muzzle flashes lit the encroaching darkness as she raked the ridgeline, the rat tat tat of rounds cutting through the Taliban's positions. Tariq did the same, their combined fire chewing into rock and bodies alike.

Meanwhile the small team of soldiers moved like ghosts, slipping through the shadows, using the Minimis' covering fire to reposition. The Taliban had been trying to creep forward, but now they scrambled for cover, caught off guard by the sudden burst of firepower.

Lecky was already on the radio, crouched low, scribbling down enemy positions between bursts of incoming fire.

"Zero, this is Alpha Two One...Contact...large enemy formation...requesting immediate extraction...over".

The reply came quickly.

"Alpha Two One, this is Zero, ETA figures four five minutes...I say again...figures four five minutes...out".

Lecky cursed under his breath but didn't waste time. He scanned the battlefield, doing a quick mental calculation based on the Taliban's spread. Then, switching frequencies, he radioed in the big guns.

"Iron Dagger this is Alpha Two One...fire mission...grid 492638...enemy company...danger close...fire for effect...over"

Then came the reply.

"Alpha Two One this is Iron Dagger...fire mission...grid 492638...enemy company...danger close...fire for effect...confirming danger close...over"

Lecky didn't hesitate.

"Affirmative. Drop it right on their heads".

"Roger...shot out...shot out...over".

Evelyn caught his eye.

"Artillery?" she called over the gunfire.

Lecky gave her a grim nod.

"Hold tight. It's about to get loud," he called out to everyone.

The Taliban were still pushing, rounds whizzing past, but the Minimis kept them pinned. The team stayed disciplined, picking their shots, working as one.

Then, in the distance - deep, booms and whines, the unmistakable sound of heavy artillery rounds in flight.

Lecky glanced at his watch.

"Five seconds".

The group stopped firing and hugged the ground, each silently praying that they would not be harmed.

The first shells hit seconds later - ranging shots, sharp, brutal impacts along the ridgeline. Dirt and rock erupted in violent plumes, the concussions rattling through their chests. The Taliban fighters hesitated, momentarily stunned, some diving for cover, others scrambling back.

Lecky was already back on the radio.

"Iron Dagger...rounds dead on target. Give 'em shit! Over".

A moment's pause. Then the confirmation:

"Roger Alpha Two One, rounds incoming...God speed. Out".

He barely had time to relay the second warning before the mountain exploded. The next volley rained down in a seemingly endless barrage, the ridgeline lighting up in a storm of fire, steel, and pulverized rock, the roar of the blasts drowning out everything, shockwaves hammering the valley.

The Taliban's return fire faltered - then stopped entirely. The few still standing turned and fled, their will to fight obliterated along with their cover.

Lecky gave a satisfied smile, lowering the radio.

"Goodnight, boys".

Silence filled the night, broken only by the crackle of burning debris and the occasional pop of settling rock. The acrid stench of cordite and dust choked the air. The soldiers stayed in all round defence, ATVs in the centre, observing as best they could into the darkness with their night vision goggles, fingers resting lightly on triggers. They weren't about to assume the Taliban had truly fled. Too many times, an apparent retreat had been a feint - a moment of quiet before another storm.

A brief discussion followed. Once the helicopter was on approach, Jake and Carter would remain as the last line of defence, covering the others as they drove the ATVs onto the waiting Chinook. They would instruct the crew to keep it hovering just above the ground, as it was a potential hot LZ, and touching down on terra firma could be a death sentence.

Jake checked his watch, then glanced at Carter.

"When the heli is in range, we flash a red torch - SOS in Morse – so make sure you've got your red filter on mate".

Carter gave a thumbs up sign.

They settled back into position, tension coiling through them. The battle might be over, but they weren't safe yet. Not by a long shot.

The thump of rotor blades cut through the night air, growing louder with every second. The Chinook was coming in from the east, its silhouette barely visible against the dark sky. Carter held up his torch, flicking it on and flashing the SOS signal. Almost instantly, the Chinook responded, dipping lower, its ramp scraping the ground as it hovered just above the LZ.

"Go! Go! Get to the heli!" Jake bellowed as he and Carter opened up with their rifles and UGLs.

The six on the ATVs revved their engines, dirt and dust kicking up behind them as they sped toward the waiting Chinook. Then, as if the gates of hell had been thrown open, gunfire erupted from all around. They were right, the Taliban had not left, their numbers doubled by the silent arrival of the force seen earlier in the valley. Tracer rounds slashed through the darkness, RPGs streaked toward them, and the Landing Zone became a war zone.

Bullets zipped past, some striking the ATVs, others smashing into the dirt. Explosions sent shockwaves rippling through the air, but there was no stopping. Each rider pushed their machine harder, closing the final distance. One by one, the ATVs leapt onto the ramp and into the cavernous belly of the Chinook.

Once on board the team ripped the light machine guns from the vehicles, raising them to their shoulders. The cabin lit up with the flash of automatic fire as they laid down suppressing bursts, aiming for the muzzle flashes all around them.

All of the enemy effort seemed to be concentrated on the Chinook as Jake looked over to Carter and winked.

"Well, here goes nothing...run!"

Jake and Carter sprang to their feet and sprinted toward the Chinook, boots pounding against the earth. The aircraft lifted momentarily, surging upward to avoid an incoming RPG.

"Shit!" Jake cursed.

The gap seemed to widen. There was no time to think - just act – as the two men launched themselves forward, arms outstretched. For a split second, it felt like they weren't going to make it. Then strong hands grabbed them, yanking them inside as the Chinook pitched skyward.

No time to breathe. No time to think.

"Give me every grenade you've got!" Taylor shouted, holding out his hands.

One by one, the team tossed him their grenades. Without hesitation, he began hurling them from the ramp, arming handles pinging away as they tumbled toward the enemy below.

Evelyn's voice cut through the chaos.

"Can I have a go?"

Taylor glanced at her, then grinned.

"Knock yourself out lady".

She grabbed a grenade, yanked the pin, and flung it into the darkness. Seconds later, an explosion rocked the plateau. She grabbed another, and another, quite obviously enjoying herself.

Jake raised an eyebrow.

"Remind me not to piss you off Miss Kane".

The fight below dwindled. One last RPG spiralled harmlessly away, then - silence. The Chinook roared into the night, disappearing into the blackness, leaving only fire and death in its wake.

CHAPTER 16

TOO IMPORTANT
TO BE LOST

The Chinook thundered through the night, its rotors chopping the air in a rhythmic, steady beat. Below them, the Afghan wilderness stretched endlessly, a vast sea of darkness broken only by the occasional pinprick of light from an isolated dwelling. For a while, no one spoke. The only sounds were the low murmur of radio chatter and the occasional metallic clink of spent brass cartridge cases rolling across the floor.

Evelyn leaned back against the bulkhead, and slowly breathed out. The adrenaline was still coursing through her veins, making her feel jittery and alive. She looked over at Jake, who sat across from her, one arm draped casually over his rifle. His sleeves were rolled up, revealing forearms smeared with dirt and sweat. Even in the dim light, she could see the faint curve of a smirk on his face.

"You throw grenades like you've been doing it your whole life," he said.

She arched an eyebrow.

"And you catch helicopters like it's an Olympic sport or something".

He chuckled, stretching his legs out.

"Not my smoothest landing, I'll admit, but definitely a Gold Medal one eh? You were full of surprises back there though".

Evelyn shrugged, but the compliment warmed her.

"I thought I might as well make myself useful".

Jake smirked.

"I think I'll call you Lara from now on, and I might even put in a word for you...you know, if you fancy a career change. The regiment is always looking for good people".

She snorted.

"Right...I'm sure I'd fit right in".

"You handled yourself better than some blokes I've served with," he said lightly, "think about it...running around war zones, chucking grenades, getting shot at. It could be fun".

Evelyn gave him a dry look.

"That's your idea of fun?"

Jake grinned.

"You get used to it".

"Well, as tempting as it sounds," she said, "I actually *do* have a job".

"Suit yourself," he said, still amused, "but I bet your next archaeology dig is gonna feel a bit tame after this".

Evelyn tilted her head, pretending to consider. Then, with a sly smile, she said, "Actually...I am looking for someone with combat experience. A head for tactics, and...most importantly...someone very, very good at getting me out of sticky situations".

Jake raised an eyebrow.

"Oh yeah?"

She leaned in slightly.

"How do you feel about a position with...let's say, a slightly more flexible approach to international acquisitions?"

His grin widened.

"International acquisitions? Sounds suspiciously like a job where we'd have to work very closely together".

"Very," she said, her voice teasing.

Jake chuckled, shaking his head.

"Now that *is* an interesting offer".

Before he could elaborate, Lecky, sitting nearby, cleared his throat.

"This is all very exciting for you two lovebirds, but what are we doing about the books?"

Evelyn let out a sigh, her smile fading.

"I keep thinking about Raiders of the Lost Ark - the final scene, when the Ark of the Covenant just gets crated up and shoved in a massive warehouse, never to be seen again".

"That'll be the fate of our books. Politicians and religious leaders don't like being told what to do...not even by God," Jake said grimly.

"Then we shouldn't hand them over," Lecky said bluntly.

"Or just hand over some of them," added Jake, "*they* don't know how many we have, do they?"

Silence settled over them as they exchanged glances.

"*We* should each keep one," Evelyn said finally, glancing at Tariq and Jake, "the others can hand over theirs. Something this important shouldn't be locked away forever".

Tariq nodded.

"I agree".

Jake leaned back against the bulkhead, arms folded.

"Looks like we've got ourselves a plan".

A sudden change in the horizon grabbed Evelyn's attention. Ahead, the dark void of the landscape began to give way to a soft, golden glow. The lights of Kabul flickered like a mirage, sprawling outward in chaotic clusters. It was a stark contrast to the vast emptiness they had just left behind.

"Home sweet home," Carter muttered.

Lecky peered out of the open ramp, giving a satisfied nod.

"ETA five minutes. Pilot's bringing us in hot".

Jake tapped his fingers against his knee.

"I suppose this is where we find out what the big wigs have to say".

Evelyn smirked.

"Let me guess - 'well done, but don't do it again'?"

"Something like that," he said with a grin.

Then he leaned forward, resting his forearms on his knees.

"So... about that job offer. You're serious?"

She held his gaze for a moment, then gave a small, knowing smile.

"Completely".

The Chinook banked slightly, the runway lights of the airport stretching out before them like a welcome mat. As they descended toward the tarmac, Evelyn couldn't help but wonder if her life had just changed forever.

The helicopter touched down with a thud, its rotors still screaming overhead as it settled into place. The rear ramp clattered down fully, and Jake stepped off first, rolling his shoulders to shake off the stiffness of the flight. The others followed, exhaustion and relief settling over them like a heavy coat, as they strode out into the artificial glare of the floodlights, revealing the huge expanse of Kabul Airport, where soldiers and ground crews moved like ants.

Even though it was the dead of night, Kabul Airport was far from quiet. Beyond the perimeter fence, the real story played out. A desperate throng of civilians, hundreds of them, pressed against the barriers, some waving documents, others simply pleading with the soldiers standing guard, their faces lit by the occasional flash of headlights or the glare of spotlights sweeping the fence line. A crackle of gunfire echoed through the city, and the occasional burst of tracer fire lit up the horizon, a reminder that their escape had been just in time. The air was thick with dust, exhaust fumes, and the unmistakable tension of a place on the verge of collapse.

Inside the secure zone, however, the atmosphere was different - controlled, methodical. A row of armoured vehicles stood at the ready, soldiers moving between them with the efficiency of men and women who had done this a hundred times before.

Colonel Salloway stood waiting near a convoy of black SUVs, his stance formal, flanked by aides and a handful of well dressed men and women – stern faced, watchful, with impassive expressions; the kind of people who carried themselves with quiet authority, accustomed to sitting in the shadows. These were not military personnel. They were something else.

As Jake and his team approached, Salloway stepped forward, offering a curt nod, his expression a mix of stern authority and genuine relief.

"That was a hell of a job...well done," he said, his voice carrying over the fading whine of the helicopter blades, "you all did exceptionally well. I don't need to tell you how close that was".

Jake, still feeling the vibration of the Chinook's engines in his bones, shrugged.

"Nothing like cutting it fine, eh boss?"

Salloway smirked, then turned to Tariq.

"And as for you, my friend, I have news. Your family is safe. They were flown out a week ago - RAF Brize Norton. They're in England now".

Tariq sighed and smiled a smile of relief.

"Thank you," he said quietly, his voice full of emotion, "thank you".

Salloway nodded but didn't linger. He gestured toward the SUVs.

"Come on. De-briefing time".

They were ushered into a secure briefing room inside the base - sterile and windowless with a long table, a few metal chairs, and a slow-turning single fan humming weakly overhead. The men and women in business suits followed them in, taking seats along the walls. They didn't introduce themselves, didn't offer names or titles. They simply watched, their presence an unspoken reminder that this was more than just a military matter.

Jake, Evelyn, and Tariq exchanged looks.

"Interested parties, then?" Jake whispered.

Coffee was poured, though no one drank it. The adrenaline was still too strong.

Salloway took a seat at the head of the table, flipping open a folder.

"Alright. I want everything. From the beginning".

And so they told him.

They recounted it all in detail, from the clues, the Garden, the people they had met, the gift of the books, what they contained, and the implications of what they had learned. Evelyn, her voice calm and forthright despite her exhaustion, explained the significance of the 'Book of Truth', her words quick and precise, as if afraid someone would cut her off before she could finish.

"The Book of Truth isn't just some ancient manuscript," she said, "it holds the potential for something...world-altering, ideas that could change everything...potentially unite cultures, challenge long held beliefs, maybe even end conflicts before they start. Not to mention the kind of knowledge that could shift the balance of power if it falls into the wrong hands".

Lecky leaned forward, arms folded.

"Maybe even the knowledge that could bring *peace* if it falls into the right hands".

Salloway absorbed the information in silence, only occasionally flicking a glance at the suited figures along the walls.

When they finished, he shifted in his chair.

"And the Garden?"

A heavy silence followed.

Jake looked directly at him, unflinching.

"It's gone".

Salloway's expression didn't change as his eyes flicked to Jake.

"Gone?"

Evelyn interrupted.

"We gave back the key. The entrance and the Garden disappeared. There's no way to find it again".

Salloway leaned back in his chair, a blank expression across his face.

"That's... unfortunate".

Evelyn studied him for a moment.

"You don't look all that convinced".

Salloway breathed out slowly, his fingers tapping against the folder on the desk.

"It's not the answer I was hoping for, no".

There was another silence.

One of the suited men finally spoke.

"So there's no chance of re-opening it?"

Jake shook his head.

"No".

The man exchanged a look with a colleague, jotting something down in a notebook.

Salloway stared at them for a long moment before speaking.

"And I assume you all understand the sensitivity of this?"

"We do," Evelyn replied, asking the question that the others were dying to ask, "which is why we want to know what happens next?"

At that, Salloway held out his hand, expectant.

"The books".

The group of eight glanced left and right at each other.

One by one, the nominated five handed them over.

Jake, Evelyn and Tariq did not.

One of the suits collected the manuscripts carefully, stacking them in a reinforced case that was quickly sealed and locked.

Salloway's gaze lingered on Jake, Evelyn, and Tariq, waiting. When no books appeared, his lips pressed into a thin line.

Jake just shrugged.

"There are only five sir".

Jake then sat back, hoping to change the subject.

"So, what's going to happen to them?"

"They'll be passed to the right people," Salloway assured them.

Evelyn narrowed her eyes.

"What *sort* of right people?"

Salloway's expression didn't change.

"The kind who can both study them *and* ensure they don't fall into the wrong hands".

It was a careful answer. Too careful. Evelyn exchanged a look with Jake and Tariq, then scoffed.

"It sounds an awful lot like a diplomatic way of saying we'll never see them again, when they were given to us to pass on to heads of religion so the world can be a better place, free of hatred and war".

Salloway didn't deny it.

Lecky sighed, shaking his head and shielding his mouth with his hand while he whispered to Jake and Evelyn.

"It looks like you were right about the big warehouse".

Salloway's eyes flicked to him sharply.

"What was that?"

Lecky smiled easily.

261 - ESCAPE TO EDEN

"Just thinking out loud...saying I can't wait to see the handing over ceremony".

The colonel cleared his throat.

"Yes...quite".

Salloway studied them for a moment longer before closing the folder in front of him.

"You've all done your part. Go get some rest. It's all in hand now; we'll take it from here".

Lecky let out a slow breath.

"What a waste".

Jake nodded his agreement.

There was nothing more to be said.

As they stood to leave, Evelyn subtly bumped Jake's arm and simultaneously cast an eye towards Tariq, exchanging a silent understanding between them.

They still had *their* copies, and they weren't about to let them vanish into obscurity. Some things were too important to be lost.

The de-brief had been short and to the point.

Salloway leaned back in his chair, eyes fixed on Evelyn and Tariq.

"There's an RAF Hercules departing in one hour. See the clerk outside - he'll ensure you're on it, but ensure you hand in your weapons first".

Tariq gave a quick nod. Evelyn hesitated just for a moment before offering a tight smile.

"Of course".

As they turned to leave, she shook her pack up and down, ensuring that the weight of her pistol was still nestled where she'd hidden it. Some things were better kept close.

Salloway's voice stopped Jake as he made for the door.

"Not you, Sergeant Allsop. Stay a moment".

Jake stiffened, as he watched Evelyn and Tariq exit the room. The door clicked shut behind them.

Salloway smiled and held out his right hand.

"Congratulations Jake, you've been promoted to Warrant Officer Class Two and are being posted to Hereford. You'll be a DS".

Jake blinked. He had expected a grilling from the officer, not a promotion. His mind whirled, caught between pride and a strange reluctance. DS - Directing Staff. That meant training the next generation of elite soldiers, instructing them on how to survive what he had just endured. It also meant stability for his final year in the Army, plus a full pension.

Jake gulped down the tangled mess of emotions and gave a quick nod.

"Thank you, sir".

"Good...tell your team to get packed up, they'll be on a flight tonight," Salloway added.

Jake didn't need telling twice, but he had a farewell of his own to give.

Outside, the airstrip was a flurry of movement. Ground crew bustled about, the loud roar of engines filling the air as the RAF Hercules loomed ahead, its ramp already lowered.

Jake spotted them just as they reached the queue. Tariq stood calm, one hand clasped behind his back, the other holding on to his pack like it contained the Crown Jewels, which it did, while Evelyn shifted her weight impatiently.

"What will I do now?" asked Tariq, not really expecting an answer.

"In England?" replied Evelyn, "with *your* qualifications you could easily be a Teacher or Lecturer, or perhaps come and work at the museum...or for me. Anyway, we're both rich enough to never have to work again".

"But where will I live? I do not know you country," he said, his thoughts only of being placed in some refugee accommodation or other.

Evelyn thought for a moment.

"I have a large house in Wye in the Kent countryside, you and your family can stay with me until you are settled. I only rattle around there by myself anyway and would be glad of the company, *and* it would be a wonderful place for the children," replied Evelyn.

Tariq was overcome with gratitude.

"Thank you Miss Kane. My family and I would be honoured".

Jake pushed his way through the line.

"Tariq...Evelyn!"

Tariq turned, cracking a rare, genuine smile.

"Jake".

Jake extended his hand, and Tariq shook it firmly.

"I hope to see you again, and give Miriam and the kids a hug for me".

Tariq smiled again.

"Inshallah".

Jake then turned to Evelyn. He wasn't quite sure what he wanted to say, only that there was something there - something unspoken, unresolved. She seemed to sense it too.

Evelyn smirked.

"I'll be starting my own company when I get home. One that tracks down ancient mysteries".

Jake raised an eyebrow.

"You'll need some cash to afford that".

She grinned and, with a sly glance around, unzipped the side pocket of her pack, tilting it just enough for him to see.

Jake couldn't believe his eyes as the golden gleam of sparkling gemstones, encrusted with the dust of centuries, stared back at him.

"The bank of Nuristan," she murmured.

His eyes widened.

"You jammy bugger. There must be millions of pounds worth there".

Evelyn's grin widened.

"Yeah... you should have caught up with us earlier, eh?"

Jake looked over to Tariq who just stood there with a smug expression on his face.

He let out a breathless laugh, shaking his head.

"Bloody hell...*you* too?"

Then, his face sobered.

"I've got one year left in the Army and I want my full pension; I deserve it after 22 years".

Evelyn rummaged in her pack and pulled out a small, clean business card. She pressed it into his hand and winked.

"Give me a ring in a year...or sooner if you want".

Jake turned it over, bemused.

"A card? In a war?"

"You never know when you might need one," Evelyn laughed.

His fingers traced the edges before he slipped it into his pocket. Then, as if remembering something, he looked directly in to her eyes.

"What about the books?"

Evelyn's smile faded slightly.

"Keep them safe. Who knows? But I think that unless we were on live TV, no one would have believed that we had even found Eden".

Jake shook his head.

"Yeah...people are bloody stupid like that these days. If it aint on social media it didn't bloody happen...morons!"

Evelyn took a step back, turning toward the plane. Then she hesitated.

Without warning, she spun around, rushed back, and grabbed Jake by the front of his shirt, pulling him towards her. Before he could react, her lips pressed against his in a kiss that was quick, firm, and entirely unexpected.

Jake barely had time to react before she pulled away, grinning at his stunned expression.

"Well, I'll see you then?"

Jake smiled to himself.

"Yes... yes, I think you will".

She smiled warmly, shouldering her pack before striding up the ramp.

Tariq, already inside, raised an eyebrow at Jake's dazed look and shouted back to him.

"I believe you have been claimed my friend".

Jake grinned and ran both hands through his hair.

"Yeah, well...she *does* have good taste".

A voice drifted back from the ramp.

"Oh, and Jake?"

He looked up just in time to see Evelyn's cheeky smile, as she thought back to their last night in the Garden of Eden.

"You've got a nice arse".

Jake opened his mouth, but the Hercules' engines roared louder, swallowing whatever witty reply he might have had. Instead, he just shook his head and laughed.

Yeah. He was definitely calling her.

Tony Squire served as a soldier for 21 years, an experience which reinforced his passion for military history and adventure story telling. His latest novel blends history, action and intrigue, following a thrilling quest set against the backdrop of the Taliban resurgence in Afghanistan. Combining meticulous research with fast paced storytelling, Tony brings the story to life, crafting compelling narratives that explore the clash between history, superstition, myth and survival.

More Books By This Author

The ANZAC Chronicles

"...UNTIL YOU ARE SAFE".
"TO OUR LAST MAN".
"OUR LAST SHILLING".

Other Titles

IN THE COMPANY OF OUTLAWS - MY LIFE WITH NED KELLY AND HIS GANG.

www.ingramcontent.com/pod-product-compliance
Lightning Source LLC
Chambersburg PA
CBHW070548120726
47909CB00007B/2287